DAPHNE DEAD AND DONE FOR

Daphne Dead and Done For

Jonathan Ross

St. Martin's Press
New York

Library of Congress Cataloging-in-Publication Data

Ross, Jonathan.
      Daphne dead and done for / Jonathan Ross.
          p.   cm.
      ISBN 0-312-05408-4
      I. Title.
    PR6068.O835D26   1991
    823'.914—dc20   90-19517
                                                                        CIP

First published in Great Britain by Constable & Company Limited.

First U.S. Edition: March 1991
10 9 8 7 6 5 4 3 2 1

1

The body, its inner spirit having been wrenched from the fleshly envelope by violence, lay empty of what had been a living personality in the utter darkness of its unexpected tomb. Having lain there for some days like a trodden-on beetle, the blood and body fluids had gravitated to the lowermost levels available to them, unpleasant processes by the bacteria of decomposition happening to the flesh and tissue that had been cleansed, cared for and deodorized in life. The lustreless eyes, lacking a living brain for the means of expression, stared sightlessly into the darkness.

Should the body's inner being have entered into a separate existence on the death of the flesh as its owner might have believed, there was undoubtedly the possibility that it was now hovering somewhere near and wondering how in God Almighty's name this had ever happened to it.

Detective Superintendent George Rogers, on occasions society's clap of doom to the murderously inclined, was in a condition when, with extremely little provocation, he could, he convinced himself, have unplugged one of the Police Authority's telephone handsets installed on his office desk and hurled it at the wall opposite to him. Not normally activated by that part of his nervous system dealing with a shortness of temper, his state was, he considered, due wholly to the regretted absence of the elements nicotine, pyridine, ammonia and carbon monoxide in his bloodstream.

Having arrived more or less intact into his fortieth year – he thought inconsequentially – his physical exterior reflected something of his condition. Overall a darkish-looking character, he was equipped with black hair, heavy eyebrows over brown eyes that could darken with the onset of anger, and a swarthy skin; all more or less complementary to his six feet two inches of forceful masculinity which, for duty occasions, he fitted into a charcoal-grey suit. If there was such a thing as a dark amiability, he had that too. Not wholly monochromatic, his teeth were an unstained white and, holding an opinion that an over-colourful exterior usually concealed a drab interior, they matched well the wardrobe of shirts he wore with muted unpatterned ties. His nose, set in a clean-shaven face of an often sardonic aspect, was his beak-shaped pride; narrow and jutting and immensely discerning of the smells of a man's villainy or a woman's scent. He was wifeless and, in his disgruntled opinion, verging on a pauperism arising from his paying out almost half his salary in the settlement of a failed marriage.

Until he had been felled by an attack of acute bronchitis, telephone throwing had been an infrequent behavioural abnormality in him, brought on only by the extremes of frustration. The onset of serious breathing problems and a feeling that his heart was fibrillating had sent him to bed, requiring the attendance of his doctor in very much of a hurry. He, an earnest bachelor who neither smoked, drank nor seemed interested in women, and who, suffering from none of Rogers's peccadilloes, hadn't in consequence much going for him in terms of carnal pleasures, clapped a plastic contrivance over the suffering detective's mouth and nose and fed him warm steam, then injected what Rogers thought to be a horse's dose of cortisone under the skin of his hand. Later, when stuffed with antibiotics and a little less pale-blue in colour he lay defencelessly flat on his back in bed, wheezing his suffering, the doctor – of a zealot's disposition and apparently knowing nothing of the sublimities of tobacco smoke – had sought from him a promise that he would give up smoking his pipe.

With his moral fibre already under siege by claims that kissing such as he would be akin to kissing an overloaded ashtray and that he and his clothing undoubtedly reeked of a particularly acrid autumn bonfire, he had been frightened enough by his attack of non-breathing to agree to give distance to what the doctor clearly regarded as the inhalation of a vapour comparable to Satan's breath.

Unfortunately for himself, Rogers held that a promise, even one made under the duress of illness, had in it something of the equivalent of an affirmation under oath. In the later weaning of his inner self from the need for tobacco's fragrant solace, he suffered, feeling no significant improvement in his fitness or any signs that he was a better detective for his sacrifice; unable anyway to prove or disprove his possession of the promised baby-pink lungs of the born-again non-smoker. He had also failed to notice any increase in the numbers of women supposed to be attracted to his recently-acquired sweeter-smelling self. It left him feeling that, apart from a hair-trigger irritability and a low level of tolerance for fools and loud noises, he was as normal as anybody else who had been abruptly deprived of a comforting life-enhancer.

As he was about to leave for upstairs and his daily conference with the Chief Constable – known unofficially as morning prayers – his unlisted telephone rang. It was Guy Izatt, editor of the county's own *Daily Echo* and one of the few outsiders holding its number.

'George,' he said. 'Do you have a Mrs Daphne Gosse of Ratfyn Road reported as missing? Possibly under suspicious circumstances?' He sounded ready for tetchiness should that be so, with his paper not having been told.

'Not under suspicious circumstances, Guy,' Rogers told him firmly. 'I would have known about it. But otherwise, hold on while I check.' Using his free hand, he called up the Missing Persons Register on his desk computer, then tapped out on its keyboard a search for the name Gosse. Immediately, the words CANNOT LOCATE appeared on its screen. 'There's nothing,' he said to Izatt. 'What's the problem?' While he had been checking he had heard the editor's impatient fingers drumming on his own desk.

'We received a written insertion by post this morning for our Personal column, apparently from her husband.' He had lowered his voice as if wary of being overheard. 'The wording was such – foul play was mentioned – that it was brought to my

7

notice and I, in turn, had the husband telephoned for confirmation. Not that I'd have run it anyway, even had he done so, but he hadn't. He denied that he'd sent it, said it wasn't true anyway and that we'd find ourselves in serious trouble if we printed it.' Izatt snorted. 'My girl who'd spoken to him said he sounded highly outraged and had slammed down on us.'

'And was she missing?' Rogers looked at his wrist-watch. Being late for the morning conference usually resulted in the Chief Constable being querulous.

'He didn't actually say, but that's probably because we hadn't the chance to ask him. Understandable in a way because we did telephone him at his place of business. While I'm not about to have a cardiac arrest about it, George, it doesn't sound right to me.'

'Say no more,' Rogers said. 'I'm already late for Chief Constable's Orders. I'll trot around to see you when I've finished trying to justify my existence to him and that should take all of thirty minutes. And would you retrieve the envelope it came in if you haven't already done so.' He closed down with his mind already pecking away at what the hell it was all going to mean.

2

The *Daily Echo*, a relatively small-circulation newspaper printed in a civilized broadsheet format, was published from a stone and glass building as soulless and unlovely as Rogers's own Police Headquarters. Its windows, fronting on a shivering winter's High Street, were crowded with the previous day's bag of photographs of the newsworthy and the prominent. To the detective's recurring displeasure his own was occasionally included, his expression seemingly always caught by the camera's lens as if about to choke on his own bile.

If editors came in a standard format, Izatt was not of that kind, being a large-bodied character in a cheviot tweed suit manifestly tailored for rough shooting in a frigid countryside and a check shirt with a yellow tie to complement the orange-coloured cleated shoes that stuck out on long legs from beneath his desk. He looked not unlike a broken-nosed bruiser recently retired from the boxing ring, his grizzled hair cut short to the stiffness of door-mat fibres, his jutting eyebrows set by a natural configuration in a permanent scowl that reflected nothing of his generally uncontentious, quite chummy temperament.

Framed black-and-white photographs covered large areas of the wall behind him, most including Izatt shaking hands with, or handing over things to, Abbotsburn district notabilities. Among the paraphernalia on his desk were two empty trays – of which Rogers felt a distinct envy – and a printed notice saying THE HURRIER YOU GO, THE BEHINDER YOU GET. Izatt, smoking a large pipe, was unfairly filling the upper reaches of the office with the tormenting incense of smouldering tobacco.

Rogers, sitting ego-diminishingly low in a leather-covered easy chair, was reading the contents of a pale blue sheet of notepaper Izatt had handed to him. Typewritten, they read, MISSING FROM HER HOME IN RATFYN ROAD, ABBOTSBURN, MRS DAPHNE GOSSE, WHOSE HUSBAND SEEKS HER RETURN. IT IS FEARED THAT SHE MIGHT BE THE VICTIM OF FOUL PLAY. *Please insert in Personal small classified column and invoice to Clifford Gosse, Firoza-bad House, Ratfyn Road, Abbotsburn.* The envelope, which Izatt had recovered from wherever it had been discarded, was of the same colour as the notepaper and addressed, also in typescript, to *The Editor, Daily Echo, 104 High Street, Abbotsburn*, having been posted the day before in Abbotsburn under a first-class stamp.

With Izatt watching him, Rogers felt that he was now expected to do a Sherlock Holmes in studying the typescript on both exhibits for a minute or so before pronouncing that it was almost certainly tapped out by two fingers and a thumb in an élite typeface, using a nylon ribbon on a three-years-old Adler Triumph or some such. He couldn't, and didn't. All typescripts looked very much the same to him although he knew that they had their differences to the expert eye and were each usually identifiable to a particular typewriter.

'I see what you mean, Guy,' he said. 'It's not the sort of thing that's done. Or, having been done, been published.' He smiled to show that he wasn't wholly serious. 'And I personally would object to his use of the phrase "foul play". They're sacred words in the constabulary vocabulary, only to be used with the utmost caution. You said he'd been contacted at his business. Who is he?'

'He owns or runs Abercrombie's, the pharmacy in the Market Square,' Izatt replied. 'The news editor put Gallagher on to it – she's the staff reporter who was chasing him – when she couldn't raise him at Ratfyn Road. I don't know the man myself,' he added, as if clearing himself of any responsibility for whatever Gosse had done.

'Nor I.' Rarely swallowing aspirins or sticking adhesive plasters on his skin, Rogers had no recall of visiting Abercrombie's or of seeing or hearing of Gosse. 'I'd like to see your Miss Gallagher to get what he said to her at first hand.'

'She's waiting outside,' Izatt told him. To Rogers's relief – and he admitted its selfishness to himself – he had laid the pipe aside on an ashtray. 'But what do you think of it?'

Rogers pulled thoughtfully at his lower lip, wondering, not by any means for the first time, how much of what he said would be misunderstood and used to promote his enquiry to the status of a murder investigation, to his subsequent embarrassment. He said, 'Assuming, as I think we should for the moment, that Gosse hadn't sent the letter to you – it'd be a daft thing for him to do under any circumstances – then we'd have to assume that it was prepared and sent to you with the intent that, however implausible was the suggestion that Mrs Gosse might be the victim of foul play, you should do with it what, in fact, you did.'

'Which, of course, gives it a greater significance.' Izatt clearly wanted more from the detective. 'Somebody else may know something he or she believes to have been foul play, which we don't.'

'A possibility, no more,' Rogers admitted cautiously and noncommittally. Izatt shouldn't make any headlines out of an indefinite possibility, though nothing that he could manufacture into news need be considered sacrosanct.

'With this bloke Gosse denying he's the author, I imagine we could go to a paragraph or so about a mystery advertisement;

no names, et cetera, but an indication that there's been some funny business going on and the head of the CID is at present investigating it.' He raised eyebrows that were soliciting assent from Rogers as a kind of insurance. 'We could, couldn't we?'

'I suppose you could,' Rogers agreed genially. 'That is, if you're not going to later worry yourself sick about Gosse or his alleged missing wife putting two and two together and seeing a solicitor about instituti ɜ an expensive libel suit against your paper.' He looked quizzically at the editor. 'And, of course, your not having anything to support that I shall be doing any more than passing on what seems to amount to an initial routine enquiry to one of my staff for action.' Seeing Izatt's growing irritation, he said persuasively, 'I'd be obliged if you'd let up on it for the time being, Guy. You'll obviously get your story at the end of the day. At the moment you've nothing but what might be an unfunny hoax done for purposes unknown to us. I'd prefer nothing is published yet and I'll give you whatever I can and possibly more when I'm satisfied there's substance in what we're dealing with.' He gave Izatt a smile. 'While I'm at it, Guy, can you tell your photographers that I'm not a bloody film actor wanting to be photographed every time I poke my nose outside the door to get on with my job?'

Izatt was equally affable. 'A difficult thing to impose, George, but I'll give it some thought while you're chatting up Liz Gallagher.' That was his way of refusing, and Rogers had to content himself with it.

The girl who entered the office at Izatt's touching of a desk bell-push had the narrowness of an apparent absence of female breasts and hipbones which she had covered artfully with a well-tailored black suit and a kingfisher-blue silk shirt. Appearing to be a year or two either side of thirty, she carried self-assurance with her like chain mail underwear and could never be imagined carrying a handbag. With her glossy black hair dropping to just short of her narrow shoulders, her unmade-up face had apparently been fashioned by her temperament to disabuse one's conceit that she would be interested in anything but the asking of awkward questions. Rogers knew her by sight only – an unsmiling face with serious eyes at the occasional press conference he attended – and, owning himself a professional disposition towards interrogation, felt that despite what might tactfully be called an excessive slenderness and what he thought he had detected to be an anti-Rogers attitude, he could at least be civilized with her.

Obviously having reservations of her own about Rogers, she nodded coolly at him and sat in a second chair, near enough for him to smell her perfume – it reminded him of hyacinths – instead of the editor's tobacco smoke. Izatt said to her, 'I think you already know Mr Rogers, Liz. Tell him about your conversation with the man we've been discussing.'

She had very white teeth in what Rogers could only classify as attractive though dark-eyed and dark-browed sardonic features and she surprised him by showing them in what he took to be a social smile. 'Less a conversation, more a ranting,' she said. 'Not being able to contact him at his home, I spoke to him by telephone at his place of business. I told him that I represented the newspaper, that we had received his message for insertion in the Personal column and regretted that we couldn't publish it in its existing form; that in any case the paper's policy was that such insertions had to be prepaid. "What message?" he said. "You've got the wrong name." I asked him again if he was Mr Clifford Gosse of Ratfyn Road and he said, "Yes, I am, but I still don't know what you're talking about." I then asked him if his wife's name was Daphne and that left me waiting for a longish silence as if he didn't quite know what to say. He finally said, "It is, although I don't know what business it is of yours." I don't think it entirely my imagination, but I fancied he was expecting to be given bad news. I said that I would read out the ad, which I did before he had a chance, if that was his intention, to say no. I couldn't see his face, of course, but I'd swear he was aghast, making strangled noises as if he had something stuck in his throat.'

'Repressed anger – annoyance?' Rogers suggested, needing some evidence to support the unseen and almost silent aghastness, and wary of being fed any shock-horror hyperbole. 'Or could he have just been surprised?'

'Not at all,' she replied stiffly, her eyebrows down, 'although he did become angry later; became offensive, in fact. And I was coming to that. When he thought fit to speak to me he asked me was I trying to be funny. That's when he seemed to be boiling up to it. I told him that I was perfectly serious and he said that he knew absolutely nothing about the nonsense I was talking and that it had obviously been sent by somebody trying to stir up trouble.' She jerked her head, tossing her hair so that it flicked against her cheeks. 'I know that one doesn't – and shouldn't – judge a person by his voice, but his was not one I'd care to have to work with. I had a feeling that he was going to shut down on me, so before he could I asked him was it a fact that Mrs Gosse was missing.' She showed her teeth again, though now not in a smile and probably reflecting her feelings at the time. 'That was when he called me an interfering bitch – and I quote loosely – ranting on about the gutter press sticking its pig's snout into other people's personal lives and private affairs, and did I in my ignorance understand anything about the law of criminal libel. Then he did shut down on me.'

Rogers had been thinking as he listened. Not much of Gosse's reaction to Gallagher's questions made him a man with something nasty on his conscience, although aggression could be defensive as well as offensive. 'Would you have expected a different reaction?' he asked her, though anticipating that she could see in what he said a criticism of her mode of questioning.

She did, bristling in immediate irritation, her eyes dark with it. 'Would you?' she demanded.

Rogers smiled, meaning it to be an emollient to the sudden discord, conscious that Izatt's pugilist's face was regarding him with what could be a friendly sympathy. 'I don't know. I didn't speak to him and you did. Would you have expected it to be different?' he persisted.

She hadn't lost what he thought to be her dislike of him, but said, reasonably restrained, 'I suspected he had avoided answering me about his wife being missing by apparently losing his temper and threatening me. But that would have been understandable if, say, she had left him for another man. That he was ill-mannered in doing it was something we expect and generally accept.'

'As we both do,' he assured her, 'and it can help at times. So, having listened to him protesting rather overmuch, do you think somebody other than he sent in the insertion?'

She shrugged her narrow shoulders almost indifferently. 'Who knows?' She then held his gaze not so indifferently, but almost challengingly. 'As I intend staying close to this one, I imagine that I may be finding out exactly what it does all mean.'

Rogers frowned. It was his turn to bristle. 'I don't believe that'd be a good idea, Miss Gallagher,' he said sternly. 'Not to get under my feet, the department's feet, and obstruct our enquiries.'

'Oh?' she snapped at him heatedly. 'Since when has there been a law saying that I shouldn't?'

'Since a long time ago, and specifically earlier this century when a King's Bench Division of judges decided on it. Acts done to interfere with the police in their seeking evidence of offences committed can amount to an obstruction, and though they appeared not to bother to say as much it could mean that you might end up in a cell.' He put on a degree or so of an affability he wasn't actually feeling towards her. 'To be honest, it's a card we prefer to keep up our sleeves and hope we never have to use. But don't bank on it, Miss Gallagher. I'm not always sweetness and light.'

Izatt intervened then, taking the pipe he had relit from between his teeth and saying soothingly, 'I'm sure Liz understands that, George, and I'm sure she won't be getting in your hair or interfering in your enquiries. After all, you wouldn't know about any of this if not for our policy of working with you rather than against you.' He gave an unconcealed wink to the girl and said, 'Thank you, Liz, you can toddle now. You've my authority to ask Mr Rogers for progress reports on any investigation he decides to make and whenever the occasion demands.'

'Yes, think nothing of it,' Rogers agreed drily, believing that he had gone a little too far in non-co-operation. 'My office will be at Miss Gallagher's service day or night. And thank you for what you've already given me.'

When he left Izatt's overheated office for the windswept chilliness of the street, he took with him the Personal column insertion and envelope for scientific examination. In the deplorably masculine habit of weighing up a chance-met and attractive woman's availability, he had also taken with him a mental picture of the fractious Liz Gallagher and himself, improbably in bed together and wasting time in directing penetrating questions at each other that got them nowhere at all. It should, he thought, as the street's cold air hit his lungs, be the time of the year when what he called his baser instincts were held in suspension in deep freeze. Only they seemed not to be where Liz Gallagher was concerned; certainly they were reanimated enough for him to hope that there would be no disruptive conflict of interests between them.

3

Back in his strictly utilitarian office of metal furniture and plastic and glass nearly everything else, Rogers had given Gosse the opportunity of confirming Liz Gallagher's assessment of his easily aroused anger by telephoning him at his shop. Apparently his response to what he regarded as interference in his affairs differed with whoever was doing the interfering. He certainly hadn't sounded pleased when Rogers told him who he was and why he wanted to see him, and was only waspish in saying that he saw no reason for discussing his domestic affairs with the police or being disturbed during his business hours, or indeed at any time, over somebody's idea of a ridiculous and pointless hoax. Rogers, tersely convincing him to the contrary, had arranged to see him at his home during his lunch break – when he would also be releasing his dogs from the house – as an alternative to a threatened visit to his shop premises.

Although the sun shone palely from high in a clear blue sky, it cast no discernible heat and a heavily overcoated and gloved Rogers, climbing into his newly-acquired Vauxhall automatic car, felt it to be much like entering a deep-freezer. He had yet to feel entirely comfortable using only one foot to operate the driving and braking pedals, his left leg apparently now considered redundant without a clutch pedal to operate. Arriving at Ratfyn Road without having tried mistakenly to change gear with the selector lever, he crawled the car along its bareboned tree'd length until identifying Firozabad House from a board posted at a drive entrance. Pulling into the kerb and parking short of the drive, he stepped out and entered the drive, passing a red Nissan saloon left in front of a closed two-car garage.

The house, probably late Victorian, had been built in mock Tudor style and now possessed a modern pantiled roof. Its glaring white plastered walls had been generously segmented into small rectangles by narrow wooden beams, the latticed windows showing darkened interiors and no movement. The arched door was of heavy panelled wood, the elaborate hinges and studs of black-painted iron. The spacious grounds in which it stood suggested that it had once stood in country house isolation before being engulfed by the town's later development. And, Rogers considered, ever ready to make assessments based on visual appearances, possibly once owned by a nineteenth-century military man pensioned off from Indian service with the British Raj.

Approaching the door, he pressed a gloved finger on an anachronistic plastic bell-push that sounded off a carillon of bells and a yapping of small dogs from its other side. The man who opened the door, apparently not having been in too much of a hurry to do so, stepped outside and closed it behind him. A guessed-at ten years older than Rogers, nature had short-changed him in fitting him out with a lumpy and squat body, giving him about an eye-level view of the detective's chest. With that and his wide blubbery mouth somehow giving an impression of froggishness, he had sandy hair and a small bristly moustache, a high-blood-pressure complexion, grey eyes behind rimless spectacles, a thin mouth and small hands and feet. Wearing a camel-hair coat with a pink shirt and scarlet tie showing between its lapels, he didn't look like the detective's idea of a pharmacist. He gave him a smile and his name and held out his warrant card for him to read.

Manifestly in no mood of *bonhomie*, Gosse glanced at the

16

warrant card and said, 'Yes? What is it you have to ask me?' His voice, a deep-seated rumble, had a slight harshness to it.

'Some questions, Mr Gosse, and none that I particularly wish to ask you standing outside.' He made that as pleasant as his words allowed.

Gosse remained unmoving. 'That's your problem,' he said. 'I doubt that what you have to say requires you to come inside and upset all my arrangements.' He didn't sound as if he liked policemen. 'Certainly not when it's about my wife.'

'I don't mind myself, although you might with your neighbours taking it all in.' That wasn't likely, given the windows-shut weather and the distances from the houses flanking them, but as a reason it was the best he could think of.

It wasn't good enough, for Gosse said, 'You apparently do mind, so we'll go to the back garden where I can keep an eye on the dogs.'

It didn't make Rogers feel very amiable, but he followed his un-co-operative interviewee through a gate between the side wall of the house and the garage into a walled garden.

A scattering of cupressus, shrubs and clumps of the dried sticks of wintering plants grew there, enclosing three sides of a shaggy leaf-strewn lawn and, apart from the felt-covered roof of a small garden shed showing above them, concealing the far end of the garden. At their entry, three small white and brown terriers ran to Rogers and snapped at his ankles, persisting until Gosse ordered them off and they reluctantly obeyed. There was a cage-like structure built around a large wooden kennel attached to the wall of the house, towards which the detective, by now needing to control a rising irritation, moved to escape from the cutting wind that was making nonsense of claims to comfortable warmth by his heavy overcoat.

'If you can give me your attention for a minute or two,' he growled, 'perhaps we can clear this matter up.' Removing a glove and retrieving from an inner pocket the typewritten notice now enclosed in a glassine envelope, he held it out by its edges for the pharmacist to take. 'Look at that, Mr Gosse,' he said, 'and tell me whether you've seen it before.'

Gosse took it and read it, his face controlled to a non-expression. 'Piffle,' he said shortly, handing it back. 'Is that all you want? Because if it is I'm going.'

'You haven't said anything about your wife,' Rogers pointed out, putting the envelope between the pages of his pocket-book. 'I take it that her name *is* Daphne? I understand you did get around to telling the reporter that.'

'I did, although what business it was of hers I wouldn't know. Or of yours either.' For an indoor man he seemed visibly impervious to the cold.

'If your wife does happen to be missing, she might well believe that it is. Is she?'

'No, she is not.' His eyes shifting had reflected a sudden deviousness. 'Certainly not missing.'

'That's good.' Rogers was brisk. 'I'd like a few words with her.'

'You can't.' A spurt of aggression was there. 'She's not here.'

'I don't mind,' Rogers said patiently. 'Tell me where she is and I'll speak to her wherever.' He gave Gosse a brief smile which he was sure he wouldn't find very encouraging.

'I don't know where she is.' His jowls were reddening, his eyes disliking the detective. 'She's never told me.'

'Yet she's not missing?' There was irony in Rogers's words and he raised his black eyebrows.

'She's left me.' He appeared to be building up to a revealing froth of anger. 'Does that satisfy you? She's been gone nearly three weeks and I don't give a damn. I wouldn't have her back anyway and the last thing I want is for the police to snoop around finding where she is.' He was watching his dogs whose ancestors, apparently, included moles, for they were digging deep holes in the frozen soil of the flower borders. That seemed to affect him rather more than did the subject of his absent wife.

'You don't equate her leaving you, not knowing where she is, with being missing?' Rogers didn't either, but that wasn't the point of his question.

'No, I don't. Nor did I at any time.'

'Why should she leave you?' Rogers was already guessing it could only be because he was such an abrasive sod. Weighing him up dispassionately, without being prejudiced by what Liz Gallagher had told him, he judged him to be a surly bugger who happened to have also been born bloody-minded, wanting

18

to ask him why any woman with her fair share of feminine intuition could ever have married him.

'Don't you think that could be my business,' he growled, his deep bass voice more effective at growling than was the detective's. For a moment, despite his lack of inches, he had looked formidable.

'Your proper business is pharmaceutical,' Rogers corrected him sternly. 'Mine is finding out what has happened to your wife, about whom somebody is concerned enough to say, admittedly in a devious way, that she is missing and that foul play is suspected. *Why*, Mr Gosse? Or don't you understand the implications there?' What Rogers, whose frozen feet he had to stamp occasionally to find out whether they were still with him, couldn't rationalize was why he was being kept out of the house. It could be that because of her absence the interior was in all the untidy squalor of a busy man living on his own; or – not so fancifully the thought came and stayed with him – that even now she was lying dead in the roof space, the likely smell of weeks of decomposition threatening, despite the cold, to be a dreadful indication to the nostrils of any visitor.

'No, I don't,' Gosse replied. 'Just what are you implying?'

'That it's certain you'd know why she left you, and under what circumstances. Do you?'

He hesitated for a while, changing emotions making his face unreadable, before saying, 'Not because I know anything of what that note suggests. If there is any of that you'll have to find out what it is from the man she went away with.'

'That took some getting out, didn't it?' Rogers said, not unkindly. 'Perhaps you'll now give me his name and where he comes from.'

'I don't know it. I don't want to, but he's likely to be somebody from where she was working and no better than she deserves.' He seemed to have reached optimum resentment in his annoyance and it had started to sound hollow. Astonishingly for the manner of his speaking, he had developed a distinct tic at a corner of his wide mouth. 'Now you know, perhaps you'll let me get on with what I came home for and not bother me with what I've put behind me.'

19

Rogers did the next best thing to refusing it by asking another question. 'I'd like to know exactly the day she left you.'

'On a Thursday, three weeks ago come tomorrow.'

'Didn't she say anything about him when she walked out?'

'I wasn't here when she went, so she couldn't, could she? When I came home in the evening she wasn't here. Then I found that she'd taken some of her clothes and things in a couple of my suitcases.'

Rogers, who had earlier decided to unleash hard words at him for the meagre information he was being doled out, decided that Gosse might now be suffering a discarded man's hell behind his aggressiveness, and be not too short of giving way to a self-pitying snivelling. Should he, even a usually under-standing Rogers would hold him in a measure of contempt. Softening his voice, he said, 'I'm well aware that being questioned by the police about the break-up of a marriage is the last thing a man expects or wants, Mr Gosse. However, some person, rightly or wrongly, has alleged that your wife has been the victim of foul play, something obviously a criminal offence. Coming to our notice, that means we have no option but to investigate, to test the truth or otherwise of it.'

Gosse, his expression showing a brooding withdrawal, the tic at his mouth more pronounced, wasn't looking at him but down at the flagstones on which he stood. His hands hanging at his sides – Rogers wasn't disposed to fret about their being a raw pink from the cold – were clenching and unclenching.

'An investigation of your wife's leaving you does mean that one way or another, from you or from other people, I intend to dig out what facts there are to be dug out. So I'm asking you, as somebody I trust with nothing to hide . . .' – he tried to make that sound convincing – '. . . to co-operate by giving me the facts I need. For example, what made your wife leave you, for surely something did? How do you appear to know that she went off with a man? Where was she working? Anything in fact that will help in my finding where she is.'

There was a silence in which Rogers was satisfied to wait. Then, looking at the detective, Gosse said in what sounded to be a more reasonable voice, 'I've nothing unlawful to hide, if that's what you're meaning.' He chewed at his lip. 'I've known

20

for some time that she's been unfaithful to me. There isn't any way that I can prove it, but I've known. I'm not a fool, you know. She's shown it in a change in her behaviour, often finding reasons for staying late at her office and leaving me here on my own in the evenings. And then, for the past few months, she's been buying and using perfume which she rarely did for me and being a lot more concerned with her hair and make-up. And the clothes she's been spreading out on lately. On top of which, when we've been together in the house – which hasn't been often lately – I've been aware that she was watching me in a rather unpleasant manner . . . as if she didn't like me any more. When I've asked her what she was looking at me like that for, she told me I was imagining it. As if I could, knowing her as I do. It'll not surprise you to know that we slept in separate rooms – she told me that I snored and thrashed around in bed, keeping her awake. Not only that, but she made no efforts to hide that she found whatever I did or suggested doing to please her, quite unwanted and even distasteful.'

He fell silent, the small muscles in his jaws moving jerkily as clearly he thought something over. Then it came out in a short burst of passion. 'No, for God's sake! That isn't all of it. I took her up on it one night when she came back late, stinking like a tart from where she'd been with him. She'd been drinking as well, which she knew I didn't agree with. She lost her temper and screamed at me and said I'd never meant anything to her; that this man had kept saying he wanted her – wanted her body which she said belonged to her and not to me – and she wasn't going to spend the rest of her life denying herself just because she was married to me. She wouldn't tell me who he was, but said that if I didn't damn well like it she'd leave me and live with him as he had always wanted her to. That's when I knew I'd moved into the other bedroom for ever and I've been there since.'

His passion subsiding, he glanced up at the listening Rogers who was wishing that he could suck philosophically on a pipe of tobacco and warm his nose at the same time, seeming to go into a change of attitude. 'The worst thing about it was that it made no difference to how I felt about her. I still do. If I knew where she was I'd go to her . . . ask her to give me another

21

chance . . .' He appeared to a somewhat sceptical Rogers to be struggling to contain his emotions in a transition from abuse to a deserted husband's bewildered lamenting. 'I did everything I could for that woman, gave her everything she wanted, and that's what she did to me.'

'Well, I'm not disparaging you for what you've said or for what your wife did,' Rogers told him, not allowing himself to be deceived by what he had decided was only a skin-deep emotion, 'but your situation is about par for the course for quite a few married men. Take my word for it, it doesn't amount to much more than a bruising of the ego and that's certainly not terminal.' He knew, having gone through the unhappy disentangling process himself. 'What sort of a woman was she before you realized that she'd gone extra-marital behind your back, so to speak? I mean, what were her social pleasures, her outside interests?'

Gosse had bristled at the detective's observation on collapsed marriages, but answered his question. 'You mean you might find her through them? I doubt it. She used to do caving and suchlike before we were married, but not since. She liked the theatre, though because I didn't she wouldn't go all that much. She borrowed from the library, always had her head stuck in a book.' He lifted his hands to his mouth and blew warmth on his fingers. 'I don't know whether it'll help because she hasn't been for ages, but she used to go regularly to some odd meetings some society used to hold in the Civic Hall. They were something to do with reincarnation, about regressing to the past, she said.' His voice held an edge of derision. 'I know they were because she used to deliberately tread on insects and snails and things in the garden and say something about liberating them into their next life.' The derision was still with him when he added, 'That's about it, if it's any use to you.'

'I'm sure it will be,' Rogers said, though he couldn't think how. 'Where did she work? At what and with whom?'

'She was secretary to a man called Henbest – and he seems to be a complete idiot – who's headmaster of St Boniface School.' For a moment he looked savage, a savageness that ill fitted his froggish mouth. 'She preferred that to working with me, which she used to for a short while.'

'Presumably she's left the school also?'

'Not presumably at all. They've been telephoning and asking where she was.'

'Why did you think she'd left you on the particular occasion she did, causing you to check on her clothing and the suitcases? Couldn't she have been coming home late?'

'She could – except that it so happened she'd put the duplicate home safe key she kept in her handbag on the coffee table where she knew I'd find it. And when I checked in the safe I saw that she'd taken her part of the money we kept in there.' Gosse had said that with an air of having scored off a slower-witted antagonist, and that interested Rogers. He seemed also to have lost his facial tic.

'At least she didn't take any of what she considered yours. That's what you're saying, isn't it?'

'She took the car.'

'Not the one in the drive, naturally.'

'Of course not. She drives a Mini Traveller. She needed it to get to the school and back. If you find her, I want you to remember that it's my car and not hers. It's registered in my name and I want it returned to me. I'm not in the business of providing free transport for her and the man she's chosen to go off with.'

So much, Rogers thought cynically, for his brief display of the spirit of forgiveness and the desire for an emotional return to marital oneness. 'You'll have to do your own car collecting if and when we find where she is,' he told him. 'In the meantime, its colour and registration number, please.'

Gosse's dislike of Rogers had only temporarily been put aside, for it showed itself again. 'It's brown and the number's AQO34S,' he said nastily. 'And I thought you people were paid to help us with our problems?'

'And so we are,' Rogers said blandly. 'It's a pity, but it doesn't include taking a car from the possession of a person who has had the owner's permission to use it. You'll probably have a reasonably recent photograph of your wife, so I'll be obliged if you'll fetch it for me. I'll see that it's returned to you in due course.' When he saw what he thought to be the beginning of a

23

refusal in Gosse's face, he added sharply, 'We do have to be able to recognize her, you understand.'

Waiting until Gosse had entered the house by the back door, which he closed behind him, Rogers walked quickly over to the garage and looked through its window. Other than a multi-coloured folding bicycle designed with a capability of being ridden by either male or female, it was empty of vehicles. Then, returning to where he had been standing, he peered through the slats of the venetian blinds covering what were manifestly kitchen windows, being able to decide that Gosse was one wifeless husband at least who failed to live in the squalid disorder of the disunited; although, of course, he could have acquired himself a cleaning woman or a more compatible substitute for his wife with no objection to maintaining in pristine orderliness a large kitchen on the side. He was standing motionless in the shelter of the wall when Gosse returned, wondering why, unlike the dogs who appeared to be enjoying the frigidness of an east wind, ancestral *Homo erectus* had made what had proved to be a monumental blunder in disposing of its warm and comfortable hair coating.

The photograph he handed to the detective wasn't a particularly good one, obviously having been taken with a hand-held 35-millimetre camera. Coloured, it showed a woman standing in the garden he was now in with two of the terriers at her feet. Apparently tall and slim, she looked sleekly and darkly Latin with narrow high-nosed features, straight black hair and what Rogers could only call an unvirtuous mouth that any man with red blood coursing through his veins would be happy to feast upon. The plain white dress she wore accentuated the litheness of her splendid body, manifestly fashioned by nature for man's unsatisfiable longing; Rogers could only speculate wildly on the incomprehensibility of how and why she had ever come to share the same bed with the froggish Gosse. She was neither smiling nor frowning and the drifts of flowering daffodils in the background indicated that the photograph had been taken in early spring. Because of something in her expression, Rogers was inclined injudiciously to take her side, willy-nilly and whatever had happened, against her husband.

Holding the photograph by its edges, he put it next to the

glassine envelope between the pages of his pocket-book. 'She's tallish?' he asked, already convinced that Gosse would have to stand on an up-ended bucket to meet her eye to eye. He had little doubt that it was this sort of thing that made so many very short men aggressive, occasionally nakedly hostile to taller men, trying to prove what was seldom doubted, that their lack of inches meant no lessening of their masculinity and ability.

'About my own height and not much in it,' Gosse said touchily. 'Does it matter?'

Returning the pocket-book to an inner pocket beneath his overcoat and putting his glove back on, he said soothingly, 'Not in the slightest. She's touching on thirty?'

'Thirty-one.'

'Are there any relatives she might contact or go to?'

'Only a sister – her name's Virginia Naylor – living at Thurnholme. My wife couldn't have gone to her because she's phoned twice asking to speak to her.'

'And you told her she had left you?' He wouldn't have, Rogers guessed, and not many men would.

'I told her nothing. It was none of her business.'

'Her address?'

'Baycliff Road. I don't know the number, not even if it's got one.'

Rogers sighed. He wasn't getting much from Gosse, but a later deepening of the suspicion attaching itself to him would give any subsequent interrogation a keener edge. And he thought he could afford to wait. He looked at him long and searchingly, seeing something in the features suggesting that were his suspicions justified, minor though they were at the moment, his having been questioned might well panic him into incautious action. He said, as if only mildly interested in whether he did or did not, 'Keep in touch, Mr Gosse, and let me know if you hear of anything about your wife.'

Gosse didn't bother to answer, but moved tight-faced to the gate and opened it for the detective to be gone. He chose neither to see him off his property nor to answer Rogers's affable 'Good afternoon', definitely not a man who would be saddened should Rogers happen to walk under a passing bus on leaving his premises.

Climbing into his car, it came to him that Gosse had not once called his missing wife by her name. Nor at any time had he detected in his face the look of haunted despair of a husband shut out from his wife's bed. He thought that both omissions would need a psychologist to provide answers to them but, nevertheless, he would, if he had time to remember, bend his own mind to wondering why.

4

Travelling the fifty or so yards to the approach to the junction with his road back to the town centre, Rogers saw an elderly man, tall and angular and bundled up in a green half-coat, woollen scarf and a Scotch plaid golfing cap, standing on the footpath and giving him a hand signal to stop. When the car had pulled in to the kerb, the man rapped gloved kunckles on the passenger window and mouthed, rather than said, 'Retired inspector. Information.'

Rogers reached and pushed open the door, letting him climb in and seat himself. The man showed his square teeth – they were too regular, too perfect, to be real – and held out his hand to be shaken. He said, 'The name's McCausland and I've been pensioned off from the Mets. If you're interested in hearing some dirt about the bloke you've just left, move on, will you? Turn right so he doesn't see me with you on his way back to the shop.'

Rogers, shaking the hand held out to him, replied, 'George Rogers, Detective Superintendent, and anxious to hear about it.'

'I've seen you about, chief,' McCausland said, his eyes on the detective a faded blue but shrewd, 'otherwise I wouldn't have stopped you.'

Checking his rear-view mirror for any sign of Gosse's emergence, Rogers accelerated his car to the junction and turned right, drawing into an over-lengthy bus lay-by having NO WAITING OR PARKING painted in large yellow letters on the ground. Switching off the engine, he could now look at his passenger, seeing the white-haired gauntness of a man in his mid-seventies or thereabouts who, not being remotely a dodderer, showed the discipline of his former calling in the manner in which he carried himself. Black overhanging eyebrows were an incongruity in his otherwise well-worn features. Rogers said, 'You're a long way off a London beat.'

'I was born here. Like an elephant, I suppose, I've returned here to die.' He grinned. 'Though, the Lord be kind to me, not yet for a few years. It took me thirty years to earn my pension and I'm set on drawing it for the same time.'

'And you're of the firm opinion that since you've left, the service has gone to the dogs?'

'Yes. Downhill all the way. You're going to be offended?'

Rogers laughed. 'No. I might even agree with you. I was checking on your having enough bloody-mindedness about it. It's the hallmark of any self-respecting pensioner. What do I call you?'

'Fred'll do, though my wife will insist on Frederick.'

'Right, Fred. What have you to tell me about friend Gosse? And why?'

McCausland adjusted the nearside rear-view mirror and settled himself in the seat, his gaze fixed on it. 'I'm watching to see when he leaves,' he informed Rogers. 'He usually goes back about two, and I know that because I live next door and in the winter I haven't got much else to do but watch the nasty little bugger. When I saw you go in there today I knew it had to be in connection with his wife.' His eyes left the mirror for a moment to stare at the detective. 'Was it?'

'Yes, I suppose it was. On the face of it she's flown the coop.' Even with a retired inspector Rogers chose to be careful.

'Ah, I knew it.' McCausland sounded his satisfaction. 'Either that or he'd croaked her. You want me to give it to you in line with the Metropolitan Police Standing Orders?'

'Not quite.' Rogers was warming to him and his potential for garrulity. 'I'd be grateful for some inspired comment with whatever you're about to tell me.'

'Right,' he said. 'First things first. I retired twenty-five years ago with my thirty in and until recently I've been employed

27

down south by a security company from who I'm receiving another pension. My original wife's still with me so I've remained fairly respectable and we moved next door to the Gosses a couple of years back. At first, although we're different generations, we were reasonably friendly, chatting over the fence sort of but not visiting or on first-name terms. I'd always thought him to be a bit of a turd, though she was better, more friendly. Then about a year ago he began giving us the cold shoulder treatment by not answering when either of us said "Morning, Mr Gosse" or whatever it was. She'd at least answer, but that was all, though it did seem at times that she wanted to unload to me in particular but was frightened to.'

Rogers interrupted him, asking, 'Did either of them know you were a retired copper?'

'Definitely not. If they knew anything, which I doubt, it was that I'd been in the security business.'

'Hold fire a moment, Fred,' Rogers said, before he could start again, 'my feet are freezing up on me.' He turned the ignition key and started the engine, leaving it to tick over and generate its version of hot air for his comfort. 'We've got to the point where nobody's speaking to anybody else,' he reminded his passenger.

'And I've just spotted Gosse on his way back,' McCausland told him, his eyes now back on Rogers. 'I was about to say that the situation was enough for Esme, being that sort of a woman, to begin to suspect me of having been caught by him *in flagrante* what's-its-name with Mrs Gosse.' He showed most of his plastic teeth. 'Me being given half a chance and I could've still managed, though I'd be worrying my guts out by now.'

Rogers laughed, believing him to still have kicking inside him much of his original goatishness, probably something to do with his black eyebrows. 'She was an attractive woman then?'

'She was temptation on the hoof, if you get my meaning. She wasn't all that beautiful, but whatever it is that women give out in waves could reach over a fence or two. God knows what she ever saw in him, but he must have been blessed in a big way by somebody at one time.' McCausland's face had reflected an appetite probably a couple of decades too young for him.

'You must be a randy lot in the Mets,' Rogers said with a fair try at looking exaggeratedly puritanical. 'For us up here it'd be next door to a hanging offence, so we don't give it a second's thought. What next?'

'This past summer when most of the windows were open, we could hear them brawling with each other like nobody's business. I've heard her yelling at him and him sounding off basso profundo as if he was getting ready to bite her, with the dogs sometimes joining in. Once, not too many evenings ago, I heard a screaming that sounded like a tom cat having a go at another, only not quite, you understand. Then I began to think it hadn't been a cat at all, but her. And that was a bit queer considering, because I hadn't heard his voice at all. I was in two minds about going there and finding out what it actually was, but what with the yelling and squabbling we'd heard before Esme telling me to stop acting as if I still wore a uniform and was forty years younger, I let it pass without me putting my five eggs in somebody else's business.'

He frowned. For a while he had been quite definitely testy. 'That's the irritating thing about wives,' he complained. 'As soon as you get a bit of grey in the thatch they treat you like a shrivelled-up old man and want to put you out to grass; too old to do anything active but look after the bloody garden. But back to Mrs Gosse. She came to us once – that was about four months back and I can give you the date – crying her eyes out and holding one of her breasts where she said he'd hit her in temper. She stayed with us for a couple of hours with no sign of him coming after her, had a cup of coffee and a whisky and Esme and her went into the bedroom to have a look at what he'd done. She told me later that it hadn't left anything worth looking at, which I don't suppose it would with all that padding she has inside it. I've never been enthusiastic about blokes thumping women and, feeling as I did then – it was about eleven at night and I'd had a couple myself – I was all for going next door and sorting the bugger out.' He scowled at what he was recalling. 'But you know what it is with us interfering in domestic disputes. What with that and Esme and her on at me not to go – she said she was already seeing a solicitor about leaving him anyway – I didn't. Nor did I report to your lot as I think I should have done, and as I was intending to if she didn't

29

eventually turn up. You would at least have known what was going on even if you couldn't have done anything about it.'

He waited as a bus drew up alongside them, intimidatingly close with its diesel engine throbbing vibrations into the shell of Rogers's car and promising to drown out speech. When it had gone, he said, 'Mind, when I happened to see chummy go in as he usually does and then you follow, I wasn't all that surprised. In fact, I thought you were going to feel his collar. Neither of us have seen Mrs Gosse since the night I thought I heard her screaming and you don't have to be too bright not to wonder just why we hadn't. You say she's flown the coop and that's probably what he told you. And she could've of course and who'd blame her, having apparently been bashed about a bit and definitely not being on good terms with him. Myself, if I was back on the job – and I did a stretch in CID – I'd be beginning to think it was something else.' His pale blue eyes had been fixed on Rogers's, telling him just what it was.

'Take it that I've been thinking it could be something else, Fred,' Rogers said easily. 'Can you fix when you heard her screaming?'

'I can, because I feel I've still got whatever it is left over from my coppering days, and I've been keeping notes of what we've seen and heard.' McCausland dived a hand behind the quilting of his coat and pulled out a woman's tiny diary, flicking over its pages. 'Wednesday the second of November; time, ten twenty-five p.m.'

Rogers did a quick mental calculation. 'Gosse said she'd left home a day short of three weeks, so your date fits her screaming and her being gone the following day. You said there was something queer about it, not having heard his voice?'

'About that and the screaming? Aye, there was.' McCausland frowned. 'At the time I'd thought Gosse hadn't returned home because when he does we hear his car. It's a quiet road and if we haven't got the box on we can hear people walking by, let alone a next-door car that has to be turned into a drive not all that far from ours. Later, quite later, I did pop outside to check and saw that his car was in the garage which he hadn't shut up. Hers wasn't, which made it all a bit peculiar as if she hadn't been in at all. Actually, we had the box on for short periods late

30

that evening so it's possible that she had gone out and he had come back without us hearing them. Possible, but as I say, I somehow doubt it.' He spoke as if he had been neglecting a duty imposed on him and Rogers knew exactly how he would feel. Handing in one's warrant card, handcuffs and truncheon on retirement rarely puts finish to a man's experiencing again the automatic responses etched into his brain by years of service in his old profession.

'And the occasion she came to your house?' Rogers asked. 'When was that?'

McCausland passed the diary to him. 'Keep it,' he offered. 'It's all in there and with nothing else I wouldn't want you to see.'

'I'm grateful,' Rogers assured him, which he was. Information rarely came in such neat and ordered helpfulness. 'What do you know about him?'

'Sod all,' McCausland said cheerfully, 'other than he's a chemist, has some terriers that do a fair bit of barking, has his booze delivered in a cardboard box each month by Shumar Vintners, has a cleaning woman in from the town twice a week when he or his wife are in and a jobbing gardener who starts some time in early spring. Oh, and she calls him Cliff.' He smiled, his eyes disappearing in creases. 'Not exactly Special Branch stuff is it, but you did ask me.'

'So I did.' Rogers and he understood each other. 'Did Mrs Gosse mention the name of the solicitor she was going to see?'

'She did.' McCausland tapped at his teeth with a gloved finger as he thought. 'Blast it!' he said. 'My memory's going. Kebab? Kilgore? Something beginning with a K and with a second name.'

'There's a Kyberd and somebody,' Rogers suggested.

'It could be.' He was still doubtful. 'It sounds familiar.'

'I'll check,' Rogers told him. 'Back to Gosse. He wouldn't let me in the house when I called, and I had to stand outside in the cold to speak to him. Any comment on that?'

McCausland nodded sagely as if that confirmed something or other. 'That's Gosse all over. It's his nature. I've seen him keep the parish vicar standing outside in the rain when all the poor old bugger wanted was a drop of sherry and the chance to screw a small cheque out of him to help stop his church from being sold off as a leisure centre or a disco dive. So I don't think he treated you any differently from anyone else.' He adjusted his cap and hooked a finger under the door catch at his side. 'I'm going now, chief, if you've got nothing else. I told Esme I was going out to buy myself a few cigarillos and that was bad enough. If I'm out any longer she'll swear blue murder I'm having it off on the side with a spare woman.'

To Rogers, it seemed that he spoke from the unlifted shadows of some well-merited and justified allegations made against him in the past. 'It's a married man's lot to be misunderstood, Fred,' he said with exaggerated sympathy. 'It's what puts the grey in our hair and diminishes any money we may have stashed away in the bank. From me, however, my thanks, and I'll keep in touch. If you do see anything you think I'd be interested in, give me a buzz will you?'

Watching in his rear-view mirror McCausland striding it back to his ever-vigilant Esme, Rogers noticed that the small violet-coloured Volkswagen Beetle he had seen parked earlier at the exit from Ratfyn Road was still there. With its nose now sticking out from the junction, he could see an unidentifiable figure in the exposed narrow segment of its side window.

Starting his engine, he drew away from the lay-by to position his car in the front of a timber lorry coming up behind him, the driver giving him an angry blast from what sounded like multiple horns for doing it. Thinking about it, he decided the Beetle's use to be too amateurish for it to be compared with the surveillance sicked on to him a couple of years back by his ex-wife's solicitor, nor a probability that his footsteps were being dogged in the expectation that it could produce manna from an obliging heaven to feed a villain whom his department might currently have under investigation. It left him with the near certainty that he was being shadowed by an about to be frustrated Liz Gallagher. And, as he used the cover of the lorry much too close behind him to turn unobserved into a side road, he regretted in a way that he was losing her company.

5

Before the fairly recent move into the present architectural abortion of reinforced concrete, glass and anodized metal designated the County Police Headquarters, Rogers's office had been situated in a building allocated for the use of a newly established top-hatted and white-trousered county police force in 1839. The building had creaked warningly, with the promise of near-future disintegration into the subterranean remains of the Roman fort on which it was held to have been built. Despite its shortcomings, it had possessed for Rogers an interesting ambience, the hidden spaces behind its walls and woodwork companionably – for him – active with mice and communities of furniture beetles, house crickets and Pharaoh's ants; its roofspace with its broken windows a sheltered breeding place for generations of pigeons and starlings. His desk had been of honest wood, a battered relic of the early Victorian era that had served many a heavily whiskered police officer, containing even in its scars and scratches a warming sense of a continuance of the constabulary tradition. None of that had helped Rogers to be a better detective, but certainly, whether the Police Authority cared one way or another, he had been a happier one.

Now his office was a sterile nothing without even an interesting ambience – nobody having yet dropped dead or committed suicide in the building – with no history to give it colour, the furniture and fittings manufactured almost wholly from inorganic materials and being therefore soulless steel, aluminium, polystyrene, polyvinyl, plaster and emulsion paints. There were no curtains, only white plastic strips on cords called venetian blinds, and a man-made fibre carpet covering only a small area of the artificial rubber floor tiles. Even the wall graph sheets, their vertical columns in red, blue and yellow showing the inexorable advance in the number of crimes committed within his bailiwick, somehow failed to reflect, as they had in his old office, the spilled blood, the agonies and the miseries suffered

by the victims of the recorded offences. All in all, he considered that his almost brand spanking new office was about as appealing a habitat as an empty coffin.

He had circulated the name and description of Daphne Gosse as a missing person, leaning heavily on the details of the Mini which would be more easily identified, less troublesome to find than a woman who, for all that he knew, could be weighted down on the bottom of the canal or buried until God only knew when under two or three feet of soil which he had found, in his experience, to be about the depth at which furtively concealed bodies were buried. Or, of course, she might be no more than in the company of a man she had, beyond doubt, found infinitely preferable to her unpleasant husband. Checking on the figures for persons missing from the county so far that year had somewhat abated the urgency of his fears. Of the eighty-two reported as missing by usually anguished relatives, all but twelve had returned home, of whom seven were adult males who had been traced or satisfactorily accounted for. Gosse had succeeded in fascinating that part of his thinking concerned with the involuntary twitchings and creasings in faces that tried hard to be held uninformative, unrevealing of probable guilts under pressure; the detective being always interested professionally in the modulation and content of words fashioned for the holding back of admissions and confessions, the camouflaging of falsehoods and deceits, and in the teeth displayed for their underwriting of a lorry load of reasons given to him why he had inadvertently picked on the saintly innocent, on the wrong man or woman for his baseless accusations. But above all for Rogers's enlightenment, the eyes that were the unconcealable mirrors of a man's guilt or innocence, of his moral honesty or its dark opposite. That he hadn't been impressed or happy with Gosse's reactions to his questions was by the way in the absence of any hard evidence of what had happened or had not happened to his wife.

A check in his telephone directory gave him *Naylor, V. I., Casa Gaviota, Bay Cliff Road, Thurnholme 231916.* He dialled the number, a woman's voice saying, 'I can't come to the telephone just now, but will you leave a message after the proceed signal.' He did, giving his name, rank and telephone number, and,

assuming that the voice had been that of Virginia Naylor, asked her to call him concerning her sister Daphne as soon as it was convenient for her. Whoever it was had sounded pleasant enough, but he thought he had detected some very no-nonsense nuances in her words. Replacing the telephone, he scribbled an instruction to WDS Millier of his department to make immediate enquiries about Miss Naylor and prepare for him a brief account of her past and present and what she had done and was doing with it.

Turning to the Yellow Pages directory and searching through its pages of solicitors, he found a modest entry for *Kyberd & Durker, 12b Parkhouse Street, Abbotsburn 620318/9*. It was the only entry under K. Neither solicitor was known to him, both advertising their legal skills in such non-criminal matters as civil and matrimonial litigation, conveyancing, wills and probates.

Needing to get things moving, he dialled their office, being put through to the Durker side of the partnership in the absence of Kyberd, for whom he had asked. Sounding to Rogers like a man with a confident self-approval of himself, he agreed, though with the usual professional caution that everything touched upon was subject to a strict confidentiality, that Mrs Gosse was indeed a client of the partnership, but did not believe that he could help a lot as his partner had dealt personally with her and was now away on holiday. Expressing concern over her apparent departure from her home – of which he was, until then, unaware – he agreed to see Rogers in an hour's time.

Almost as cautious himself, no man to accept wholly that which might appear to be unassailable and unarguable truth, Rogers did a quick check on the local membership list of the National Association of Retired Police Officers, finding McCausland's name, address and former force details as he had been given them. Finally, he put all the names he had been considering – including Liz Gallagher's, just to prove to himself how impartial he could be – through the force computer for a record check and came up with nothing.

About to grope from habit in his pocket for the pipe he had foolishly discarded, and cursing without passion his doctor for extracting from him so rash a promise, he reached instead for his internal telephone and dialled his second-in-command's office number. Finding him in, he asked for his immediate attendance.

Detective Chief Inspector David Lingard, heir apparent to Rogers's chair when, or if, it ever became unoccupied during his own service, was a dandy in his dress and deportment, patterning himself in many ways on his admired Beau Brummell, though he had now been dead some hundred and fifty years. With a slim and sinewy body that could deliver physical destructiveness when used against the unwisely aggressive, wet blond hair cut expensively with a contrived shagginess, daunting blue eyes that chief officers of police were reputed to accept as a qualification for rapid promotion, and narrow patrician features. His suits were of impeccable cut and stitching, the waistcoats complementing them of coloured, embroidered and patterned fabrics. His white silk and fine cotton check shirts were hand cut, modishly high in the collar and long in the cuffs; his ties always silk and unpatterned, and each matched by a silk handkerchief to hang with casual disarrangement from his breast pocket. He used a miscellany of snuffs such as Attar of Roses, Golden Cardinal, Macouba and Brown Rappee, pinching the grains from a tiny ivory box and inhaling them into his narrow nose with panache.

Entering Rogers's office, he waved a hand in cheerful salutation, sat himself elegantly in the visitors' chair and said, 'You sound as if you've a problem, George.'

'Probably an overrated one, David. And parts of it about to become yours.' Rogers sketched out the facts relating to the receipt by the *Daily Echo* of the insertion notice about the allegedly missing Daphne Gosse and the salient points of his interviews with Gallagher, Gosse and McCausland. 'There you have it,' he finished, 'and it's a toss-up whether she's just upped and left her husband or, God forbid, she's dead and buried.'

Lingard was in the mood to be flippant. 'You're the one who's seen the obviously repellent Gosse,' he drawled, 'and that must be an advantage. But he does seem to me to be the sort of chappie to have cut the lady into bite-sized pieces and fed her to his dogs.'

'What an extraordinary analytical mind you do have,' Rogers

said ironically. 'I never thought of that. What odds would you give that he'd killed her at all?'

Lingard stroked his nose, in him a rare sign of indecision. 'Unless you're holding back on me, I'd say evens. Mainly because I don't like the implication in that personal column notice. Somebody knows something – or thinks he does – and wants us to dig into it.'

'Or she,' Rogers said. 'It reads very female-ish to me and I've been thinking of somebody like her sister. She's a Virginia Naylor, living at Thurnholme, and I'll be seeing her when I can fit her in. But that doesn't mean I'm hooked on its being her. While I'm not getting a rush of blood to the head about it, it might even have been put in by Gosse himself to mislead or to promote the action it did.' He passed a deck of head and shoulders photographs of Mrs Gosse to Lingard. 'I've had those copied and blown up from a snapshot, David, and they're for showing around wherever. So drop whatever you're doing and set in motion some research on both her and her husband. We want to know where they come from and for how long they've been here; how long married and the identities of any previous spouses or lovers either has had.'

'There's a reason for supposing they had?' Lingard queried. Having put the photograph away, he had withdrawn his ivory box from the pocket of a moss-green waistcoat decorated with golden fleurs-de-lis and inhaled snuff generously, scenting the air around him with Attar of Roses.

'Only the workings of my naturally indelicate mind so far as he's concerned,' Rogers admitted affably, 'though it's often been proved right. So far as she's concerned, the nasty suspicions he loaded on to me were probably justified. She used to work in her husband's shop, so put one of our better-looking DCs on to chatting up one of the female staff without Gosse getting to know. For you, it's St Boniface's to interview Henbest, the headmaster. Use a little diplomacy with him for she's said to have been his secretary with a penchant for working evenings, and secretaries who work evenings always bring out in me the darkest of suspicions.'

'Name me somebody who doesn't,' Lingard murmured, keeping his remark circumspectly below the level of audibility.

Aloud, he said, 'You've come to some sort of a conclusion about her being alleged to have left behind the home safe key, but taking only the money she considered hers and not the lot?'

'I've thought about it,' Rogers agreed. 'The trouble is that while an honest woman would have done it, so might her husband had he killed her. He'd have been a fool not to have thought of it to support any story he'd have to tell about her having left him.'

Lingard wasn't about to give his own opinion on that, but said, 'Since she's been gone for three weeks, I'd have thought on the hypothesis of her having been murdered that her body would have surfaced somewhere. If not murdered, then having gone absent without leave, surely she or her car would have been seen or heard of by now. Either being so far a non-event, it's . . .'

'The car,' Rogers interrupted him. 'Before I forget it, and assuming it hasn't been dematerialized. While you can hide a body reasonably easy, unless you've an unoccupied garage or shed, your car, even a Mini, has to be dumped in deep water or in a deep enough hole in the ground. I'd go for our canal and the use of the Underwater Search Squad to look for it. I just hope that being in it doesn't poison them.' It was probably a vain hope; the canal's water, apart from being de-oxygenated, was almost permanently foetid and discoloured by the discharge of industrial chemicals.

'Which means you're asking me to lay it on?' Lingard felt all his old lust for Rogers's job where, it seemed from his particular seat, he could dish out all the largely mind-numbing chores to his own second-in-command.

'In between whatever else it is you have to be doing,' Rogers said expansively, knowing precisely what Lingard was thinking. 'So there's no terrible rush, just so long as you get it started straight away and restrict it for the moment to the obvious access places.' He cocked an eyebrow at him. 'Are you still on speaking terms with that cousin of yours at the Yard?' Lingard's cousin, a Chief Superintendent in a department unhelpfully designated E17, had access to what he called matters of higher concern.

38

Lingard was wary, his eyes unreadable. 'It depends on what you want to know for,' he prevaricated.

Rogers grimaced. 'I hate to have to do it – in fact it's why I'm getting you to do it for me – but it wouldn't be the first or last time that one of our lot reaching his seventies found himself still in breeding condition and wanted to do something about it. Such as a bit of extramarital fornication. Mind you, David, this is purely precautionary, but I believe in the interests of impartiality that our retired McCausland – he's a Frederick, incidentally – should be checked to confirm he's as clean as a whistle. Which I'm sure he is. You can get all his details from NARPO records and your cousin can dig around some of his older colleagues to find out what he was like when off duty and probably not accountable. *Comprenez-vous?*' Rogers's French was limited and suspect, but he thought it added an occasional confidentiality to what he said.

'Only too well,' Lingard replied, standing and regarding his senior with unconcealed cynicism. 'Does this Virginia Naylor you've chosen to see instead of the hairy males you've pushed over on to me happen to be stunningly beautiful, unattached and believed to run a well-stocked kitchen and bar?'

'Now that you mention it, David,' Rogers said imperturbably, 'she must be, and do all of that.' He put on what he thought to be an altruistic expression. 'It's a fact of life you should remember for the future that we senior officers have to set an example by taking on our own shoulders the more distasteful jobs.'

With Lingard gone, Rogers telephoned Guy Izatt at the *Daily Echo*, asking him mock-seriously to inform Miss Gallagher that there was no real need for her and her car to cause an obstruction at road junctions doing her surveillance job on him, because should she want any update on his investigation then it might be available at some time or another that evening in the Minster Hotel.

He was in no mind to be overly confiding to Gallagher – he felt he had nothing to be confiding about anyway – but hoped that she might have gathered a useful item or two herself and be willing to pass it on. Not desperate yet, but beginning to feel pushed for time, he was willing to consider the most unlikely sources of information. And this chiefly because one of his beliefs was that if a murder investigation had not produced a clear suspect within forty-eight hours, then the chances of doing so later were dismally minimal.

6

Pewter-grey clouds were sweeping in from over the coast only a dozen or so miles from the town, bringing with them a sharp-edged nuzzling wind that blew dust and paper rubbish against Rogers's trouser legs as he entered Parkhouse Street. It was manifestly going to rain or snow, which, Rogers considered, might be preferable to the frigidness either would supersede, but not by enough to make him feel euphoric.

Finding a notice board neatly scripted *Kyberd & Durker, Solicitors*, attached to the green-painted wall of an open passage separating the business premises of a rating surveyor and an electrical engineering company, he entered the only door at its end and climbed steep carpeted stairs to a landing. Amid a small jungle of potted rubber plants there were two doors, one of them with ENQUIRIES painted on its frosted glass upper half. Knocking and entering, he was smiled at by an over-lipsticked girl who was working a typewriter at a desk behind a small counter. In the far wall of the office were two doors; one was goldleaf-scripted *Hugh C. Kyberd*, the other, *Michael Durker*. Shown his warrant card and withdrawing the smile apparently kept in reserve for fee-paying clients, she tapped on the second door, pushed her head and shoulders inside, said something inaudible and then held the door open for Rogers to enter.

Durker, standing from his desk and holding out his hand to be shaken, was not in appearance the archetypal solicitor Rogers had imagined he would meet. Big, with a rugby-player's frame, he wore a hound's-tooth-check suit with a pink shirt and a red bow-tie, able with his height to meet the detective's searching stare eye to eye. He had tightly-ridged brown hair, a wide mouth suggesting that it was over-full of teeth, and a snub nose that supported black wire-framed spectacles, all somehow combining to give him the superficial appearance of a boyishness yet to need the use of a shaver. This could be dispelled by the pale-grey eyes, which held nothing in them of boyishness, but rather the calculating and withdrawn coolness seemingly handed out as legal equipment to graduating solicitors. His green-leather-topped desk had none of the profusion of bundles of documents tied with pink tape that Rogers was used to seeing, but the meticulous neatness of a rack of trays containing a sparseness of papers, an onyx pen stand and two or three manila files. Behind him were two shelves of books, most in the uniform green binding of law reports.

There was no welcoming smile and, releasing Rogers's hand from the brief handshake, he said, 'Please sit down, superintendent.'

Sitting on a leather-seated wooden chair near a window overlooking the blank brick wall of a neighbouring building, Rogers said, 'While I hadn't mentioned it when I telephoned you, it appears that in Mrs Gosse being missing from her home for some three weeks, there's a possibility, a suspicion if you like, that she has come to some harm. The circumstances of her background make it important that I gather what information I can about her private life, the people she knew and those with whom she associated.'

On resuming his seat, Durker had raised his eyebrows, then pushed himself away from the desk, leaned backwards with crossed legs and clasped his hands together over his stomach. 'You've some evidence for your supposition, of course?' he asked, manifestly not very impressed with what Rogers had told him.

'A suspicion, as I said.' Rogers believed already that his path was to be a stony one. 'But enough, I'm sure, for you to be reasonably forthcoming about her reasons for wanting to leave her husband. Matters such as domestic violence or his having had an adulterous affair on the side. Or whether *she* had one if it comes to that.' He beamed encouragingly at the solicitor.

'But your suspicion is not quite enough, superintendent, as you must know.' Durker was talking down to the detective, an attitude likely to have repercussions he wouldn't enjoy. 'Mrs

41

Gosse is Mr Kyberd's client and he's away for a break. I don't believe there's anything I can do but to note the situation and your interest for when he returns.'

'And when would that be?' He let his dissatisfaction show.

Durker gave him an elaborate shrug of his shoulders. 'Mr Kyberd will call me when he decides.' Then he said acidly, 'I certainly don't propose disrupting his holiday over what may yet resolve itself into an unimportant triviality.'

'That's not good enough,' Rogers said sharply. 'Since when has a person missing been a triviality? We have here a client of your partner's who could possibly be dead as the result of a criminal act and . . .'

Durker had held his hand up, cutting him off short and saying with a put-on pomposity, 'When you are able to assure me that she is – for you certainly haven't yet – then there is a possibility that we may consider breaching client confidentiality and pass to you whatever information we believe relevant.' He definitely wasn't liking the detective and it showed.

Rogers stared, bearing down on him with his will. 'I find your attitude difficult to understand, Mr Durker, seeing that it's your partner's client who is possibly a victim and not yours.' He was tightlipped in his annoyance, his swarthiness darkening. 'I'd prefer to ask him myself, so if you'll tell me where I can contact him I'll do it. If so be it necessary, over your head.'

Durker had removed his hands from over his stomach and was tapping his teeth with the knuckle of his thumb, his eyes, narrowed at Rogers, showing what looked like a specially promoted anger. 'That would be most unwise of you, superintendent, particularly as he's away because he has not been too well lately, but I'll let it pass for the moment. I had briefly discussed Mrs Gosse's case with Mr Kyberd and I'll concede this; if you'll tell me what there is about a woman leaving her husband that has given rise to what you appear to hold as a significant suspicion that she has come to some harm, then it may be possible for me to at least tell you whether there is anything in the file relevant to it.'

'Information was sent to one of the local newspapers referring to Mrs Gosse being missing and suggesting quite specifically that she might be the victim of foul play,' Rogers said, by no means intending to be too informative when Durker was plainly going to concede only a little, and that under pressure. 'This was passed to us, and I have since seen Mr Gosse who has confirmed that she had left home three weeks ago, although he thought it unnecessary to report the fact to us.' He scowled his irritability. 'You think that of no significance? That we should ignore it, do nothing about it?'

The solicitor did what was probably the only thing he could do and disregarded Rogers's challenges, saying derisively, 'The information was anonymous, of course? And I certainly don't see any particular significance in Mrs Gosse leaving her husband, not in view of the matter about which she consulted Mr Kyberd. Unless, naturally, there's something you haven't chosen to tell me?' With no reply coming from an expressionless Rogers, he frowned and said, 'As you wish. I'll give you what I promised. Mrs Gosse is the plaintiff in divorce proceedings under consideration. As I told you, she is being represented by Mr Kyberd and the proceedings have yet to result in an appearance in court. That is the most to which you are entitled.' He straightened in his chair, looking at the detective and then at the door, manifestly expecting him to accept that and leave.

Rogers, recognizing dismissal when he heard it, did his own disregarding. 'That's a hell of a lot of client confidentiality that you're leaning on for the preliminaries to a divorce, isn't it?' he pointed out. 'Particularly for a woman who may never need them.' He lowered his eyebrows. 'You do appreciate that my investigation is in the interests of your partnership's client, not against her?'

'I need no reminding of the situation,' Durker said stiffly. 'If that's all you require, no doubt you'll excuse me. I do have work to attend to.' He reached as if to retrieve a document and leap into action by signing it.

Durker was the second man Rogers had met that day who had made his dislike of him obvious. He accepted that it was because he was a police officer and not – he hoped – because of any personality defect or physical obnoxiousness. It wasn't anything that worried him, for he had never been a man who needed to be liked by everyone. Just, he always qualified, by those obliged by their sex to wear skirts, bras and heady perfumes.

'It isn't all I require by a long chalk,' he growled. 'I don't suppose you'd be breaching any lawyer's code of conduct in telling me who is representing Mr Gosse?'

Durker hesitated, suffering the sarcasm, though losing none of his stiffness. 'To the best of my knowledge he is not at present represented.'

'Has Mr Kyberd been in recent touch with Gosse?'

'I don't know. I don't think so.' Durker had hesitated before saying that. It probably meant that Kyberd had.

'While she is not your client, I presume that you've seen Mrs Gosse when she's called here? Or should I ask your receptionist, who certainly must have?'

'I have seen her. Once, I believe.' He was back to tapping his teeth with his thumb which Rogers chose to regard as a sign of unease.

'You interviewed her?'

'No. I merely passed the time of the day with her.' He stirred in his chair. 'I want to make it clear that I'm not accustomed to being questioned by policemen in my own office and I resent it.'

In a way, Rogers felt sorry for him, his boyish face so repeatedly failing to support whatever masculine resolve he needed to use in the interview. 'Yes,' he agreed amiably, having risen above his irritation and swallowed his intended retort. 'I imagine you do, but I'd hate to believe you were being per- versely unhelpful.'

Durker's eyes blinked behind his spectacles. 'I'm being as helpful as my duty as a solicitor permits,' he said, more disgruntled than angry. 'That and no more. Quite frankly, superintendent, if you are convinced that some harm has befallen Mrs Gosse, I'd advise you to direct both your questions and your activities in other directions and not waste your time and mine in matters which can have no bearing whatsoever on her alleged disappearance.'

Rogers, ever a believer in the exercising of tenacity, said, 'I'm wondering whether Mr Kyberd would approve or agree with your being so secretive about a woman who, for all we know, may be dead. I repeat, if you would tell me of his present whereabouts I'd like to speak to him myself. I would, of course, respect any wish he made to be left alone should he tell me so himself.'

A dull flush rose from behind the solicitor's pink shirt collar and for a moment he looked as if about to shout at Rogers. 'I shall do nothing of the sort,' he ground out. 'However, to rid myself of your imprudent questioning I'll speak to Mr Kyberd and obtain his authorization, if that's what he wishes.' He stood to show that he was ending the interview. 'If I get a positive response, you'll hear from me.'

Rogers, knowing that he wasn't to get Kyberd's address and never having expected that he would, lifted his own length from his chair. 'Thank you,' he said formally. 'I shall, obviously, inform you of any development in our investigation for Mr Kyberd's information.' Then, keeping the sarcasm from his voice, he added, 'I'm sure Mrs Gosse would be pleased, whether she's dead or otherwise, to know that you and your partner can find it in yourselves to help us discover what has happened to her.'

An early darkness was creeping into the clouded sky and it was beginning to rain when he left the passage for the street. It didn't surprise him, for it fitted very aptly the interview he had just concluded with the uptight and unhelpful Durker.

7

Having been saddled with the undemanding chore of interviewing the headmaster of St Boniface's School, Lingard had done his homework on him. Nothing was recorded against his name – Henry Tobias Henbest – at the National Identification Bureau, and nothing was known locally to his detriment. Held in high regard as an academic, he held the degrees MA and PhD and had been headmaster and principal of St Boniface's Private School for twelve years. Now sixty-eight years of age, he was a married man with an adult son and daughter.

c. 1

Lingard drove to the school in his car, subjecting her reluctantly to the late afternoon's rain drumming on her canvas hood – which occasionally leaked – and to the wet grit and mud thrown up against her mudguards by the wheels. She was his cherished veteran Bentley, in his belief a *grande dame*, still unwrinkled and stunningly attractive with her racing-green livery, long strapped-down bonnet, dinner-plate-sized headlamps now at full beam in the growing gloom, wire-spoked wheels and a deeply throbbing engine in the heart of her. It was a departmental witticism of sorts, unknown to Lingard because nobody had the courage to pass it on to him, that had nature made it possible for man to mate with a car, then beyond doubt the devoted Detective Chief Inspector would surely have done so.

During his drive through the wet streets, he mulled over his telephone call to his chief superintendent cousin – in Lingard's opinion an arrogant sod, who considered his own department the hub of the criminal investigation world. He had made it clear that in making the enquiry about ex-Inspector McCausland's antecedents – not, he had said sniffingly, that he could promise to pass on the result – he was doing for a force he thought of with obvious disdain a favour of some magnitude. On top of being insufferably overbearing, he usually wore what Lingard regarded, in his turn disdainful, as machine-made shirts and woollen pullovers instead of waistcoats.

Parking the Bentley on the forecourt of the school, floodlit by a conveniently sited mercury street light, he locked the doors – theft of her being his ever-present worry – and took in the building looming squatly above him. Standing in the elbow of a tree-lined road of mostly Victorian houses, it was a slate-roofed, three-storeyed specimen of a mid nineteenth-century building in oxblood-red brick being progressively stifled by a rampant ivy. Above the pedimented door, and illuminated by a hanging lamp, was a carved armorial bearing of a lozenged shield with two phoenixes supporting it over the word RESURGAM.

The panelled door was glossy with blue paint and equipped with an oversized brass knocker that, in the absence of a bell-push, was presumably to be used. The attractive young woman who answered what Lingard considered to be an uncivilized

46

and uncalled for noise came from a small cubby-hole of an office inside the door and was, presumably, the missing Mrs Gosse's successor.

Being expected and having shed his raincoat, he followed her along a corridor which, to him, had the smell of the small boys who must have been only recently dismissed, together with that of treacle pudding. At its end he was shown into a room which appeared at first glance to have walls totally hidden beneath shelves of books and framed group-photographs of facially identical, uniformly dressed schoolboys holding cricket bats, squash and badminton rackets, hockey sticks and rugby balls. There was a huge desk with, on it, a jumble of more books, wooden trays of papers, pens and pencils and, what he thought to be a visual joke, a large stuffed owl wearing a mortarboard.

The headmaster, a tall, angular, grey-haired and cadaverously-featured man in a navy-blue suit of many creases, stood from the desk and shook hands with the detective, then resumed his seat. He didn't actually creak but wasn't far from doing so. Lingard's first impression was that he looked a man too old to be interested in any woman but his wife, and possibly not even her, or to have had Mrs Gosse interested in him. In a quick assessment, he guessed him to be a likeable man he could trust. That is, as much as a policeman could ever trust anyone.

'Please sit down, Mr Lingard,' he said, 'and tell me how I may help in this worrying business.'

The elegant detective, sitting on a hard and slippery wooden chair with an uncomfortable runged back, had already, over the telephone, given Henbest the few facts he thought he should have concerning Mrs Gosse's disappearance. Careful in the circumstances not to do too much damage to his syntax, he said, 'Thank you, sir, I'd be grateful if you could fill me in – I mean, give me an account of her employment here, how you found her as a woman, and whether she ever said anything that might throw light on her leaving her home as she did. The kind of information that might assist us in finding her.' He gave Henbest a smile as if to say that this must be simple stuff for him to comment on.

Henbest put the tips of his knobbly fingers together and

looked grave. 'I fear the worst, I'm afraid, but perhaps when you've heard me you will assure me that my fears are groundless.' He looked down at his blotting pad for at least thirty seconds before starting, as if composing what he was to say. 'Mrs Gosse,' he said, appearing to be addressing the back of the owl's head, 'has been employed here as headmaster's secretary for two years and three months. Professionally, she has given the school complete satisfaction and I would have no hesitation in recommending her employment elsewhere in a similar situation. In addition, I should say that she was an exceedingly nice woman and well favoured. What you would be interested in knowing, I'm sure, is that she left the school at five-thirty on Wednesday the second – of this month, naturally – with nothing said by her to indicate that she would not be coming in the following morning as usual. Further, in retrospect, I see that that evening was an unlikely one on which anything could have occurred.' He frowned at that and shook his head. 'When she failed to arrive on Thursday morning, I telephoned her home, thinking that she might not be well. There was no reply to my call so I telephoned again when I thought she or her husband could be home for lunch. Her husband answered my call . . . a quite unpleasant man, I must admit.' He made an exasperated *tching* sound with his tongue and a pink stain appeared over his cheekbones. 'I gave him my name and asked was it possible to speak to Mrs Gosse. He said, unpardonably abruptly, that she wasn't there. When I remarked, quite courteously, that I was worried because she had not arrived at the school that morning, he said, "So what? I don't know where she is either," and disconnected from me.'

'Those were his exact words?' Lingard queried.

'I recall them clearly,' Henbest assured him. 'But to go back to him; in the next few days I had my senior form mistress telephone Mr Gosse, though, alas, with no further information being given us other than that he wished to repeat to me that he did not know where she was and could not help us in what was none of our business.'

He directed his noticeably penetrating grey eyes at the mostly silent, but plainly interested Lingard who was content for the time being that the headmaster should do the talking. 'You might possibly wonder why I did not report Mrs Gosse's mysterious absence to the police, particularly as I have already expressed the fears I hold about it. Well, initially, I had assumed from what she had confided in me and from her husband's attitude towards her absence, that she had at last decided to leave him. Against that, and I'm reluctant to admit it for it does show a degree of personal selfishness on my part, is that I was quite disappointed in her, for I would have expected her to tell me she was going and not leave me without secretarial help.'

He released his hands from their almost prayer-like touching and shifted in his chair, then chose a coloured pencil from a cardboard tube of them and began to scribble geometric figures on his blotting pad. He made a face, as though pushing himself to a resolve. 'One other matter at the time decided me in believing that she had left her home of her own accord. I would not mention it did I not now fear, as apparently do the police, that some ill has befallen her, whether of her own volition or not. Do you understand paranoia as a disease, Mr Lingard?'

'Not nearly enough,' Lingard admitted, knowing that he was now about to be told. Through the window behind the head-master's desk, he could see that darkness had fallen and hear the rain that beat against the glass.

'I have a little experience of it – not professionally, naturally. Many years ago I had an aunt who was dear to me and close, and who suffered from it. I saw the different stages of the disease until death took her away.' His face reflected a sadness still remaining with him. 'I really am not speaking as an expert on this matter because I am not qualified to do so, but what I tell you is the truth as I saw and heard it. So, with Mrs Gosse, I heard what I took to be the early symptoms in what she said to me, mainly about her husband. She certainly believed that the actions of those closest to her were in some way directed maliciously at her. But contrariwise, she had no over-marked responses to whatever minor setbacks and frustrations came her way, her personality remaining pleasant as it has always been. You'll wish to know how this manifested itself to me, of course?'

'It would help,' Lingard said, being still in the listening mode.

He dug into a waistcoat pocket and withdrew his ivory snuff-box. 'Do you mind?' he asked with a straight face, showing it to the headmaster with its lid open. 'I have to take it to keep my sinuses in good fettle.'

For the first time Henbest smiled. 'I do occasionally take it for my own.' Accepting it as an invitation, he dropped the pencil he was holding and reached forward, taking a sizeable pinch of the snuff, inhaling it into his bony nose as the surprised Lingard joined him. 'Attar of Roses and, my guess is, by Fribourg and Treyer, though my dear wife would certainly not approve of my taking it.'

They were fellow addicts, both feeling a little guilty at having anything to do with the mostly proscribed tobacco, but each understanding the other's need for it. 'However, back to Mrs Gosse,' Henbest said. 'It would be wholly understandable should she have decided to leave her husband. She was not happy in her marriage, and that is something of an understatement, for she said that she had knowledge of his having a quite serious affair with another woman. A married lady, she implied, who was still living with her own husband. She told me on a number of recent occasions that Gosse had been – how shall I put it? – tyrannical in his treatment of her. She unbent so far as to say – if I understood her properly – that in one or more of his rages with her he had threatened to kill her. Or, at least, do her a serious physical injury.' He shook his head, looking dubious. 'I am not, I must emphasize, quoting her actual words, but certainly the meaning of them by unmistakable inference. With it went her insistence that she was terrified when with him, yet she had always maintained she was too frightened to leave him. It was all very distressing, particularly when the poor girl would break down and weep, because she wasn't the kind one would normally associate with tears. And I was of little comfort, Mr Lingard, not being one of nature's confidants. It was, I feel, that which suggested to me what might be the onset of paranoid delusions. She had also told me on a different occasion that she had discovered – she didn't say how and I did not ask – that he had been secretly giving her hyoscine; which, if true, I am sure wasn't given to her as a medication. This, she said, she had associated with her occasional periods of a complete loss of recent memory. That, I must admit, I hadn't noticed in her.'

'I take it you knew that he was a pharmacist?' Lingard asked. The only thing he knew about hyoscine was that it was a poisonous derivative of the Deadly Nightshade plant and one or two others, though it seemed highly unlikely that a homicidal pharmacist would have to have recourse to what seemed a primitive form of plant poison extraction.

'Yes, of course. But that would only explain its availability, would it not? And, if true, would that be consistent with her arriving at school not too long ago with a quite nasty bruise on the side of her face, quite near the eye in fact?'

'That too,' murmured the detective. Louder, he asked, 'Did she say that it had been caused by her husband?'

'I did comment on it, thinking that it might have been caused in an accident, but she merely said that yes, it was painful, and was so obviously reluctant to discuss it that I took it no further. But that reluctance told me everything and I knew that it was caused by no accident.'

'In view of that – it's evidence of a sort, isn't it? – and the threats she had complained of, did you ever consider giving her any advice? Such as seeing a solicitor or, if it was thought that the threats of violence and the dosing of her with hyoscine had substance in them, complaining to us? Taking it to its extreme, it's a little late, isn't it, for her to wait until she's either missing or dead?'

'I do see that now.' Henbest was beginning to look unhappy. 'In particular as I then had some possibly unworthy doubts about her having the protection of a private detective because of her husband's threats.'

'Tell me about that.' Lingard was hearing doors banging, as if the school were closing down. It was after five-thirty and he was probably keeping the headmaster from things he would rather be doing. He held out his snuffbox, thinking it a palliative against the possibly impending demolition of at least one or two of the virtues with which Henbest might have credited his former secretary.

'Thank you . . . it is exceedingly generous of you.' He pinched generously at the scented grains of tobacco and sniffed

51

them into both nostrils. For a moment, until he returned to the subject of Mrs Gosse, his expression was one of contentment. 'She told me,' he said, 'that because of the fear she had of violence from her husband she had hired a private detective who was an ex-policeman. He was to follow her in his car on the dark evenings when she left the school. She herself came here regularly in a small red car and she gave me the impression that this man would follow her to her home or to wherever she was going that particular evening. Naturally . . .'

'I'm sorry,' Lingard interrupted him. 'That was what you were referring to early on, when you said the last evening she was with you was the most unlikely one on which she could disappear?'

'Yes. She actually made some remark I had until now forgotten about not keeping her detective waiting. But it would have no significance should she not have gone missing that evening. Had she?'

'We haven't confirmed exactly when,' Lingard said lamely. If Rogers had told him, his mind had mislaid it somewhere on the way here.

'I see. However, one incident, probably not unconnected with that, did bother me a little. There's an open yard at the back of the school we use as a hardstanding car park for the staff. One evening about two months ago, after she had finished here at her normal time of five-thirty, I had occasion to go to the back – it was a little before six o'clock – and to my surprise I saw her car parked there. Then I heard a man's voice – quite an educated one, but being unforgivably offensive – behind the wall of the yard. He was speaking to Mrs Gosse, for I heard her say something in reply; not that she sounded frightened, you understand, but worried as if she were telling him to keep his voice down. It was a situation I would have preferred to avoid, but I felt obliged to find out whether Mrs Gosse was being threatened.' He was pulling at one of his fingers, making it give out muffled cracking sounds. 'I coughed rather loudly to indicate to them that I was there and walked out to where they were standing under one of the alder trees we have at the back. They were apart, as two people in conversation would be, and they both stopped talking and were looking at me, presumably to see what I wanted. I must admit that they succeeded in making me feel as if I'd intruded on a most private matter, which I suppose I had. I could see from Mrs Gosse's bearing and expression that she was not about to welcome my interference into whatever was going on between them. The man looked at me with what I had to accept was quite undisguised insolence, and perhaps with menace. He was such, too, that I could have done little or nothing had he been offering violence to Mrs Gosse.' He gave Lingard a self-deprecating smile. 'I then retired, as one would say, to my study, hearing Mrs Gosse's car being driven from the yard a few minutes later. Now, I suspect, you are going to ask me what explanation she gave me the following morning, and all I can say is that I chose not to speak to her about it.' He cleared his throat, looking as if he had committed a major *faux pas*. 'I am not a man who welcomes what might be embarrassing confidences, and as whatever she was doing outside the school was none of my business, I took it no further.'

'Presumably you had a good look at the man?' Lingard said. 'Could you describe him for me? So that if I tripped over him I'd know who I was apologizing to.'

'I can,' the headmaster said. 'I made a particular point of remembering him in the event of something like this happening. I would guess his age to be about thirty to thirty-five, and from his dress to be in one of the professions. He would be an inch or two below six feet and what you would call of a wiry build. You know? A normally slim man fined down by hard exercise or athleticism. He was Mediterranean-skulled, what you would call round-headed, his hair intensely black and close to the scalp in small very tight curls. Almost negroid, you understand, though he was definitely not negroid himself. At first glance I took him to be negligently unshaven, but on later reflection and having regard to the rest of his appearance I accepted that the stubble I had seen was what is now called a designer beard. Though my acquaintance with him was happily brief, I judged him to be a man of violent passions. Would that be what you wished, Mr Lingard?'

'I'm most grateful,' Lingard said, thinking that the description had been beautifully honed by a good intelligence. 'May I take it that you heard only the tone of the conversation and none of the words?'

'No, you may not.' Henbest looked just a little pleased with himself. 'While there were only a few words audible as I came within earshot, I did hear him say something about her being a cheating and deceitful bitch, which I'm sure is quite untrue, while she protested that he was mistaken and in doing so called him Simon. I remember that quite easily for it is my son's name.'

'That sounds immensely useful, Mr Henbest,' Lingard said. 'There's more?'

'I'm afraid not. May I take it that the gentleman I saw could not have been Mrs Gosse's private detective?'

'So far as he's concerned,' Lingard said, holding back from expressing any derision at the absurdity of it all, 'I'm afraid I don't believe what she told you for one second. It would have been an impossibly ridiculous situation with her still living with her husband. For this so-called detective fella to be effective in riding guard on her, he would need to live in the house with her, and eat and sleep with her. All this, of course, unless she believed somebody other than her husband was set on attacking her. Or, an absurdity, believing that Gosse had arranged for a contract killing.' He gave the headmaster a half-smile to soften any implication of credulousness on his part in what had been said to him. 'Do you think she was lying?'

Henbest was biting at his bottom lip. 'I think it to have been part of what I see as her illness. It's not beyond the bounds of possibility that she really believed herself threatened.'

'I meant about the hiring of a private investigator,' Lingard said gently. He could believe the headmaster to possess an unworldly innocence that could be envied. 'There are just four such agencies in Abbotsburn. None is owned by, or employs, an ex-police officer, and none, I am quite certain, would undertake a protection job in the circumstances you've just mentioned.'

Henbest shook his head. 'Accepting that as I must and do, I still find it difficult to believe that she lied to me.'

'One other matter before I leave you in peace,' Lingard said carefully, not wishing to tread too hard on toes which could be, even though improbably, vulnerably exposed. 'I understand that Mrs Gosse remained here until late in the evening on a number of occasions. Would that be . . .'

He stopped when he saw the headmaster again shaking his head, this time vigorously and saying vehemently, 'I don't know from whom you received that information, but it is simply not so. I really must emphasize that Mrs Gosse was never required to work past five-thirty, and on no occasion did she. May I ask who said that she did?'

Lingard could see what he took to be righteous indignation in Henbest's face and he hurriedly said, 'I'm sorry, but I'm powerless to do so; you know, regulations and so forth. Of course, I do accept without question your statement that she didn't.' He stood smiling from his chair, his buttocks numbed from contact with hard polished wood. 'I'm grateful for your very considerable help, and I'll see that you'll be kept in the picture about Mrs Gosse.' He retrieved his snuffbox from his waistcoat, holding it out opened to the headmaster as if for the first time. 'It seems to be bucketing down outside,' he said, 'and this'll keep the viruses or whatever at a respectable distance. Can I tempt you to join me?'

Climbing into his Bentley, now gleaming wetly, he thanked the stars under which he had been born that he had never married for someone to stamp a female prohibition on any of his simple pleasures as so unmistakably had the headmaster's wife. And such a nice civilized chap with it, he had judged, though he couldn't help but wonder at his sudden vehemence in denying that his secretary might have worked some occasional overtime for him. And with it – a mere fancy – a recall of the word *Resurgam* under the armorial bearing, which could be applied to the possible optimism of an elderly man if, as he recollected, it meant 'I shall rise again'.

'You've a filthy mind, Lingard,' he told himself as he switched on his headlights, put the Bentley tenderly into gear and drove out from the forecourt.

8

Rogers sat at his desk, always homing back to his office after a spell outside, his head stuffed with both the useful (he hoped) and useless (he feared) information, this to be reduced to printed detail, which often took longer to do than it had taken him to collect it.

While he felt without conviction that the circumstances of Daphne Gosse's leaving home pointed to her being the victim of a killing, he could be so easily discountenanced. Firstly: were it found that she had been murdered, then, with somebody's hindsight, it could be charged against him that he had pressed his investigation neither as hard nor as comprehensively as it had warranted. Secondly: were she to surface unharmed, proved to have left her husband of her own volition, then he could be charged with having caused resentment and embarrassment by an overzealous and heavy-handed enquiry into what would, with the same hindsight, have been nothing to do with the police.

A note from one of the switchboard operators left on his desk in his absence said *Miss Naylor, calling from Thurnholme at your request, left a message to say that she would be out for the remainder of the evening and that should you wish to speak to her concerning her sister she will be available for that purpose on board the Bark of Bodwyn between 9 and 10 tomorrow morning.*

The Bark of Bodwyn was the replica of a royal naval carrack that had sailed from Thurnholme in 1578 to be immediately sunk offshore with all hands by an ill-met roving Spanish warship. Her guns and metal artefacts had been recovered from the sea in the 1970s and a replica of the ship herself built to accommodate them by a local benefactor. Moored in the harbour, she was used as a museum of local naval antiquities and as a tourist attraction. That Virginia Naylor wished to be interviewed there made him frown his puzzlement.

An unnecessarily loud knock on his door posted notice of the arrival and entry of Detective Inspector Coltart, returned after a three-year secondment to the Regional Crime Squad and having now been sent for by Rogers. He was a massive man with sandy hair, small green eyes, an unsmiling mouth and a voice that, when used, rumbled deep in his cavernous chest. In movement, he lumbered like an army troop-carrier and was about as subtle in his contact with other people. His brown suit, reputedly purchased in error from a drunken tent manufacturer, draped his frame like the loose hide on an elephant's hindquarters. A born-again non-smoker from way back, he repressed whatever neuroses he suffered as a bachelor by chewing at pencils and wooden toothpicks. 'Sir?' he said, his taciturnity being properly accepted as indicative of deep thinking.

'Sit down, Eddie,' Rogers said. He had great confidence in the solid and reliable Coltart whose weight, in sitting, made the steel and plastic visitors' chair creak, and he told him shortly of his frustrating interview with Durker. 'I'm not to be put off by Kyberd being on holiday, for I'm sure he'll be a lot more accommodating than his partner. It's not going to be easy, but I want you to find where he's spending his holiday. The telephone directory gives his address as Windswept, Luggate Heights, and I've had his number rung a few times with no answer. That's expected, of course, if he's away as Durker says he is. Be careful how you do it. I don't want anybody wrongly assuming that we're after the blood of a respectable solicitor who's probably quick on the draw with a suit for defamation of character or similar. You've enough?'

Coltart nodded. 'Enough,' he said.

'Good, because while you're about it I also want a rundown on his background.' Sending him off, he added, 'Waste no time, Eddie, because I've a horrible feeling Mrs Gosse is going to confound me by turning up dead and done for. And while you're dabbling with Kyberd, see what you can find out about Durker. All I know about him outside his office is that he lives in Queensbury Street. I might have to see him again and I'd like to know what makes him tick.'

Darkness had fallen early and thinking it practical to eat before something serious and blood-stained was reported, caus-ing him to spend the rest of a black night empty-stomached, he put on his trenchcoat and ran for his car in cold drenching rain to do something about it at the Minster Hotel. An ancient hostelry, its decaying stonework probably already blotched with moss and lichen when it moved into the eighteenth century as a staging post, it boasted a restaurant reputed to employ no waiter who was not at least a sexagenarian. And, Rogers always maintained, none the worse for that in terms of old-fashioned service and civility. The service and food were enhanced by napery of heavy starched cotton, embossed silver-plated cutlery and fine quality china. Its soups – particularly its incomparable vichyssoise – were superlative, its charges falling only just short of being acutely painful. Heavily beamed, with two capacious log fires, the restaurant was almost full when Rogers entered it and went to the table he had been careful to have reserved.

He was well into the destruction of a baked trout studded with heavily charred almonds when he saw Liz Gallagher standing in the doorway, her black hair spotted with rain and carrying a blue showercoat and a dripping umbrella. He waved her in and, on her approach, stood, feeling unexpectedly pleased to see her.

'I took it for granted that I'd find you in the bar,' she greeted him with what he might take, should he wish, as being mildly derisive.

He smiled, and said with heavy irony, 'That's not at all a bad approach for somebody badly in need of information. You'll join me? At least for a drink?'

When she said 'A whisky with water, please,' Rogers nodded his head at the waiter who had taken up station behind her and who had been handed her showercoat and umbrella.

Both seated and within the enclosing ambit of light shed by the small pink-shaded lamp on the table, he became aware of her dark eyes reading his features. Staring back at her and conscious that their minds were meeting at a level yet to be categorized, but apparently half-way between social politeness and friendliness, he wondered what it was about her off-putting sardonic expression and physical meagreness that fitted in with his concept of a sexual attraction where, he uncharacteristically felt, the body seemed not to matter. Well, not overwhelmingly so, he qualified to himself, but for a woman who chose to drive a violet-coloured Volkswagen – and who surely must possess an exuberant temperament – probably enough. 'You'll see I've not finished with my fish,' he pointed out, breaking off his stare, 'so may I do so while you unload some of the information I'm sure you've turned up since you decided to stop breathing down the back of my neck.'

'On a quid pro quo basis, naturally.' She was too clever to take up his remark about her following him, nor did she choose to shrug it off as something he should accept without complaint.

'For the little I have,' he qualified. He didn't particularly like being watched eating with her kind of studied intent. It might contain in it an unspoken criticism that it was being equated with a dog's gnawing audibly at a biscuit.

The half-smile she gave him showed that a wider, more expansive one could transform her features into a pleasant attractiveness. 'That's exactly what Guy said you'd say, but also that you were capable of being softened by sweet words.'

'It could be that Guy knows his stuff,' he said, trying to fillet a now one-sided trout. 'Do what he says, Miss Gallagher. It might work.'

The waiter came, leaving her whisky, a small highly-polished glass jug of water and a finger bowl containing a few ice-balls at her elbow. Diluting the whisky to what must have been near tastelessness, she lifted the glass to Rogers and then sipped at it. 'I found out about the boat,' she said, watching for his reaction.

He only just avoided showing one. 'Ah,' he said, as if it had confirmed what he already knew. 'It's still there then?'

She raised black eyebrows. 'Of course, shouldn't it be? I mean, you did know, didn't you?'

'About where it is?' he felt limited to answering, not chancing to suggest whose boat, though he guessed it could only be Gosse's.

'Yes.' She almost let her amusement show.

'Tell me about it,' he said, already sensing that he was on to a loser. 'You could have some fresh information I'd find useful.'

She frowned at him, though not ill-naturedly. 'You're a big fraud, aren't you. Guy warned me you could be as devious as they come, and you don't really know what I'm talking about, do you?' Exposing his dissembling seemed to have warmed her to him.

He conceded defeat and looked discomfited. 'No, dammit, I don't. But then, I never could fool an intelligent woman. Whose boat are you talking about and where is it, because I haven't caught up with it yet.'

He thought he had caught a lightly breathed 'Oh, lovely, lovely,' but couldn't be certain. With her eyes glinting with what appeared to be wickedness – it could have been mischievousness, he couldn't tell which – she said aloud, 'It belongs to Gosse and it's a four-berth bilge keeler if you know what that is, which I don't. It seems to be kept at Ullsmouth because he's a member of the Fouled Anchor Sailing Club there. If you're going to ask me for verification, it's in one of our issues eighteen months back when he came in second in a race the club organized and which we covered in full because we'd sponsored a slice of it. It's useful?'

'It could be,' Rogers agreed, 'and I'm grateful. You've the name of the boat?'

'*Ephedra*,' she replied promptly. 'I also looked up what it means because I guessed you weren't going to know and you'd probably ask.'

'You're a mind reader,' he said drily. 'So it's not a woman's name?'

'It's the name of a drug, a medical one, an alkaloid used as a heart stimulant and for the dilation of the bronchial muscles among other things. Good heavens! How could anyone normally know that one's bronchia actually had muscles?'

'If they have,' Rogers grunted, 'I've never noticed them.'

'That was a rhetorical question that didn't need an answer,' she said. 'The pharmacopoeia I read up on said it was, so it is so. It also said that it's the name of a leafless desert shrub.' She quirked her mouth at him. 'Knowing he's a chemist, that wasn't too difficult to research, was it?'

With his fork held poised midway to his mouth, he said, 'You'd make a good detective. There's more?'

'God forbid,' she shuddered delicately. 'I mean about being a detective. I've some fairly trivial and gossipy stuff about Mrs Gosse that I was given on the promise I wouldn't disclose my informant's name or any information that would identify him. And also, that you'd respect *your* source, which is me. You agree?'

'God's honour,' he promised, using what he remembered as a schoolboy's oath. Then casually, 'If it's one of your paper's staff I probably wouldn't wish to anyway.' He had said it deliberately, seeing the flicker in her eyes that had given him his answer.

'You *are* a tricky bastard, aren't you,' she told him calmly, realizing what he had done and almost certainly knowing that she had given away the origin of her own source. 'That serves me right for listening to Guy.'

'Don't fret,' he said affably, 'it's all part of the job and I'm not tricky on reneging on promises. The promise I made to you as a source, I mean. There's a chance I'll run up against your colleague anyway, and if I do it'll somehow be made clear to him that we were told his name other than from you. Now tell me about Mrs Gosse.' His had been a large fish and his appetite, now minimal, felt as if he had been feeding it trout for several consecutive days. He liked to think that he was reasonably Spartan in all his appetites.

She was rubbing a neatly manicured fingertip around the rim of her whisky glass, making a just audible musical squeaking noise. Rogers thought that it might be one of her ways of camouflaging the effects on her of life's minor annoyances. She said, 'Before she married Gosse, her name was Daphne Naylor, and she was employed by him in his shop. It was then that my informant, who has since married into ultra-respectability . . .' – she gave him a wry smile – '. . . had a fairly heavy affair with her. He used to go potholing with her and they also did some microlight flying together. I gathered from him that she was quite a handful at times and rather given to outbursts of bad temper and name-calling should she not get her own way. She was, he said, either completely fearless, or too feather-brained to appreciate a dangerous situation when she was in one, or just plain unbalanced. He said that he could quite easily look after himself in potholing, but as far as he was concerned with her flying – he was supposed to be giving her lessons in the microlight he owned then – he was forever astonished that she

61

hadn't killed herself and him with her. She'd already done some hang-gliding and obviously knew something about it, and my informant's refusal to continue with what she considered quite superfluous lessons was the beginning of their quarrelling and eventual breaking up. I think that he was later grateful to be rid of her, for he told me that it was a petrifying experience to be in the same aircraft with her, never knowing what impulse in her would put them both in danger and he unable to anticipate or do anything about it.' She lengthened her face in pretended discontent with what she had said. 'It isn't much, is it? All stuff that's over the hill, though it might throw some light on what she had inside her head.'

'Interesting,' Rogers said, 'though I don't know that I'd have liked to do any rock climbing with her.' He was acquiring a respect for a woman whose photograph probably did her wild spirit less than justice. 'Do you know whether she took up with a less apprehensive boyfriend afterwards?'

She pushed out her lower lip. 'I wasn't doing an Agony Aunt interview,' she said, reasonably mildly considering, 'so don't get all hot and bothered about him. He's one of our more respectable staff members and a Seventh Day Adventist on top of it. I'll ask him if you insist, but I don't believe he'd know or choose to tell me if he did.'

'I'm not insisting on anything,' he said amiably, 'but try it. Is that the lot?' His trout was now a fleshless skeleton and he wanted nothing more but coffee.

'Apart from what you are about to tell me, yes it is.' She was still fiddling with her whisky glass, having repeatedly diluted its contents until its amber colour had fled.

'Don't bother to take your notebook out,' he said. 'I'm sorry, but much as I'd like there to be, there isn't going to be much from me. What little I have is either unimportant, unchecked hearsay or potentially slanderous.' He was amiably pleasant with her because that was an aspect of himself she seemed to have the temperament to draw out. 'Will you have a coffee with me while I sort out what I can give you?'

Ordering two coffees and deciding that she would respect any remarks he made as confidential until he said otherwise, he disclosed what he knew about the missing brown Mini Travel- ler, gave her a three-second viewing of the blown-up photo- graph of Daphne Gosse – she said, 'She is rather attractive, isn't she?' – and told her that he believed, without any likelihood of evidence coming forward to support it, that it had been Mrs Gosse's intention to divorce her husband, which therefore heightened by inference the probability of her having left him of her own accord.

'And that's it?' she queried when he had finished, not visibly unhappy about the paucity of what he had told her.

'There is just an odd shot,' he said. 'Assuming she's toddled off with an adulterous boyfriend, where – as a woman without a police-oriented mind – would you suggest we start looking?' He wasn't expecting a useful answer to such a disingenuous question, nor could he, but thought that it might encourage her into a closer co-operation.

'I do wish you wouldn't underrate my knowing how the police service operates,' she replied tersely, though only slightly irritated. 'I do know that a detective superintendent wouldn't waste his time over a married woman he believes has only left her husband for another man. Not with a situation that warrants no more than the filling out of a form and feeding it into the force computer.' She made a noise in her throat that could indicate strong disagreement. 'If you hadn't believed there was some substance in that Personal column ad we passed on to you, you wouldn't be sitting here now and squeezing what you can out of me.' Not waiting for whatever answer he might be contriving from that, she said accusingly, 'And more to the point, there has to be something relevant to Mrs Gosse's disappearance in your speaking for such a long time to that man you picked up in your car.'

He laughed away any suggestion of importance she might be attaching to his conversation with McCausland. 'A wholly mistaken assumption,' he said. Bending his facts a little, his face straight, he explained, 'He's a police pensioner who's long gone past noticing anything much. He wasn't any help and isn't, anyway, the kind of man to be overly gabby. Certainly not with investigative reporters. Not even with one so attractive and persuasive as Miss Gallagher of the *Daily Echo*.'

'That's a put-off and doesn't get you absolution,' she said. 'I was told that Mrs Gosse has a sister with whom she was very close.' She was gazing at him searchingly. 'You know?'

'I know of her.' He thought she was trying to catch him in his dissembling again. 'I know where she lives and I've already made an appointment to see her. Until I have, I'm afraid she has to stay under wraps.'

He didn't want any more questions to ward off, any likely to disrupt the growing warmth between them. He said, checking the time on his wrist-watch, 'I'm sorry, but I do have to go. So, please, no more questions for the moment.' He changed the tone of his voice to a more friendly one. 'Liz – if I may call you that – I really am grateful for what you've told me. If you're free tomorrow evening and wish to, I'd appreciate it if you'd join me here for a meal.' He added hastily, 'That is, of course, unless there's somebody who's likely to object. And if there is, we can always call it a press conference. Or a working breakfast if that should be more convenient.'

She stared at him quizzically. 'You're being too nice and, I think, a little obvious. But why a breakfast, working or otherwise?' There was now amusement in her voice. 'I mean, it *is* only a meal you presumably have in mind? Not our making love together?'

Rogers recognized that he could back off quite easily from a situation – if there were a situation – that he hadn't consciously provoked, but he was damned if he would. He liked her and he was going to accept that their warming attitudes to each other – instant attraction and a need to do something about it was never out of the picture for him – and the almost non-committal suggestion in her words, could mean what, in fact, he was wishing them to mean.

'Do you know, the thought never entered my head,' he said with a grin that she could accept as a lie to it, 'but now that you mention it . . .' He trailed off in what he thought was a fail-safe situation that left its consummation in her hands, though he knew as definitely as he ever would that the matter was already settled. Then he added, holding her gaze, 'Let's say nineish tomorrow for the meal, shall we?'

'I'll be here,' she said, although now managing to look

irritatingly enigmatic like most women did on the approach to somebody's bedroom door.

It was still raining when they left to collect their respective cars. For Rogers, it dampened nothing but his hair and trench-coat now that he thought that he could happily look forward to the promise of something he had always found to be far more fragrant and psychologically uplifting than the day-to-day mechanics of a possible murder investigation.

9

At a quarter to ten, a dampish and wholly sober Rogers was sitting at the bar counter of the Headquarters' Police Club and glumly drinking a non-alcohol lager, not the most exhilarating activity in the world, but better than returning too early to his wifeless apartment. But only minimally better, for, the bar being well attended, the air held within its walls was over-hot and blue with the haze of cigarette smoke. He was presently – only temporarily, he hoped to God – a man without life-supporting alcohol, tobacco or any approvable access to a sexual relation-ship. He felt the need, he had been dourly thinking, to go outside and howl at the moon – had there been one that evening, and had it not been raining so hard.

When Lingard entered the bar in search of him, the prospect of a further discussion on Mrs Gosse's disappearance was almost a relief. His second-in-command took the stool next to him and ordered a Pernod. 'You look as if you're about to lay a square egg, George,' he said easily.

'True,' Rogers growled, thinking that it might be nice, and would certainly be a change, to see him dressed not so decid-edly dandified. 'But only since I saw you coming through the door. Aren't you chancing your arm with that stuff?'

Lingard's drink had arrived and he poured iced water into it, giving it the appearance of skimmed milk. 'I have it judged to a millilitre,' he said, 'if you're thinking of one of our friendly colleagues sticking a breathalyser into my face.'

Its pungent aniseed smell had reached Rogers's nose and he made a face indicating his distaste. 'Frog's rotgut,' he said dismissively. 'Before you fall over, tell me something useful, such as what have you brought out from St Boniface's.'

Lingard gave him what he had since written down in his pocket-book after the interview, with his opinion, having then distanced himself from any influence Henbest might have exerted on him by virtue of his immediate presence and personality. 'I liked the old boy,' he finished, 'and I wouldn't argue if you said that he was far too naïve and kind in his assessment of Mrs Gosse. On top of which, he was a man who I thought protested too vigorously against the suggestion that she had danced attendance on him for an evening or two.'

'I was half-way towards believing Gosse when he told me that she was undoubtedly having it off on the side with an unknown seducer,' Rogers said reflectively, 'so don't scrub him off our list too impulsively, though I'm more inclined to agree with you about the stubbled man with the bad temper. You've given him the treatment?'

'Naturally,' Lingard assured him. 'A full circulation under Identity Sought. It shouldn't take more than a month or so to unearth him from a county population knocking on four hundred and sixty thousand plus. Provided, that is, we don't have anything else to do.'

Rogers knew that his second-in-command wasn't being too serious. 'I'm credibly informed that half the adult population are females,' he said, 'and I doubt that many of them are called Simon and have designer beards.'

'Something I overlooked,' Lingard smiled back at him. 'Give me until tomorrow.'

'Before I forget it, had you considered friend Henbest as our mystery writer of personal ads?'

'A pox on it!' Lingard said under his breath, visibly put out of countenance. 'Sorry, George. I'd put my mind on the hyoscine business and overlooked it. At the time I thought it an odd thing to allege; in particular, the loss of memory bit.'

'Yes, it is.' Rogers was reaching back in his memory. 'I researched on the stuff three or four years back when we were sorting out who'd poisoned that chap Knostig with it. Remember? If I can recall, it's used medicinally, so Gosse wouldn't have any problems about getting his hands on it. It's poison, of course, and you could find it much too easily in a salad of Henbane, Woody Nightshade and Thorn Apple among others, if you care for that sort of thing. Nor does it take much more than a grain or two of it to be lethal.' He mused on that, knowing it to be only man's general disinterest in wild plants that made unusual the use of such easily acquired deadly poisons. 'The loss of memory – if it's true – is interesting because somewhere in the back of my mind I've a recollection of the barrister who defended Crippen the poisoner making an issue of his use of the hyoscine that killed his wife. He argued, if I'm remembering correctly, that it was given to her not only to make her unconscious, but also unaware later that she had been unconscious, while Crippen, presumably, was doing his stuff with Ethel le Neve. Ah,' he said, clearly faced with an imponderability, 'I've missed out there, haven't I? If all that's so, how would Mrs Gosse *know* that she'd lost her memory or, in fact, had been given hyoscine? She wouldn't, would she? Which, at the moment, doesn't help much unless we can work out if and why Gosse did it, because it sounds about as daft as her saying that she was being guarded from an attack by her husband by a private investigator. You'll be checking on that in the morning, I'm sure?'

'Egad, George, it's already under way,' Lingard protested. He drank an inch of his Pernod, then charged his nostrils with Attar of Roses. 'As was the searching of the canal until darkness closed it down and the squad was send home to thaw out and be fumigated. We start again at first light, but I say now that from what I've been told it's turning out to be a fairly hopeless undertaking.'

Rogers had never thought much of the supposed moral felicities of no alcohol, no tobacco and the unnatural denial of occasional fornication so, watching Lingard's noticeable enjoyment of two of those heinous vices, did not particularly do so now. 'I'm beginning not to like the sound of it, David,' he said, determined on a little pessimism. 'I've a premonition – one with dark grey clouds hanging all over it – that something nasty's going to happen and not about to do us any good. Though under different circumstances I might doubt the bulk of what we've dug out about Mrs Gosse, there's enough that's acceptable in it to make the back of my neck prickle. Paranoiac or not, nonsensical as it may sound, she's said it. If we don't do something about it and she really has been murdered, then some brainy bugger not too remote from the Chief Constable is going to be wise after the event and jump on us for not reading the sacrificial chicken's entrails the right way round.' He eyed Lingard appraisingly, knowing precisely how he was going to feel. 'So, on top of searching the canal, I want a bigger effort with more men and aimed at extending it to other likely places.'

'Such as?' Lingard questioned, his narrow face inscrutable in passing back to Rogers what he knew had at best to be guesswork.

'For God's sake, David! Somewhere a body can lie undiscovered for three weeks. We're not looking for somebody's lost handbag. She must be about nine stone of flesh and bone and difficult to hide for too long if she's dead.' The question had irritated Rogers, though only by its unanswerability. 'Any woods and copses we happen to have left to us. The moors. Waste ground that's knee-high in rubbish or has been used for fly-tipping. Under somebody's bloody bed, or in his coal-shed. Anywhere, just so long as we make the effort and are seen to be doing things that somebody believes are useful, even though they're getting us nowhere and are never likely to. You work it out and get it organized.'

He drank some of his denatured lager, then told Lingard about his interview with Durker. 'It's our bad luck,' he said, 'that he's an uptight bugger suffering from an excess of lawyer's lockjaw, and I doubt that I'll get any more change from him in the future than I got this afternoon.'

'But you're not leaving it at that?' Lingard asked, knowing he wouldn't, that somehow it meant another chore for himself.

'Not for one moment,' Rogers grunted. 'It's Kyberd I want to see and intend to, so I've put Coltart on to finding where he is. I get my holidays spoiled often enough, so why shouldn't he? You've the run-down on Gosse I wanted?'

'I gave the detail to Sergeant Hawkins – he's known in the

department, if not to your eminence, as Passion Hawkins, by the way – since when I've heard nothing. But,' he added confidently, 'I'm sure that he's most of the way there with one of Gosse's girls and with some no doubt interesting intelligence to come.'

'In the meantime,' Rogers claimed unblushingly, 'I've dug out some information that Gosse keeps a bilge keeler boat at Ullsmouth, so I've put the Section there on locating it and reporting back. It's almost certain to have been laid up for the winter so there should be no difficulty there.' He didn't think it worth remarking on what else he had learned from Liz Gallagher about Mrs Gosse. Somehow he knew that Lingard, though he might not mention it, would put the wrong construction on his meeting her in the restaurant of the Minister Hotel.

'Do you know why Ullsmouth, when Thurnholme is miles nearer and has more facilities?' Lingard had pointed out what Rogers had already tossed around in his mind. Ullsmouth, not much larger than a village, was situated on an estuary, a sea inlet at the mouth of the River Ull. Further from Abbotsburn than was Thurnholme, its use was confined largely to river craft and it was correspondingly less popular with those people who found pleasure in getting soaked to the skin or being violently sick in hard-to-handle small boats.

'I have thought since,' Rogers said, 'that it could have been more convenient, less open to discovery, for Gosse to meet and associate with the married woman his wife mentioned to your headmaster. That's assuming, of course, that he'd be less well-known at Ullsmouth than he might be at Thurnholme.'

'The boat a temporary coffin for a dead Mrs Gosse?' Lingard suggested.

'It's a thought,' Rogers agreed, 'though her being found there – I'm sure she'd be beginning to smell very sick-making by now – wouldn't give Gosse much chance of coping with some rather unpleasant questions. Still, we shall see sometime tomorrow if all goes well.' Smothering a yawn, he finished off his lager with a grimace and climbed from his stool, convinced that the hubbub coming from a double handful of off-duty policemen drinking the genuinely alcoholic was giving him earache. 'I'm

69

for bed, David, to sleep off my feeling that somebody somewhere is busy lighting a firework under our rear ends in order
to compound our confusion.'

Splashing his car through the dark late-night streets, he was
wishing that he hadn't mentioned to Lingard what had been in
fact an offshoot, and a highly imaginative one, of what would
be a short-lived pessimism about almost everything coming
within the survey of his awareness. As a student graduated
from the force's tough and difficult driving instruction school,
it was ingrained habit that he kept himself informed through
his rear-view mirror of whatever was happening behind his
exhaust pipe. Such as the small car, an unidentifiable dark mass
with narrowly spaced headlights, which had been kept several
car-lengths away while turning with him through the last four
uncontrolled junctions.

Approaching and reaching the Head Post Office, he used his
direction indicators and pulled into the kerb, climbing out into
the rain and going through the motions of posting his pocket-
book. The car following him had been halted way back, inconveniently midway between street lights. Though he could give
it only the briefest of glances, he thought it had to be the
obviously unsatisfied Liz Gallagher's Volkswagen. It was, he
complained to himself, disappointingly anticlimactic in what it
could have promised his investigation.

Re-entering his car, apparently without arousing any suspicion in Gallagher that she had been detected in whatever she
was up to, he drove away, seeing the small car pulling out and
following behind. She had a lot to learn about trailing behind
the sources of what she and her paper considered to be
publishable news. And with her now in his mind, he thought
that for himself – never a man fast with a trouser zip – there
had to be a life of occasional friendly intercourse beyond the
frettings and frustrations of his job. If she chose to put herself,
unwitting of his half-formed intention, within the orbit of what
he considered that life of occasional friendly intercourse should
be, then bad luck, Gallagher, or good luck, Gallagher, whichever she would eventually determine it to have been. Because
of what she was doing, he felt that he could be uncharacteristically ruthless with her. Well, nearly so, he qualified, as he

braked to a halt in the resident's parking space he held outside his apartment.

Not looking to see what she was doing about parking, he dismounted from his car, locked its door and, before crossing the pavement, looked up through the veil of rain at the apartment block as though locating a particular floor. The entrance to the building was deeply porched and, entering its darkness, he stood out of immediate sight against the corner wall, amusement on his face.

When he was near believing that he had been mistaken and was preparing to admit he was a fool, he heard a woman's footfalls approaching from outside, climbing the four steps and then pausing. After a few seconds of silence, a slender rain-coated figure, recognizable even in the semi-darkness as that of Gallagher, stepped cautiously into the porch, passing close enough to the almost stopped-breathing Rogers for him to smell the unsettling perfume she wore. A column of three white cards at the side of bell-pushes on the door frame, displaying the names of the occupiers of the apartments, was dimly visible and she peered closely at each card as if trying to read the names.

From behind her, Rogers broke the silence by saying sternly, 'I think you'd see better if you used a torch, Miss Gallagher,' the touch of his finger on her shoulder as light as a whisper.

She had jerked around with a sudden small shriek, her eyes wide with shock, her hand flying to her mouth, then beginning to show a growing indignation. 'Damn you!' she cried shakily. 'You frightened me.' Fighting back from the shock, her eyes on his, she snapped at him, 'Do you understand what you could have done? I might have dropped dead for all you knew! Or damned well cared!'

'And for all I knew, you might have been somebody aiming to stick a knife into me,' he said, exaggerating a little, realizing that she hadn't at any time been about to collapse on him. 'I thought we'd arranged to meet tomorrow, not tonight.' He was drily mocking. 'Couldn't you wait?'

She was recovering fast. 'I don't think that's funny at all. You weren't all that open with me this evening and I was right in believing you'd be off interviewing somebody you didn't want me to know about.' She looked hard at him, trying to see in the deep gloom how he had taken that, then said less aggressively, 'I imagine I should apologize, though I can't be too terribly sorry in view of what you didn't tell me. I do still have my job to do and I never said I wouldn't go on doing my own investigating.'

'And I'm sorry that I frightened you, together with an admission that you made a nice professional job of shadowing me,' he said, lying for the sake of her pride. 'But my not baring my bosom enough for you isn't much of a justification for haunting me, is it? Not so soon after I thought we'd come to a sort of friendly agreement.' He shook his head, trying to look rueful and admiring at the same time. 'Still, let's forget that, for I must admit you've managed to hit the right button tonight. Actually, you've followed me to the home of a significantly dodgy character who's been the subject of my close interest for many years, and who is definitely connected with what might have happened to Mrs Gosse.'

She stared at what she could see of him in disbelief. 'Do you mind if I doubt I can trust you when you're being so generous with your information? Why are you telling me this?'

'I never lie to anyone for whom I have a liking,' he protested, smiling his good will, sure that she could hear it if not see it. He produced a pen torch from inside his trenchcoat and shone its narrow beam on the middle card of the column that gave his name as the occupier. 'Read it, Liz. You can interview him yourself if you wish.'

She read it, remaining silent for long seconds before turning back to him. In the reflected light from the torch her eyes had softened and she looked as though she had recovered most of her damaged assurance. 'I've made something of a fool of myself, haven't I? she said.

'Not really, but I am off duty and conceivably of no present interest to the *Daily Echo*. So unless you were planning to do a Mata Hari on me, I'm afraid that you're on to a loser.'

'You think that I might be?' She was suddenly serious, a little forbidding.

'My witless humour,' he said amiably, unvaliantly backtracking from any serious suggestion of an in-bed intelligence gathering.

72

'I see.' Her face was expressionless. 'You do live here?'

That was something he could have been waiting for. Having read the card, she manifestly knew that and it was over to him. 'My one and only dust-ridden hovel,' he said lightly, his door key ready in his hand. 'I share it with a couple of house plants, a music centre and a sideboard of strong drink. You've probably noticed it's raining outside and not a night for travelling abroad, so would you care to join me? Possibly in getting sloshed as a defence against the evils of our society?'

She stared at him again – this time it felt as if his heart was interfering with his breathing – a woman full of serious and intense silences. 'I think I'd like that,' she said gravely, 'if it's all right to leave my car where it is in somebody else's parking space.'

'You must, I'm afraid, do your own bleeding about that.' Then he murmured 'Dammit' soundlessly to himself as he fitted his key into the door lock and ushered her in. Being already there, he had once again been robbed of the opportunity of uttering those immortally profound words, surely first said by a fig-leafed Adam to Eve, 'Your place, or mine?'

10

It had been what he should have expected, Rogers supposed as, furious with that which foul circumstances had again dumped on his lap, he began dressing himself.

In his cramped apartment, which he believed originally to have been built and furnished for living in by necessarily tasteless dwarfs, he himself had started on his intent to seduce with a large measure of undiluted whisky, Liz Gallagher staying with her single watered-down parody of an alcoholic drink. She had, she explained initially, to remember that later she would be driving her car in a running of the gauntlet of night-shift police officers, few of whom would be over-extended to the point where they would wish to miss checking a solitary motorist out in the small hours.

Rogers had accepted this to mean that she had changed her mind – a not uncommon trait in women finding themselves on the verge of co-operating in matters of sex – and intended to stay only for a social drink and a few polite pleasantries. During them, however, she had told him that after their earlier conversation she had telephoned her Seventh Day Adventist informant, asking him if he knew whether the then Daphne Naylor had transferred her affections from him to another man, and, if she had, did he know to whom. He had said yes she had, and to a married man he refused adamantly to put a name to, though he had seen them out together often enough. That, Liz said, had been final, and Rogers was not to push it further unless he wished to risk losing whatever collaboration he and she seemed now to be enjoying. 'It might have been that man was you,' she had said, transparently with her tongue in cheek. 'Then how would you have liked your name given?'

Having seated her at one side of an uninspiring electric fire and himself on the other, he had left himself with a problem in the manner of moving a piece in chess, to somehow get Liz and himself to occupy the same air space. A difficult manoeuvre, he guessed, believing that at some time she had been badly bruised emotionally and understandably seemed not to have too high a regard for the male animal. In between their exchanging somewhat awkward flippancies she had, several times, stared searchingly at him, as if asking herself whether a once sated detective superintendent could be trusted not to run off with her handbag should she have possessed one, and palpably being unable to decide on the answer.

Rogers had tried to reflect in his face all the virtues of his profession and a subtle sort of rejection of what she appeared to be thinking. In his adolescence, his first attempt at securing a more intimate relationship with an older girl – she had had red hair and freckles and a father in Her Majesty's Diplomatic Service – had resulted in the freezing rebuff, 'What on earth do you think you are doing?'; which was then unanswerable, did terrible things to his ego from which it had never completely recovered and now tended to dissipate any masculine urge to hairy ruthlessness he might otherwise have had. Not, he thought behind the geniality he was creaming over her, that she was being particularly forthcoming herself.

He had then stood, saying, 'Would you care for another whisky?'; trying this time to look deprived.

She, placing her unemptied glass on the carpet beside her, rose from her chair, her dark eyes unfathomable as she moved to stand in front of him and said in a quite normal voice, 'I think not. Not a drink, anyway.'

She was then so close to him – he could feel the heat of her body and believe that he could taste her perfume on his lips – that it had been made easy for him. And then surprising him with the sinewy strength in the arms with which she held him and the thinness of her almost breastless body which went on to give him so much. Apart from his accidentally kicking over the glass she had earlier placed on the carpet they were occupying in their furthering of a closer co-operation between the press and the police, he knew that for both of them it had been a surprisingly pleasant, wholly civilized and uncommitted experience. And he did think that she rather liked him, though he had a minor reservation when she murmured something about his being very definitely user-friendly.

After she left him – he never knew, and didn't wish to know, what problems she might have found in collecting her car from someone else's parking space – he took a quick shower and dropped as naked as he had left it into bed.

When the telephone bell hauled him up from the dark velvety depths of undreaming repletion, he was fuddled and partially hung-over, and for quite some time couldn't understand that it was half-past three in the morning with the duty chief inspector at Headquarters telling him that there had been a fire in a house in Ratfyn Road and that the householder, a Mr Clifford Gosse, had been found battered to death in his sitting-room.

Having put the receiver down and disconnected, he hoped that he had been sufficiently understandable in the stupor of his sudden awakening to have ordered the chief inspector to put into effect the routine calling out of the services and personnel he might need in the preliminary stages of a murder investigation; also to put into operation the informing of those who had a need to know, that he was on the job and presumed to be bright-eyed and functioning on all cylinders.

11

The only advantages of being dragged out of bed in the early hours that Rogers would accept were that it had stopped raining and that the air was untainted and didn't smell of something chemical. The moon at which he had earlier needed to howl in frustration had the sky to itself, and he hardly needed his headlights in its ashen illumination of deserted wet streets. Reaching the residential area of the town where roads and avenues replaced streets, he imagined he could feel the shut-inness, the quiet breathing sleep of those whom he sometimes facetiously called his parishioners.

Fully awake now and believing that, given luck, he might reach his next birthday *compos mentis*, he turned into Ratfyn Road, passing a fire appliance on its way out. A good omen that, he thought with an unusual optimism for four o'clock in the morning, and perhaps it also wouldn't be too obvious that in his hurry he hadn't waited to shave his whiskers. Parking his car behind two police cars outside Firozabad House, he climbed out, noting that one was occupied by its driver, who would be routinely waiting at his open radio connection with Head-quarters Information Room. There were no curious spectators – which was understandable – but he did see slight movement in darkened windows on the opposite side of the road. A uni-formed PC, placed on guard at the gate, saluted Rogers as he passed through it.

Inspector Llewellyn was standing in the drive waiting, and Rogers joined him in a moonlight that seemed to give off chilliness, bathing the white-painted house in a leprous lividity and casting deep shadows. Yellow light shone from the win-dows and from the open front door, which looked as if it had been attacked by a fireman's heavy-duty axe. Holes had been broken in the glass of the upstairs windows and two on the

76

ground floor had been smashed in a welter of lozenged glass and lead strip, showing fire-blackening on the white plaster above them. A gutted easy chair with its foam stuffing protruding had been thrown out on to a lawn trampled to muddy grass.

'Give me a run-down on what's happened before I go in to see the body,' Rogers said to the heavily moustached and blue-jowled Llewellyn.

Putting it together from the inspector's volubility, it appeared to Rogers that a Mr Robert Pryke, living in the same road, was returning in his car with his wife to his home at twenty to three that morning when he saw flames in the ground floor windows of what he knew to be Gosse's house; obviously, he had said, the curtains were ablaze. He had stopped his car and sent his wife on home, then reversed to the drive's entrance. From there, he ran to the door and banged on it to rouse the occupants, but had no response. There were no lights on and none was switched on. He tried to open the front door but it was locked, as was the back door when he ran around to try that. While there, he heard the dogs barking and he opened the door of their cage, though when they made no move to leave he left them to go when they wished to.

Pryke had said that he had then rather panicked, throwing pebbles up at the bedroom windows. When that had met with no response he ran to his own home – it was only three buildings away – and told his wife to dial 999 for the fire service. Returning to Firozabad House he met a Mr Frederick McCausland who had obviously come from his bed because he was wearing an overcoat over his pyjamas. He said that he had been awakened by Pryke's banging on the doors, and was then doing the same thing himself. It was he – McCausland – who broke the glass in the upstairs windows by throwing large stones taken from the garden at the rear, trying to wake Gosse who, he said, was probably on his own in the house.

McCausland had, Llewellyn said, caught up the dogs and taken them to his own house next door, returning as the fire tender was arriving. Pryke had, on its arrival, moved his car to his home, then also returned to the scene. Both men had left when the fire was quite quickly put out, during which time the body had been discovered. Both were then asked to hold themselves available for later questioning.

Llewellyn had, before this, arrived there with a PC, prepared to arrange whatever control would be needed at what was then a not too unusual house fire. That a man had died in the house was discovered only when one of the firemen, checking out the final damping down of the fire, had found the body wedged behind a sofa which had been almost untouched by the fire, though burning papers had been placed on it. When he – Llewellyn – had entered the room and looked at the man's body, it was clear that he had been fatally injured by repeated blows to the head. He had then fetched in Mr McCausland who had told him he was a neighbour and a retired police inspector from the MPD – that had patently been a gold-plated seal of approval in Llewellyn's eyes – and he had immediately identi-fied the body as being that of Clifford Gosse, in whom, he had said, he was sure Superintendent Rogers would be extremely interested.

'You seem bent on leaving me with nothing to do,' Rogers said amiably, 'though I suppose I'd better have a look at the body now that I'm here.'

Following Llewellyn, he stopped at the forcibly opened door and examined its mortise lock, finding the key to be still on its inside with the latch bolt extended in the locked position. It had been a handsome door, now splintered beyond satisfactory repair.

The hall with its flight of stairs leading to the upper floor appeared untouched by fire, though smelling strongly of smoke, its carpeting marked by the muddy boots of firemen. But the worst smell, the foul stench of drenched ash, came from the open door of the sitting-room in which the blaze had been first seen.

Entering it, Rogers saw that the actual destruction by burning had been largely confined to what was near the windows, though all four walls and the ceiling had been coated with a greasy brownish-black that shaded to saffron on the side away from the blaze. There was charring and scorching beyond the fire's apparent seat in the two now curtainless window embra-sures, and soot had covered the furniture, furnishings and pictures with an opaque film of wet nastiness. The missing curtains had been transmuted into heaps of slushy ash below where they had hung. Other soft furnishings, burned and unburned alike, had been pulled down or off and hosed into unidentifiable shapelessness.

A small bureau that had been charred and blackened had had its desk flap opened. On it was a scattered disorder of paper ash. Below it, on the carpet, was more paper ash, as there was on the seat cushions of a sofa set diagonally across the corner farthest from the windows.

'Arson without a doubt,' Rogers muttered, not intending to illuminate the strikingly obvious, but merely to confirm it to himself. Louder, he said, 'I'm surprised it didn't finish off the whole house.'

'The fire sub-officer was sure that the furnishings, though possibly not the curtains, had been treated with a fire retardant,' Llewellyn said. 'He seemed surprised too, though he thought that the fire had just been started when Mr Pryke saw the flames.'

'Which means that whoever started it wasn't too far away and Pryke might have passed him without knowing. And the fire was almost certainly not premeditated, otherwise petrol or paraffin would have been used on the furniture, not burning paper.' Rogers was thinking past that. 'So it'd possibly be intended to cover up what would probably have been the also unpremeditated killing of Gosse. You said he was behind the sofa?' He moved to it over the water-sodden carpet – its colour had been deepened to what could only be called a blackish green – and looked into the triangle of space now occupied by death.

For Rogers, any dislike or antagonism he felt for a person was invariably made a nothing when he saw that person dead, incapable of any defence and somehow to be pitied in what the detective saw as the last and most feared extremity; particularly should the ending have been slow and painful. And Gosse's ending could have been both. Now soaking wet as a result of the hosing, he lay on his side with his shoulder jammed into the angle of the skirting boards. His face, for the most part the left side, was a picture of dreadful ruin; bloody and disfiguring flaps of torn skin, swollen purple contusions, all testifying to the savagery of the attack on him. If there was any expression that death had left in what had been his features, it was fear, though the half-closed eyes were dulled in their apparently earnest scrutiny of the back of the sofa. The flesh on the back of the left hand was torn and bloody, the fingers curled; clearly, in Rogers's opinion, a defensive injury. There was little soot on his flesh or on his wet pyjamas and his feet were bare. While there were driblets and smears of blood fouling the shoulders and collar of the jacket, the minimal amount of it on the carpet under his head made it likely that he had been bludgeoned elsewhere in the house. That supposition would be confirmed or disputed when he was more or less taken apart in the mortuary by Dr Twite, the Home Office appointed pathologist, who was said – with only a little exaggeration – to wield his scalpel like a two-handed broadsword.

Breaking what had been a contemplative silence and recovered enough to be almost cheerful, he said to Llewellyn, 'We'll shortly be having the Murder Bus arrive and an inundation, I hope, of CID personnel who'll all be extremely irritable at being dragged from their beds. You stay outside and hold them in check until I've found something for them to do. When Dr Twite, Mr Lingard, the coroner's officer and Sergeant Magnus arrive, push them through to me if I haven't surfaced by then.'

With Llewellyn gone, Rogers moved slowly around the room in a search for the usefully significant, cursing the soggy ash-covered carpet for what it was doing to his recently bought Oxford shoes and socks. There were filing compartments in the opened bureau, which at a guess had held the papers with which the blaze had been started. Those papers, having gone through fire and the flood of a fire service's hosing, would plainly give little or none of their contents under laboratory testing. Of the two drawers in the bureau, one held only a telephone directory and a *Yellow Pages*. The other contained a cased portable typewriter, which he removed for later examination and a comparison of its typescript with that used for the personal advertisement application sent to the *Daily Echo*.

Moving from the bureau, he found part of what he thought

must be the instrument of Gosse's disfigurement and death when he used the toe of his shoe to straighten out a rug that had been bundled into the centre of the room. It was the upper half of a broken walking stick, its handle the solid brass head of a duck. A visual examination of the duck's head revealed no obvious signs of blood though it was smeared with dark wet ash and rug fibres. Swinging it in his hand, he felt it to be heavy enough, the flat beak sharp enough, to have caused the havoc inflicted on Gosse's face. Whether it belonged to him, or had been brought in by his killer, was a question Rogers decided to worry about later. Its presence in the sitting-room seemed to be against his theory that Gosse had been bludgeoned elsewhere in the house, and that was something else to worry about later. Now knowing what he was looking for, he found the bottom half of the stick lying against the kerb of the hearth.

If Gosse drank alcohol or smoked, there was no evidence of it in the sitting-room. Rogers couldn't help but think that if he had done neither, nor had sexual access to his wife, then life for him must have been definitely on the dark-grey side. There was no photograph of either of the Gosses, a lack he would some-how have to remedy.

The dining-room and kitchen revealed nothing of interest, not even the unwashed dishes and remnants of Gosse's last meal. Again, there was no evidence that Gosse had ever comforted himself over the loss of his wife by hitting the bottle. Rogers was beginning to feel profoundly sorry for him.

There were three bedrooms upstairs. The largest contained a double bed, one side of which had been slept in, and from which a lonely Gosse had manifestly risen to go downstairs to his death. If he had earlier done any entertaining of another woman, there were no signs of it visible to Rogers. A second bedroom with a neatly made-up bed in it, a small wardrobe of a woman's clothing and a dressing-table loaded with an array of cosmetic jars and tubes, was almost certainly the room to which Gosse had complained his wife had moved to escape his snoring. To Rogers, leaving behind clothing and cosmetics seemed not the action of a wife departing freely in the absence of her husband. The third bedroom – he did no more than put his head around the door – was obviously unused, smelling of stale air and containing an abundance of dead flies.

While doing his first-arrival searching, he had, unrewarded, made visual checks on the windows in all rooms for signs of insecurity or of a breaking and entering. He finished at the rear door opening out from the end of the hall passage; its cylinder lock being still with its bolt in the locked position and its key hung on a hook on the back of the door. Rogers was satisfied as much as he could be that no forcible entry had been made anywhere, and it seemed a high-level probability that either the killer had possessed a key or Gosse himself had opened one of the doors to allow his killer's entry. Theoretically, the latter seemed the more probable, until his mind raised the question; would a man already in bed answer a knock on his door, or let in an expected visitor, without first putting on a dressing-gown and slippers?

Impelled to check, he returned to Gosse's bedroom, finding a dressing-gown hanging behind the door and a pair of leather slippers beneath his side of the bed.

Returning downstairs, he hoped that he hadn't missed anything of obvious significance. If he had, it would certainly be found by Sergeant Magnus, an experienced and gifted scenes-of-crime searcher to whom the macroscopic and the almost unfindable were old friends.

Cars arriving in the road and the sound of voices in the drive interrupted the flow of his thinking and he returned to the hall, still feeling reasonably amiable but prepared to give vent to some irritation at what he considered an unnecessary delay in their arriving.

12

Dr Wilfred Twite, BA, graduate in Morbid Pathology, a gourmand and an unashamed predator on other men's wives – all of whom must have had a perverse thing about oversized pathologists wearing Mexican-style moustaches and side-whiskers – had demanded the removal to elsewhere of the sofa and was now sitting hunched on his hams, interesting himself in the outer shell of the dead Gosse. He was grossly fat – how in the hell did he ever manage it, Rogers had often wondered – and, when not called out at four-thirty on a cold and dark morning, was cheerfully ebullient. Dressed quite unlike the conventional medical man in that most of his clothing was expensively trendy in pastel colours and unusual patterns – he was now in an off-white fur coat that made him resemble a squat polar bear – he used clothes, in Rogers's opinion, as a visual aphrodisiac for his unlikely conquests. Unconventional as he was – slapdash evisceration being the name of his game – he knew how to find exactly where in the internal mechanisms of the body death had managed to pull the plug.

Wearing clear plastic gloves, he was feeling with fat fingers the flesh of the skull beneath the wet sandy hair, screwing his eyes against the smoke rising from the scented cigarette held in his mouth.

Rogers, standing behind him and holding the beam of a powerful handlamp on what Twite was doing, waited for his provisional finding on what was manifestly obvious; which left him free to engage most of his mind in trying to work out why, not how, Gosse had died. Being light years away from accepting that this was a case of a householder being killed because he had disturbed a homicidal burglar, Rogers was no nearer to having any idea of the real motive. Of one thing he was almost certain, Gosse's death had to be connected with his wife's disappearance. It had in it, he decided, an implication that disaster had also visited her, and it might be proper to consider her in the past tense. As for Gosse, whose mutilated face had lost all traces of the froggishness it held in life, his earlier antagonism and unlikeability could be sympathetically attributed to his worries about his missing wife eating large holes in his liver; possibly also worries about his business, his bank balances, and his hair falling out. And now all for nothing when death had made a futile nonsense of it.

Twite pushed his bulk upright, grunting his discomfort, and began to strip off his gloves. Lighting a fresh cigarette from the stub of the one he had been smoking and coughing wheezily, he said with a before-breakfast humour, 'If he hasn't been fed a dose of cyanide beforehand, old son, then it's going to be a finding of death from multiple injuries to the head. The blows to the face would be painful though not fatal, but there are two grossly depressed fractures of the skull that are possibly comminuted, and almost sure to have caused intracranial injuries that would be. He's as bad a case of a thoroughgoing beating as I've seen for some time. And that walking stick you found is likely to fit the bill for doing it.' While talking, he had been examining his shoes for signs of fouling and, from his expression, had found them.

'I can see he's been whacked about,' Rogers said. 'Perhaps more than was needed to shut him up, if that was the intention. It could be that there was personal animosity, or, perhaps, to ensure that an unexpected recognition went no further. Would you agree right-handed blows?'

'I'd be certain if, as I think, they were delivered from the front with both fractures being in the anterior parietal bone.' The pathologist was showing signs that he wanted to be away, and that was nothing new.

'You've a provisional time for his death?' Rogers asked. He thought cynically that he could now give ownership to a simplistic theory that pointed to Gosse having been killed by a short-tempered right-handed man or woman who, having regard to the walking stick, might limp, and who could be a smoker because he or she had handy in his pocket or her handbag a lighter or a box of matches.

Twite said, 'I'd say about the time the fire was started. But his having been exposed to a slight roasting and then given a good soaking, I could be wide of the mark. If you've finished with me I can confirm it or not after breakfast, which, no thanks to you, I damned well haven't had yet.'

'You're overdoing it, Wilfred,' the detective said, amiably sardonic. 'When did you ever do a post-mortem for me so quickly without being bribed or threatened?'

'Testes of the most corrupt to you, old son,' Twite replied. He and Rogers were friends of long enough standing to be able to cheerfully insult each other. 'Immediately after breakfast –

say eight o'clock? I've a five-star conference to attend at ten, so get your friend along to the mortuary *tout de suite* if you want him done today.'

When he had gone, driving away at a foolhardy speed in his elderly shark-snouted Citroën Safari, Rogers went outside to the oversized coach parked there for the use of the investigating team. When used by the CID, it was called the Murder Wagon, though it was officially designated as the Major Incident Mobile Office. There was for Rogers a satisfactory noise and movement behind its frosted glass windows and from the small compartments into which the interior had been divided, referred to exaggeratedly as offices. Sitting at a blotting pad-sized desk in the marginally larger compartment allocated to the senior officer in charge of whatever it was that justified the Murder Wagon's being called out, he hastened the writing up of his notes in his large scrawling italic and reviewed the action he had taken so far.

On Lingard's arrival, he had been detailed to organize door-to-door enquiries in the road at first light, in the meantime ensuring that no very early riser or night prowler escaped without being questioned. He was further required to arrange, also at first light, for a party of PCs to quarter and search with metal probes and a couple of police dogs every inch of the rear garden, with all those taking part to be psychologically primed to expect that a woman's body, probably badly decomposed, had been buried there. Further, they were to anticipate that Gosse's killer might have left footprints somewhere in soil softened by the earlier rain. The photographer had exposed coloured film of Gosse's body and the room in which he had been found, in close up and at wide angle. That completed, access had been allowed to Detective Sergeant Magnus to put the contents and inner structure of the house through the analysis of his close regard, together with an instruction first to check on cupboards and cabinets, the freezer and pantry, and, in particular the roof space or attic, for the dead body which might not anyway be found in the garden. It was all precautionary stuff that had to be gone through, arming Rogers against later questions motivated by hindsight from those in authority outside the force who would have had him open every cavity wall and rip up every floorboard in the house in his search for evidence.

Assured that McCausland would be waiting in anticipation of being interviewed, Rogers sent one of the floating DPCs to ask him if he would attend at the Murder Wagon. Being shown into the office, McCausland looked decidedly crumpled, though fully dressed, the plaid cap he wore seeming to be one of his permanencies. Stubble showed white on the creased flesh of his chin and jowls, and his eyes were heavily pouched. He managed a toothy grin as at Rogers's invitation he sat his stringy gauntness on a small flap like a shelf hinged to the wooden partition.

'I knew you'd have to call the Yard in before the night was through,' he said affably. Pouched though they might be, his faded blue eyes were alert, taking in everything of his surroundings, as well as apparently sizing up Rogers's attitude.

'Thank you for coming along.' Rogers, though maintaining geniality, put aside excessive matiness for a proper investigative attitude. 'A very busy man I hear; concerned in trying to wake up Gosse when his place was on fire and later identifying him for Inspector Llewellyn. Would you like to fill me in on the details?' In the oppressively claustrophobic office he could smell uncensoriously that his visitor had drunk a gin or two or more. He supposed that it didn't matter much what anybody drank in their seventies so long as it wasn't an excess of cocoa.

'There was something before all that,' McCausland said, 'though it mightn't be important because I dream a lot and I don't think I was properly awake at the time. I'm not a heavy sleeper and it was the next door dogs barking that woke me up. That was unusual, for though I know that terriers are noisy little sods, I've never heard them bark at night before. When they kept on like dogs do when there's more than one of 'em sounding off, I got out of bed to find out what was going on, seeing that that poor bloke Gosse's garden and his kennel are visible from our landing window.'

He was silent for a few moments, obviously sorting out what he was about to say. His black eyebrows, lifting skywards at the outer extremities and mobile in his use of them, looked an incongruity against his white hair and stubble. Rogers noticed that he hadn't again referred to Gosse as a nasty little bugger, which was understandable. 'There're tallish conifers and a six-foot wooden fence at the end of his garden,' he continued, 'and a narrow service lane over the other side that can take a Mini and not much else. I've got to be honest, chief, but it's a strong possibility that this is all a load of tit because I couldn't have been completely awake and I wouldn't want to mislead you. As you've seen for yourself, the moon's full on tonight and I saw, or thought I did, that one of the conifers was shaking as if someone was touching it and there was a shadow – a long shadow like a man's – coming from behind it until it moved and was gone. Then I heard, though not too clearly because the window was closed, what I took to be scraping noises as if somebody was scrabbling to get over the fence, only I couldn't see anything moving then and it could have come from any- where.' He shook his head, screwing his mouth in a grimace. 'Because the bloody dogs had stopped barking and I'm no longer a copper, because I wasn't so sure about it anyway and Esme was bitching about being woken up, I got back into bed. I see now that I could have waited and, bloody freezing though it was, listened to see if a car would be started up.'

'You're thinking that whoever it was would have come here by car, leaving it parked in a nearby road?' Rogers prompted him, knowing it was a policeman's reasoning that anybody bent on villainy would do much to avoid being surprised on the job without wheels.

'*If* I heard someone,' McCausland qualified, 'and *if* he didn't live hereabouts, when he'd be better without one.'

'You didn't mention this to Inspector Llewellyn,' Rogers pointed out, careful to avoid making it sound like a rebuke.

'No.' McCausland obviously wasn't taking it as one. 'It was only just before you sent for me that I decided to mention it at all because, honest to God, I really was half asleep when it happened and I'm still not sure I saw what I think I did, or whether I dreamed it.'

'That's me first thing in the morning; bleary-eyed and fogged up with lost sleep,' Rogers said, and it so often was. 'I think I'll accept that you saw it. Can you make a stab at what time it was?'

McCausland gave a short barking laugh. 'Time? I don't think then that I knew where I was, let alone the time. On top of which, I couldn't have been back asleep for more than a few minutes when Esme woke me and said that the dogs were at it again and that somebody was kicking up a hell of a row by banging on Gosse's door. So this time I put on my overcoat and shoes and went down to sort out whatever noisy bastard was doing it. There was nobody there, but I had a hell of a surprise to see that there was a fairish old flare-up in the lounge. I thought then that whoever had been kicking up the row was the one who'd started it. I ran back and shouted up to Esme to dial emergency for the brigade and then tried to raise Gosse by chucking rocks through what I took to be his bedroom windows. Bob Pryke came along shortly afterwards then and said he'd also been trying to wake him – which explained the row, of course – and that the fire brigade was on its way because he'd rung them too. Which they were, for they arrived almost straight away and just in time to stop us bashing in a window to find out what Gosse was up to.'

'When did you last see him, by the way? Apart from when he was dead, naturally.'

'When I was with you yesterday, though I must have heard him garaging his car at about seven last evening.'

'Had he had anyone call on him that you saw or heard?'

McCausland shook his head. 'Nothing,' he said. 'There was a film on the box I wanted to see and when that finished we went to bed.'

'I hear you're looking after the dogs?'

'There's nobody else to do it, is there? The little sods are in the lounge with Esme and she's making more fuss of 'em than she's ever made of me.' McCausland smiled, making it a humorous exaggeration.

'You wouldn't know of anyone in the road who might not have loved Gosse, would you?' Rogers asked poker-faced, almost adding 'Apart from yourself, of course', but holding it back. 'Or someone about here who might have been feeling more emotional than neighbourly about Mrs Gosse?'

'It's no to the first, though I wouldn't necessarily know. People around here tend to keep their own counsel and I don't blame 'em, for I suspect quite a few are having one thing or another off on the side. So far as she's concerned, work it out for yourself on the basis that to a long-serving married man, other men's wives must always look to be more attractive, more sexy. I wouldn't say that having had Gosse for a husband she'd consequently take her knickers off on her own doorstep, but there's always the probability that she had.'

'A succinct account of the human condition,' Rogers observed drily. 'I'd never worked it out to that extent. There's anything else?'

'No, except that I'm walking on my chinstrap.' He did look as if about to fall off his seat. 'If you've finished with me I'd like to get back to bed,' then adding glumly, 'If those bloody dogs aren't already in it.'

'You're a fraud, Fred. You probably think more of them than your wife does.' Rogers stood from his desk, ducking his head to avoid banging it on the low ceiling. 'I'm grateful,' he said. 'You've been a great help and we must get together in the club one evening.' He smiled. 'That is, if you can still convince your wife that you're only going out to buy yourself some cigarillos.'

Thin daylight was paling the sky behind the dark mass of the moors when he saw McCausland out of the coach. He still had Robert Pryke to see, though that would be much of a formality, and now an examination of the fence and the soil beneath it to check whether McCausland had been dreaming or not. When he had finished with both he felt that he could, with a relatively clear conscience, hand over to Lingard. Facing another day without a pipe between his teeth, he needed a shower, a breakfast and the time to titivate himself for his interview with Virginia Naylor.

13

Rogers's precautionary measures taken at the scene of Gosse's death were, so far, unrewarded. Sergeant Magnus had found no body or parts of one, nor any evidence that there had been a past concealment of either anywhere on the premises. While shallow depressions, roughly the size and shape of shoeprints, had been found adjacent to the garden fence, they were characterless and unlikely to be identifiable to any suspect's footwear. Further, there were no marks on a fence that was middling old, scarred and lichen-covered that could be definitely attributed to a recent climbing of it.

While the probing of the garden soil had not been completed when he left, what had been done had produced nothing. Which had been comparable with the result of his interview with Robert Pryke, who could add nothing of consequence to what Rogers had already been told.

Gosse, the oblivious cause of a day promising to be the *couleur de merde* for so many, was now in the mortuary waiting for Dr Twite to finish one of what were reputed to be his gargantuan breakfasts before using scalpel, chisel and power-saw in separating flesh and bone to get at and dissect his organs.

While Rogers was arranging with the duty chief inspector for a press release, he hoped – a frailty with little promise in it – that Liz Gallagher would separate Rogers the occasionally imperfect man from Rogers the detective superintendent, and not expect to be given preferential treatment in the passing out of official information because of the previous evening's over-the-top exchange of pleasantries. He feared that she would, women possessing a logic of a different kind from men's, and he was bracing himself for the flak of future dark-browed recriminations.

Calling in at his office before returning to his apartment to refurbish himself, he sorted through an accumulation of papers left on his desk, mostly the returns on his farmed-out intelligence gathering. Among them was the expected biodata report compiled by Woman Detective Sergeant Millier on Daphne Gosse's sister. Millier, an attractive blonde with a too attractive mouth, was sexually potent enough to be a disruptive element in a largely male department, unwitting of it though she appeared to be. Worse, she had clearly set female sights on Rogers which, apprehensive always of falling foul of disciplinary regulations, he could do nothing to encourage, keeping so far as he could his official contacts with her on reasonably harmless paper. As now.

Virginia Audrey Naylor was, Millier reported, an unmarried woman of about 35 years of age. She was a joint owner of the villa *Casa Gaviota* with a Miss Mary Finche-Roche, the two women sharing the same accommodation. They were both former commissioned officers in the Women's Royal Naval Service, graduating together from the Britannia Royal Naval College. Miss Naylor was currently employed part-time as a curator on the replica naval ship *Bark of Bodwyn*. She was not known to have any regular male associates. Miss Finche-Roche was a graphic designer employed full-time in Abbotsburn. She, too, appeared not to associate with any specific male person. A car, a red Alfa Romeo Spider convertible, registration number unknown, was garaged at the villa. Nothing was known against either woman; both of them being held in high regard by those who knew them.

Though he found himself only a little wiser about the persona of Virginia Naylor, he at least knew why he was to interview her on board the *Bark of Bodwyn*.

In his apartment, before he shaved and took a shower to remove the smell of death and smoke from his skin, he had to clear away the debris of his last night's entertaining before his chapel-going cleaning woman let herself in and clucked her tongue over the dirty glasses, the whisky-stained carpet and the dying fragrance of Liz Gallagher's perfume, all pointing to what would be, in her already confirmed opinion, his flagrant licentiousness. The chores done, he concocted and breakfasted on his latest *chef-d'oeuvre* of, he hoped, salmonella-free scrambled eggs with black unsweetened coffee, though not without a feeling of guilt that he was being relatively idle while his subordinates were soldiering on.

It was close to nine-thirty when he put his foot on the brake pedal of his car in descending the hill dropping steeply into Thurnholme Bay. The risen sun was an acid yellow in the palest of blue skies, its heat not noticeably reaching that part of the earth occupied by Rogers and his car, its light throwing weak and indeterminate shadows from the naked trees lining the road.

From his vantage point he could see the *Bark of Bodwyn*, with whose exterior he was familiar, hemmed in by tethered and gently swaying small boats, and moored in a corner of the liquid green rectangle that was the inner harbour. Around the harbour and rising steeply on the amphitheatrical slopes of the town were the tiers of white and pastel-coloured guest-houses, shops, pubs, retirement cottages and, in Rogers's opinion, environmentally degrading amusement arcades, with the huge multi-storeyed RAC and AA approved hotels taking over the headlands and lofty vistas.

Without its summer visitors, Thurnholme was a quiet, almost placid, well-ordered town and Rogers was able to park his car virtually in the shadow of the *Bark of Bodwyn*. Though not a large ship her hull, pierced by a single row of closed gun ports, was bulky and swollen with her stepped decks supporting bow and stern turreted wood castles high above his head. The mainmast and the secondary masts before and behind it held on their spars furled canvas sails. Painted black with her elaborate ornamentation picked out in dark crimson, the Tudor roses gilded, she appeared as sinister and piratical as her original probably was. Moored by rope cables to iron bollards, she swayed almost imperceptibly on the harbour's heaving water.

He climbed railed wooden steps promising no easy passage to the deck to the tottering elderly or the careless young. A door with a board attached to it saying in red pseudo-archaic lettering *The Thurnholme Bay Museum of Naval and Maritime Antiquities* opened on to stairs leading almost vertically below. Descending them, he found himself in an extensive open-plan chamber illuminated by skylights set in the decking above. With the exception of a small enclosed room at the far end, its door marked *Miss V Naylor, BA., Curator*, the butt-ends of the three masts passing through the flooring to the bilges were the only deck supports visible. Traversing the bare wooden planks to reach the curator's door, bending his head to avoid cracking his skull on beams, he passed eight-feet-long iron guns lashed to timber baulks, small heaps of rust-pitted iron balls, a World War II mine painted green, anchors, rigging blocks and coils of decomposing rope. There were ancient compasses, sextants, unidentifiable pieces of rusty metal and Spanish coins in glass-topped cases; flags, pennants and ensigns, being displayed colourfully on wall boards.

She called out 'Come in' to his knocking on the door, in the no-nonsense-from-you voice he had heard on her answering machine, standing from her desk in what was obviously her office and shaking his hand before reading the warrant card he held out to her. Telling him to sit down – it sounded like an order – she sat back in her chair, clearly weighing him up as, in return, he was her.

A woman plainly unlikely to be unsettled by his swarthy masculinity, Virginia Naylor was in every inch of her six feet an obvious former WRNS officer. Dressed in a navy-blue suit with a turquoise silk blouse, she carried the gold-rimmed spectacles through which she had examined his warrant card on a black cord around her neck. Her features were strong and attractively hawkish, her hair dark brown and worn in a short Egyptian cut with a heavy fringe covering her forehead. Her richly curved body, top-heavy on breasts and seen in its ripeness when she stood, was magnificent, yet surprisingly failed to trigger any response in a Rogers normally susceptible to such a female stimulus.

'I'm grateful you could spare the time to see me,' he said, noticing her eyes to be a deep orange and indicating to him she was a woman not to be asked foolish questions. 'I take it you already know that your sister Daphne Gosse has been missing for the past three weeks?'

'Yes.' She retrieved a small blue packet from a drawer of her desk and shook out a cigarette, putting it between her lips and snapping open a gold-coloured lighter at it. 'You, of course, wish to question me about what I know of it because so far you've not traced her. Is that right?' She was neither pleasant nor unpleasant towards him, but seemingly guarded.

'So far, not,' Rogers admitted. 'Will you tell me first what you know about her marriage to Mr Gosse?' There was a periodic creaking in the timbers of the ship and the floor – he supposed it to be called the deck or whatever – moved uneasily beneath his chair.

Distaste had shown in her face on hearing Gosse's name.

93

'Fortunately I've only met him once, but that was enough for me to know what an utterly contemptible character he was; what a fool my sister was to marry him! Had she listened to me, she would have left him long before this.'

'Why should she, Miss Naylor?' he asked, optimistic enough to believe that she was a woman from whom he would not need to chisel out information.

She frowned. 'Because of what she told me. She rang me now and then, usually complaining of his behaviour, my being her elder sister and, I imagine, the only one to whom she could complain. I understood that quarrelling between them was frequent and that for the past seven or eight months he had used violence against her. I do have to say that when I'd seen her there were no marks or bruises to indicate that the assaults were terribly serious, but none the less it was never the conduct of a gentleman.'

Rogers thought that she was choosing her words with care rather than being mannered. 'And you believe she's left him for that reason?'

'Naturally. Are you believing differently?' There had been signs of her bristling then and she blew out cigarette smoke jerkily.

'Not at all,' he denied. 'But even so, we do have a duty to confirm that she left her home of her own volition. You spoke to Gosse after she'd gone, I understand?'

'I wished to speak to her and on the two occasions I telephoned he said she wasn't in, that he didn't know when she would be, but that when she was he would tell her that I'd called. I assumed from his manner that she had gone and I didn't bother telephoning again.' Her orange eyes narrowed. 'In any case, he is such a detestable brute that I'd rather not have spoken to him at all.'

Rogers creased his forehead. 'Why should you accept that she'd gone mainly from his manner? Why not assume until you knew differently that she hadn't gone anywhere, but might still be in the house?'

'Simply because I did,' she said sharply. 'As I've already told you, I had reason to know that she would eventually go.'

There had been an unease there and he noted it. 'I see,' he

said, though he did not wholly. 'While I'm not suggesting it happened, didn't the possibility occur to you that she might have been the victim of a more serious assault and was unable to speak to you?'

'No. Why should it?' she questioned, apparently untroubled. 'I can't believe it so far as my sister is concerned. You appear not to either.'

'True,' he acknowledged mildly. 'Though while we often don't know, we do tend to fear the worst. I'm sorry to have put it to you in that form.' He changed course, deciding not to worry her unnecessarily by telling her of her sister's screaming in the night. 'You said you had visited her occasionally. I presume you'd have met Gosse in the process and formed your own opinion of him?'

'I met him once when I was home on shore leave.' She was terse, in the tone of her voice the suggestion of an unforgiving nature. 'I thought him then an ill-bred and unpleasant bore with a quite contemptible attitude towards my sister and to women in general. I have not had reason since to change my opinion of him.'

'Obviously Gosse wouldn't be there when you visited your sister. You were avoiding him?'

'Naturally, and particularly so as I went there to continue my efforts at persuading her to leave him.'

'What were her reactions to those?' Though she wasn't appealing to him in any sexual sense, he was finding it difficult to keep his gaze from the abundance of bosom seeming to be straining to get out from behind the buttoned-up jacket of her suit.

She frowned, either because she caught Rogers staring at her, or at his question; it was for him to guess which. 'Earlier, not too sensible. The silly girl couldn't make up her mind and dithered about it. Later she did, and went to see a solicitor about obtaining the divorce I had been urging her to get for months.'

'You know who? The solicitor, I mean.'

'She did tell me the names, but I've completely forgotten them. There were two, I know, and they were somewhere in Abbotsburn.'

'Do Kyberd and Durker ring a bell?'

'Vaguely,' she said, 'but I honestly couldn't swear to it.' She chewed on a very attractive bottom lip for a few moments while he wondered on what highly significant item of information she was making decisions. Then she said, 'There's something else, though I hesitate to tell you because it may not be helpful to you and I feel that it rather smacks of family disloyalty.'

'It's often called privileged criticism,' he said lightly, not knowing whether it was or not, but making it a matter of little concern. 'You're probably over-exaggerating it, anyway.'

'Possibly.' She wasn't sounding too convinced and for a moment worry showed in her expression. 'I have to trust that you will treat what I tell you with respect for both my sister and myself. She appears to have had a completely irrational infatuation with some man who she refused to name, resulting from which she is pregnant; I believe about three months or so. This, while needing her divorce proceedings to be dealt with soon, would also certainly require her to leave her home before her condition became noticeable.'

'She told you this?'

'Naturally, a week or more before the time you said she was missing.'

Rogers was seeing the light on that. 'Because you telephoned Gosse, she obviously hadn't told you that she was leaving. I can see that in your position you must have expected that she would. Is that so?'

'Yes, but also not doing so until later would be consistent with her character. She is rather a scatterbrain.'

'And she hasn't in fact been in touch with you, although I imagine that this could now be called later?'

'No, she has not.'

'Returning to this man she was infatuated with,' he pressed her. 'Surely she said something that might suggest who he was? What he did for a living, for example? Where he lived? Whether he was single or married, and whether unobliging in intending to do something about her pregnancy?' He cocked an eyebrow at her. 'You know, these questions *are* discussed in crises of this kind.'

For a moment he thought that she was about to bristle with

annoyance. Then she said, 'She did mention some time ago that she was seeing a man who painted. I believe that he wanted to paint her portrait and I rather gathered there was something going on between them. Whether he is the same man responsible for her pregnancy I don't know. She certainly didn't say. I think she saw that the whole business was extremely distasteful to me.'

'There's been talk of her having a seemingly unpleasant association with a man called Simon who wears a designer beard. Might that be him?'

She shrugged. 'He could be, though she never mentioned that name to me. But please, she is my sister and I shouldn't really be discussing that side of her life.'

Rogers thought he could recognize a closing door when he saw one. 'As you wish,' he conceded, 'but apropos of that sort of thing, I understand that Gosse was having an affair with a married woman.' He cocked an eyebrow. 'You knew?'

'Daphne mentioned it, yes. There again, she gave no name, being quite obvious that she didn't care one way or another about it.' Clearly unsettled, she had stubbed out her cigarette in an ashtray with a navy ship's crest on it, lighting another immediately.

The smoke, entering Rogers's bronchi and lungs, was reminding his not yet stifled addiction to pleasures still unforgotten and he was beginning to suffer. He said, 'But definitely married?', thinking of a cuckolded husband understandably vengeful with a rising blood lust to heat his anger.

'So she said,' she answered, with a manifest lack of interest in whatever Gosse did.

'I'm given to understand,' he said, choosing his words carefully, 'that Mrs Gosse was concerned enough about her husband's threats of violence towards her to hire a private detective as a bodyguard. Would you know that to be a possibility? Something that she'd be likely to do, and to tell you that she had done it?' He had already seen astonishment and incredulity in her expression.

'That has to be absolute nonsense,' she answered with forceful emphasis. 'What on earth good could that do?'

'My own opinion exactly,' he said dismissively. 'Forgive my

asking, but are you very close to your sister? I mean, it isn't always the case.'

Not answering immediately, she stared at him as if he had asked her what kind of underclothing she wore. Then she said stiffly, as if rebuking him, 'I don't believe that either of us approved the other's way of living, Mr Rogers, though I fail to see how that can be relevant to your investigation.'

'That was a preliminary to something else I have to ask you,' he said, giving her a smile he hoped wasn't to be taken as being obsequious. 'Not in itself unlawful, not even improper, I imagine, but a notice was posted to the *Daily Echo* for entry in its Personal column. In effect, it said that Mrs Gosse was missing and suggested that she might be the victim of foul play. The sender of it is so far unknown. Needless to say, it wasn't published but passed to us.' In saying that he had been meeting her steady gaze on him, seeing no recognition or awareness in her eyes, though some apprehension. Being satisfied that she was not the author of the notice, he withdrew from his intended questioning of her concerning it and said, 'I tell you this because it does explain why I feel that Mrs Gosse's disappearance may not be entirely of her own seeking.'

Behind the steadiness of her regard of him she looked shaken, wounded. 'You really think that something has happened to her?'

'I don't honestly know.' He kept any suggestion of doom and disaster from his voice. 'It's what I'm trying to find out and hoping it hasn't. It's why I've been questioning you, so is there anything else you can add to what you've already told me?'

'I think not, though I would like to reflect on what you've said and see if anything comes to mind.'

He stood from his chair, remembering not to crash his skull on the beam above him, and prepared to leave. 'I'd be grateful,' he told her. 'There is one more question. In your visits to your sister's home, did you ever notice a walking stick with its handle in the form of a brass duck's head? Or, if not, did you know or were you told that Gosse owned one?'

She shook her head, looking blankly at him. 'No,' she said. 'Is that something I should know?'

He hesitated, deciding against telling her of its use, or of

Gosse's death anyway, though plainly this was an occurrence that would cause no particular distress to her. Death could cause a reversal of opinion about its victim, bordering on the soft and forgiving side, and telling her beforehand might have influenced adversely what she was prepared to disclose about Gosse and her sister. Now it was too late to do it without offence. He said ambiguously, 'Not really. It would only have been useful had you known.'

She hadn't asked for elaboration on any of the questions he had asked; her curiosity apparently muted. She had not, in fact, lived up to her no-nonsense voice. Promising to keep in touch should he discover anything about her sister, he took the hand she held out to be shaken, once again regretting that the chemistry of sex was missing from the brief contact and suspecting that whatever femininity she possessed was being wasted, like water dribbling into dry sand. He would have felt less sad had her living-in companion been somebody masculinely bearded and hairy and one whom he could honestly envy for having a nightly proximity to her abundance of bosom.

14

Detective Inspector Coltart, his huge frame encased in a fur-collared leather coat, was discovering why the solicitor Kyberd's house had been called *Windswept*. It was perched on rising land known as High Moor in a high-priced and therefore exclusive area; the houses occupying it commanded a lofty view of the sea a few miles distant and with it an exposure to the bitter winds sweeping inshore.

The house concentrating Coltart's attention was situated at the end of a narrow ridge bulldozed out of the sloping landscape. Built of weathered grey stone with a green-tiled roof steeply pitched to shrug off snow, it had a Victorian-style conservatory built at its southern end and a separately sited two-car garage. The grounds of the house ran parallel with the ridge; interspersed clumps of trees, now starkly skeletal, proclaiming the area's exclusivity. A thick laurel hedge passing one side of the garage concealed a panoramic view of the town below.

Despite his bigness, Coltart had no surplus fat on him and he felt chilled in the legs and face from the frigid breeze that hunted him through the leafless trees. The sun, he thought, must be doing nothing that morning but warming itself. After he had rung and knocked at the front and rear doors and obtained no answer, he checked the house's exterior, finding the curtains drawn close at the ground-floor windows and venetian blinds shut behind what were evidently the windows of a kitchen. Were Coltart going on a holiday, this was how he would leave his own home, did he happen to live in one and not in lodgings. The garage had an automatic door and a small window obscured by the laurel hedge. Squeezing past the hedge he looked through it, seeing only half the darkened interior, but certain that nothing longer than a Mini could be in there, and perhaps not even that.

Going out into the road where he had left the CID car, inconspicuously nondescript and rarely remembered clearly enough to be later described, he walked to the next house, fifty or so of his strides away. Entering the drive he saw a long and narrow paddock with panel fencing forming a windbreak along its length. Though not a golfer, he recognized what was obviously meant to be a short grass fairway flanked by deep- and semi-rough fringes. A flagged green halfway along its length was surrounded by bunkers of different shapes and depths. A short stocky man dressed in a hip-length windcheater, whipcord trousers and what the detective would call a ratcatcher's flat cap, was standing in one of the deeper bunkers belabouring the ground with a short iron in splashing a ball on to the green in a flurry of white sand. Hearing Coltart approach he turned, showing his face, as red as if glowing from an internal fire, with a bristly grey moustache and startlingly blue eyes, *in toto* giving him the image of a retired military man.

'Good-morning, sir,' Coltart said in his subterranean growl. 'I'm a police officer and I'd be glad of a few minutes of your time.' He held out his warrant card to be read. 'Can I have your name, please?'

'Jarvis, Major Jarvis,' the man said; then solemnly, 'And you're about to ask me why I'm out here in the cold on a one-hole golf course and acting in a suspicious manner?'

'How did you know, Major?' Coltart put on his tough look which went with his rough-hewnness, knowing that his leg was being pulled and reciprocating with elephantine humour. 'The place is surrounded by armed police officers, so you'd better come quietly.'

'Good man,' Jarvis said, grinning. 'I imagine that I would, seeing the size of you. How can I help?'

'I've been next door to try and see Mr Kyberd about an enquiry with a lot of urgency behind it. I understand that he'd have returned from his holiday by now, but he hasn't so far been back to his office and I can't get hold of his partner.' His approach was sounding more feeble than he had expected and he put on an expression of bafflement. 'I wondered, if he's back, whether you, as one of his neighbours, would know where he is?'

Jarvis stared hard at him, his eyes showing a sudden shrewdness. 'Ah,' he exclaimed. 'He *wasn't* on holiday then?'

'He wasn't?' Coltart said, foxed by the unexpected answer. 'Why do you say that?'

'Because, old son, you don't seem very good at hiding that you know he mightn't have been, and because I've been thinking it myself for a couple of weeks.' He pushed a small black instrument into his windcheater pocket and climbed from the bunker, his club still in what looked a formidably powerful fist. Facing the detective and showing his teeth, he said, 'Give me a good reason to open up and I might tell you what I know.'

'Like I said, I was believing he was back from his holiday,' Coltart rumbled, having nothing he could disclose, 'but if he isn't back it does leave me wondering.' He frowned. 'You think something's happened?'

'All I'm thinking is that the signs are he isn't on holiday.' Jarvis lowered his voice although they were separated from the rest of humanity by a hundred yards or so of very cold paddock. 'I'm his keyholder and when he goes away he tells me. Without fail and always with due notice. Now he's gone and hasn't told me and, anyway, I've never known him to go away in November.' There was an air of offence having been taken at this omission.

'Isn't that something we should be worried about?' The detective fixed him, not aggressively, with the small green eyes that could cause acute discomfort in the villainous. 'Hadn't it occurred to you to do something about it?'

'The answer to that, old chap, is I've lived long enough to know not to jump in with both feet until I can see what I'm doing.' He beamed at Coltart, but there was a measure of irritation behind it. 'And long enough to know that solicitors and their ilk – jolly upstanding chaps though they must be – are frightfully quick on the draw over conclusions wrongly jumped at by well-intentioned chaps such as myself.'

'I think I know what you mean.' Coltart put sympathetic understanding in his voice. 'But now you do have the opportunity of unloading it on to me. Whatever you tell me will go no further than my detective superintendent's ear.' When he read in Jarvis's face that he was with him on that, he said, 'When did you last see him and after that catch on to the fact that he may not be where he should have been?'

'I'm a little rusty on dates, but it was a day or so either side of two weeks ago when I saw his car pass my gate with him presumably on his way to the office. I didn't see or hear him return – which would almost always be about six-thirty unless he stayed away for the night – though that doesn't mean that he didn't.' He rubbed the ball of his thumb on a closely shaven and glossy chin, his expression thoughtful. 'I can't recall when I realized he'd not been about the place; one doesn't, does one? Two or three days later? That'd be fair enough. In some ways he was a noisy chap, often banging car doors at night and first thing in the morning, making a hell of a din. That sort of a thing – though I'm not complaining – so I suppose I should have missed him earlier.'

'Did you think of going in and checking the house to see if he was there? That all was in order?' The detective, to whom the obligations of a duty imposed were imperatives, thought that as a keyholder Jarvis might, before his visit, have done some

102

useful wondering about whose car was parked outside his neighbour's house and what he, Coltart, had been doing prowling around it.

'I wasn't at all worried, old son, though I did go round there as routine and see that everything was secure. I didn't go inside because I've no remit to do so, I hold the key for emergencies only.'

'You'd know if the car was in the garage, wouldn't you?'

'I didn't think of it,' he admitted, 'but in any case it's locked by one of those infra-red thingamabobs.'

'You're friendly with Mr Kyberd?' Coltart suggested. 'I mean, you having the key to his house?'

'Oddly enough, not particularly, but being the next-door neighbour I suppose it'd be the form to ask me in case the house was on fire or burgled while he was on his hols.'

'You know where he'd go?'

'The Grosvenor Hotel at Preston Magna,' he said promptly. 'That I do know. He fishes trout there, apparently stands waist-deep in the river for hours and chucks flies at 'em. I've never known him go anywhere else in the six or seven years I've held his key. He's always told me when he'd be there so that if anything serious happened he could be contacted.'

'He goes with his wife?' Rogers hadn't mentioned his domestic situation so Coltart had to do some fishing on his own.

'He hasn't got one; well, not one that lives with him. She went off with her brood about four years ago. He's never said anything about her or the kids to me or my wife and we never asked, but she never came back.' He stared knowingly at the detective. 'You could say he was a sort of bachelor, couldn't you? Leading a bachelor's life kind of thing. Is that anything you'd be interested in? On the QT of course.'

'You mean a woman?' Coltart said heavily, disapproving of any but those who reminded him of his dead mother.

'Several, I think. He'd bring one of 'em back some evenings, and if she left before the next morning I never heard anything of it. But jolly good luck to him, however it was.'

'You saw any of them?'

Jarvis shook his head briskly. 'No, but it's quiet up here and sound carries, bounces off the rocks, I imagine. Ladies being

103

brought back by him or delivered by taxi and escorted indoors aren't often doing it in dead silence.' Anxiety suddenly clouded his face. 'You're sure this isn't going any further?' he asked.

'Positive,' Coltart assured him. 'How old is he?'

'Forty, possibly pushing forty-five, with his hair on the turn to grey, but I'm guessing.'

'If Mr Kyberd didn't go on holiday and he has a problem in being somewhere else,' Coltart said, 'I'm sure my chief is going to want some information about him and his life-style, his habits – stuff like that.' ·

A mixture of emotions seemed to be struggling for expression in Jarvis's face, an uneasiness that suggested sudden cold feet clearly being one of them. 'Hold on, old chap,' he protested. 'I did say we weren't particularly friendly and as I know nothing to his detriment – all solicitors being bloody fine chaps and honest with it – what can I say that could be interesting to you?' His reluctance to disgorge what he obviously thought might be slanderous statements was growing.

'It was just ordinary information I asked for, major,' Coltart said, as if he had been misunderstood. 'Not necessarily any mud-slinging, although I know if you knew of anything that smelled you'd tell me.'

'I don't, and that's the point,' Jarvis hastened to assert. 'I mean, those ladies I mentioned, they could have been his sisters, his aunts, all frightfully proper and above-board, and I haven't suggested otherwise, have I?'

'Of course you haven't,' Coltart assured him stolidly and untruthfully.

'I thought not. I've never been in his house, never been asked, in fact, and that shows I'm no intimate of his. He isn't the type I'm likely to be too friendly with anyway, him not playing golf or being interested in it. He's a quiet, very decent sort of a cove and you'd never know what he was thinking, though no doubt like the rest of us there's some hidden fire in him somewhere.' He laughed immoderately at that, adding hastily, 'I'm joking, of course. What I can say is that he's moderately well-off, but then solicitors always are, wouldn't you say? And with nobody to spend it on but himself.'

'He smokes? Drinks?'

'I think I may have seen him smoking a cigar in his car once. Drinks? I wouldn't know, would I?'

'What car does he smoke his cigars in?'

'A Rover. It's in metallic green with a black roof covering.' Jarvis, looking pointedly at his one-hole course, was fidgeting, showing signs of impatience with the continued questioning, and the detective was expecting to be told to bugger off at any moment.

'Its registration number?'

'I can only remember B something something PQ.'

'How was he looking when you last saw him? Fit and well? Or, perhaps, ailing?'

Jarvis looked at him as if wondering what the catch was. 'Normal as he always has been. Absolutely. Why do you ask?'

'There's always the possibility that a man can be taken ill, don't you think?' Coltart scratched at his mind for what else. 'I've never met Mr Kyberd,' he said. 'Could you make a stab at his age and describe him in case I do run into him?'

'H'm.' Jarvis sucked at his teeth. 'I'd say he was batting on forty-five or thereabouts. About my height and build, though perhaps not quite. Brown hair getting a mite thin on top, but quite a handsome looking fella . . .' – he snickered – '. . . something like me on a good day. Let's see, it'd be eyes you'd want, too. Middle-brown, I think, and no beard or moustache. He's got one of those sharp pointed noses you could open a tin of sardines with.' He creased his eyes at the sun. 'I reckon that's about as far as I can go.'

Coltart wondered whether he had gathered enough information for the sometimes testy Rogers and decided he probably never would, that being a perfection rarely achieved. He said, 'Thank you, major, I think I'll know him even on a dark night. I'm sorry to have kept you from your practising. I'll get along : . .'

Jarvis chopped his words off short. 'That so-called practising,' he said crisply, his complexion turning a deeper red, 'happens to be something that'll revolutionize the game of golf. The secret's in the short approach where nine times out of ten the game's won.' Seeing, presumably, the lack of comprehension or interest in Coltart's eyes, he demanded, 'I take it that you do play?'

'No,' Coltart said flatly and undiplomatically, holding all golfers by definition to be touched with madness and beginning to move, having a telephone call to make and needing to be gone. 'I never did see any point in bashing a little ball around a field and then chasing after it.'

Later, he thought that he hadn't made too close a friend of a man who he suspected had held back on giving his all about a neighbour; and whose only reward for what he *had* given was the detective's brusque dismissal of a game with which he was patently obsessed.

It wasn't until Coltart reached his office that he thought belatedly, smacking the heel of his hand at his forehead as he did so, that he should have persuaded Jarvis to use his key to allow him access to Kyberd's house, to confirm whatever it was that Rogers would now almost certainly think up that needed confirming.

Getting the telephone number of the Grosvenor Hotel at Preston Magna – it was some sixty-odd miles away in a different county – from Directory Enquiries, he dialled it. Without disclosing who he was he asked to speak to Mr Hugh Kyberd, a guest at the hotel. Kyberd, it seemed, though a long-time and well-known visitor, was not then there and had not been expected.

Coltart, closing down, wasn't sure that Kyberd's not being there was what Rogers wanted, and he spent time looking at the blank wall of his office, trying to work out exactly what could be going on and why.

15

A telephone message form left on Rogers's desk told him that Sergeant Blackstone, in whose section Ullsmouth lay, had called to inform him that Gosse's boat *Ephedra* had been located at the Fouled Anchor Sailing Club. A locked brown Mini car without number plates had been found near by and might be the car sought in connection with the missing Mrs Gosse. Telephoning him back and telling him of Gosse's death, Rogers detailed Blackstone to meet him outside the club in an hour's time, then disconnected and began sifting through the growing accumulation of papers in his IN tray.

A brief note of three items from Lingard, still active in investigating the killing of Gosse, told him that the garden appeared not to be concealing the body of Mrs Gosse, nor indeed any other body but that of a small dog buried for what appeared to have been months, and that both garden and house were now being held shrink-wrapped and vacuum sealed pending further instructions. The search of the canal and, as Lingard flippantly put it, the remaining acreage of Rogers's bailiwick, was proceeding with so far nothing to report.

Passing on a message from an unnamed source not unconnected with New Scotland Yard, Lingard reported that the also unnamed subject of the enquiry had retired from the force twenty-five years earlier equipped with the rank of Inspector, a Long Service and Good Conduct medal and a character assessment given as 'Excellent'. An unofficial and shared assessment, culled from retired senior officers, was that he, being a married man, had been morally suspect in that he was known on a number of occasions to have been reprimanded without entry on his record sheet and verbally cautioned because of his alleged sexual entanglement or suspect associations with women; two or three of them being the wives of serving colleagues, one a policewoman sergeant, and an unnumbered few known to have not too sweet-smelling reputations.

Rogers knew that McCausland must have been an unusually lucky man to have survived to draw his pension, for he had been serving in the decades when casual fornication and, more seriously, adultery by a police officer were considered only a degree or so less depraved than necrophilia or the abominable crime of buggery. A man, Rogers thought wryly, who in the present decade would be held to be more deserving of admiration than censure.

When he left his office for Ullsmouth – somehow he had missed ever visiting it during his service – it was with an

107

unexpected craving for a smoke of tobacco, this provoked in passing on his way out a member of the public thoughtless enough to have a pipe between his teeth and to allow its intoxicating aromatic smoke to reach Rogers's nostrils. Driving his car on the narrow valley road that ran alongside the river, heading for the sea, he was shut in by the forest of trees rising on either side of him. Where the land flattened out on the approach to the river's mouth there were houses, a small grocery store, the Goat and Compasses inn, and a yellow-brick chapel with broken windows that looked as if it had been deconsecrated sometime in the last century. It was mourned, it seemed, by the keening of herring gulls standing one-legged on its moss-grown guttering. The few cottages lining the river side of the road added to the sense of isolation Rogers felt there, visualizing them as being occupied by silent people waiting behind closed doors for the winter to pass. Beyond them he could see the sailing club's premises, a long green-painted wooden pavilion identified on its nameboard by a black anchor looped with a length of rope. It faced a dwindling river with an ebbing tide leaving a widespread prospect of pewter-coloured mud flats.

The uniformed and lanky Sergeant Blackstone, one of the decade's contemporary young men with his spider legs and no perceptible buttocks, was waiting near a telephone kiosk standing on a finger of shaped rock reaching out over the river bed. Rogers, pulling up behind the section beat car, climbed out and looked around him at the deserted village. Acknowledging Blackstone's salute, he said ironically, 'I'd have expected you to have done something about crowd control, sergeant.'

'Sir?' Blackstone replied, his forehead creased. He was a solemnly earnest young man – vaguely dim-witted in Rogers's opinion – and prissy in his attitude; a university graduate pointing his nose resolutely in the direction of a future chief constableship. 'I'm sorry,' he added, in case by some distortion of logic it was something that he should have considered.

'No matter,' Rogers said straight-faced, thinking that he was going to make a brilliantly obtuse chief officer should he ever get there. 'I think we might manage between us. I'll look at the boat now, and the car afterwards.'

A padlocked five-barred gate gave entrance to the sailing club's strip of foreshore and the two men climbed over it, Blackstone telling Rogers, whose bones were creaking doing it, that the club's so-called commodore, who had pointed out the boat for him and who knew that they would be visiting, had refused to be present. Nevertheless, the sergeant was able to remember, despite Rogers's doubts, where Gosse's bilge keel cruiser was situated in the line of single-masted boats parked on cradles or launching trolleys above what appeared to be the high water mark.

Curious to see what a bilge keel cruiser looked like, Rogers gave it a landsman's scrutiny. Its hull, about twenty-four feet of it, had been painted a now oxidized navy-blue, with *Ephedra* in pale-blue minuscule lettering, and not all that difficult even for the sergeant to identify. A small propeller stuck out from its stern and the two metal keels on which the boat stood spread-eagled were bolted on at an angle on opposite sides of the belly. The low profile cabin was white and pierced by a mast rising from its centre, the rigging cables and wires lashed to it. Standing low on its keels, the boat was effectively screened on both sides from casual observation.

Rogers grasped with both hands what he had heard referred to as 'gunnels' and heaved his thirteen stones on to the cramped deck, followed by the rather more willowy and less weighty sergeant. First looking into the cabin through the side window, he saw what were manifestly folded sails occupying two padded benches. Moving down the single step to the double-hatch entrance to the cabin, he found it to be securely padlocked. As almost certainly, he reflected ruefully, recommended by the police crime prevention officer. 'You must have a tool or two in your car,' he said to Blackstone. 'Please get one and force that padlock for me.'

'Force it, sir?' The sergeant looked disconcerted. 'Wouldn't that be unlawful without the owner's permission?'

Rogers stared at him dead pan. 'Whose permission are you going to get? Gosse's, who is at present in the mortuary though undoubtedly anxious to have a chat with you about it? Or Mrs Gosse's, who's been missing for three weeks and who just could be down below us as dead as her husband?' He spoke tersely, with, he thought, a non-smoker's irritability. 'Don't be a twit, sergeant. Just go and do it.'

Waiting for Blackstone to return, Rogers stared down at the expanse of wet grey mud which seemed to symbolize Ullsmouth while he tried to speculate without much guessing. Apart from its foul stench, small circles were appearing in it accompanied by audible plops, suggesting that some evidently insensitive organisms actually lived in the noisome sludge. That led to the depressing thought of what it would be like to be buried in the stuff. Nothing of it helped his theorizing about the probability of finding the possibly decomposing body of Daphne Gosse – a horrifying condition in any corpse, that always raised his gorge – necessarily coupled with the thought that were it so then it had somehow to be connected with the subsequent killing of her husband. It was all too full of ifs for a man used to dealing in observable facts. Were she to be presumed alive somewhere else, possibly with the man she was infatuated with and pregnant by, that still left too many unquantifiable propositions to make sense, a significant one being why should her Mini car, stripped of its number plates, be dumped near her husband's boat?

Blackstone, returning with a jack handle, interrupted Rogers's profitless speculations and, under his sardonic gaze, wrenched the padlock free of its fastening. 'You'll probably find that's a civil tort you've just committed,' Rogers told him as he opened the flaps of the hatch. It was a frivolous remark calculated to have the sergeant leafing anxiously through his law books when he returned to his station.

There was no stench of corrupt flesh to greet him, and he was uncertain whether to be relieved for his gorge's sake or seriously perturbed because of the collapse of one of his tentative theories. Stepping down into the cabin's cold, stale and oil-smelling air, cursing all boat builders who designed their ceilings without concern for anyone standing over five-and-a-half feet in height, he could see that there was no real prospect of hiding an adult's body successfully in the cramped dimensions of the boat. Even with only Blackstone, now standing in his shadow, it seemed vastly crowded with overcoated men.

110

A search turned up a couple of sets of yellow oilskins, navigation charts and tidal tables, a deflated rubber dinghy, and an untidiness of paraphernalia that Rogers believed was needed to be able to mess around in boats. There were a few tins of food stored in the locker of a galley smaller than a bachelor's wardrobe and, in plain view on a small table bolted to the decking, two car keys attached to an enamelled medallion bearing the Mini logo.

Those, he guessed without thinking too deeply about them, were going to pose him a problem by just being there; telling him nothing at the moment, yet surely indicating something significant he should recognize. Putting the keys in his pocket, he said more amiably than he felt, 'It seems that you don't have a body in your section after all, sergeant. Not unless it's been overlooked in the car.'

Blackstone chose not to rise to that one. 'I think it would be difficult not to see,' he replied seriously, 'and it isn't in the boot because I checked it. There is a kind of sponge bag thing on the floor of the back seats.'

Rogers turned and moved outside the cabin. 'Did you ask your commodore chap if anybody had seen any visitors to the boat since it's been beached?' he asked.

'I don't expect he'd know, sir,' Blackstone equivocated. 'He lives a mile or two back up the road and as I said he doesn't seem all that interested in coming here, being that he's very old.'

'He probably came here to die,' Rogers said, not too pleased with the sergeant's lack of initiative. 'It seems that sort of a place. See him again and this time ask him questions. Make sure that he shows some interest in one of his club members who's happened to have gone on before him. Is he the one who told you about the car being here?' He put a steadying hand on the side of the boat and jumped as lithely as he could to the ground. It wasn't bad, but his forty years were showing their limitations.

'Yes, as a sort of afterthought.' Blackstone followed his senior with all the irritating ease of a much younger man. 'He was told about it by one of the villagers nearly a week ago, but left reporting it until he saw one of us down here.'

'See if you can find out who from and how long it'd been there. It could be important.' Rogers followed him across the road and along a path through closely growing trees. 'And before I forget it, you'd better do something about replacing that padlock you smashed before you leave here. I'm sure you wouldn't wish to compound your tort with anything more serious, and I want the boat left secure.'

The Mini, having that air of resigned lostness common to abandoned cars, stood shrouded in shadow beneath a pine tree, its brown paintwork and glass dust-covered and freely splashed with the white droppings of birds probably roosting in the branches above. The number plates had been unscrewed and removed, and the tax disc which would show the registration number was missing from the windscreen. None the less, the car had to be that belonging to the missing Daphne Gosse, though it might take a few hours to prove it without doubt. Its appearance gave no clue to how many days and nights it had been sitting there. In Rogers's experience, loose-bowelled birds were attracted to cars wherever they were parked, and much of the splashing could have been done before the car had been driven to Ullsmouth.

One of the keys he held fitted the driver's door and he opened it. There was nothing inside but the sponge bag already seen by Blackstone. Patterned with tiny cream roses, it contained a nail-brush, what appeared to be a dried-up and stiff face flannel, a small bottle containing a little pink moisturizing cream and a used red lipstick. There were no driving documents of any description in the fascia compartment and the unlocked boot contained nothing but the spare wheel and a lifting jack. Fitting his bulk into the driver's seat – he noticed that it needed little adjustment to give his legs operating room – he used the ignition key and choke, the engine starting from cold with no trouble.

Taking the sponge bag and relocking the car, Rogers left the modestly unfortunate sergeant – conscious that he might have been a little unkind to him – to somehow find another padlock in what seemed to be a completely God-forsaken village, occupied only by unseen phantom presences, beached boats and herring gulls.

112

Driving back to his office and feeling cold and hungry, his lungs apparently playing up for a fix of nicotine, he reckoned that he could have done without the illogicalities raised by his visit there. Somebody – it could have been Daphne Gosse, of course, if her legs were long enough, which was something he didn't know – had possessed not only the keys to the Mini, but also a key to the padlock securing the boat's cabin. Could the bloody woman actually have left her husband, as Gosse had alleged, of her own accord? And if she had, why abandon her car in Ullsmouth after removing the means of its immediate identification, locking it and securing the keys in her husband's boat? In *her* boat as well, he supposed. Where would she go? And how? Or had somebody else done those things? Dumping her unconscious or dead in the river on an ebbing tide, to be swept out to sea. How did it all tie in with her husband having his head smashed in by an intruder, entering – God knows how – three weeks after she had gone missing? And when it came to establishing a motive, why had he been murdered at all?

Having no answers worth mulling over, he conceded a temporary defeat and said to nobody in particular, 'Sod it! Let me think about it some other time.' He was, he knew, very close also to conceding defeat in a quite different matter, now believing how utterly reasonable and understandable it would be were he to stop *en route* and buy a very small packet of tobacco, dig out one of his old pipes and smoke it as just one tiny life-enhancing concession to his apparently imperishable, undying addiction.

16

The walrus-moustached and homosexual proprietor of the Solomon and Sheba pub was known by Rogers to be working hard at his bar meals – and temporarily losing money at it – in an effort to get an approving entry in the following year's Henri Fabius pub food guide. Since he now served the best seafood platter in town, Rogers gravitated frequently to his refurbished eating tables, on the occasion of his return from Ullsmouth inviting Lingard and Coltart to join him there for an exchange of information. Though not feeling particularly virtuous about it, he had resisted surrendering to his latent craving for tobacco, but it had been a close-run thing.

Seated in a shadowed corner of the bar where they would not be overheard, he managed the art of presenting disjointed fragments of information as a coherently whole narrative to Lingard and Coltart between eating pieces of battered and deep-fried fish with what was now called *sauce tartare de maison*. 'If you think about it,' he said, pushing away his plate, 'the Mini, the keys to it and, presumably, the sponge bag represent the only material things we have met with that can possibly be connected with Mrs Gosse. Everything else we know about her is what we've learned from being told by fallible observers with possibly prejudiced views. One says that she is, or was, recklessly fearless to the point of being daft, even unbalanced, in potholing and microlight flying, in which she apparently risked her own neck and that of others a few years back. Her husband tells us that she was two-timing him, which she undoubtedly was because her sister says that not only was she heavily infatuated with some presumably unlucky cove, but that she was three months pregnant to boot.'

He lifted an interrogative eyebrow. 'Haven't we heard of putative fathers becoming rather desperate and doing something nasty about it?' When he received no visible support on this, he said, 'Ah well, perhaps not in this free-wheeling age of ours, but there could be exceptions. But back to Gosse, who also said that she was capable of being generally unpleasant to him, screaming at him, denying him what we might decently call a lawful access and generally telling him to get stuffed if he didn't like what she was doing. Mind you, Gosse wasn't in any position to be wholly disapproving, having had, it now appears, a doxy of his own and being in my opinion a mean and surly bastard with all the manners of a bush pig. Another observer of the human condition, our friend McCausland, who, hearing Mrs Gosse scream a couple of times after nightfall and then have her come charging into his house crying her eyes out and complaining that Gosse had hit her, had quite understandably seen her merely as a victim of domestic violence.'

He scowled a little at that, and continued: 'Then we have an informant at St Boniface's School where she was employed. He saw her, obviously uncomprehendingly at the time, as a paranoiac with delusions of persecution. One he mentioned in particular was that she was being secretly given doses of hyoscine by her husband; another, that she had been forced to hire a private detective as a bodyguard against her husband's intent to do her violence. You've managed to check that out, David?' he asked Lingard.

Lingard had long finished the tournedos Rossini which he hoped his senior would be paying for, and was drinking his coffee. 'Egad, George,' he protested as if offended, 'don't put that down to me. That was nonsense, as I knew it was at the time. The agencies I checked thought I was bonkers for even asking, and if it's any comfort I don't believe the hyoscine bit either.'

'Nor, I think, do I,' Rogers said, 'and I hope some bright bugger doesn't prove us wrong. Have we identified the designer-beard chap Simon yet?'

'If Gosse had not inconveniently got chopped,' Lingard drawled, 'I think I'd have been a bit closer to having done it than I am now. Priorities rule, George, as you've often said.'

'So they do,' Rogers agreed. 'It was but an enquiry, no more. But when you do get around to him, you might as well consider him to be a portrait painter as anything else, and there can't be too many of them around here. Mrs Gosse's sister says that there was something going on between her and one such, and that she was pregnant, though not necessarily by him. There's a report about it on my desk, so have a look at it when you get back there. Have either of you any useful ideas about the Mini and the locked-away keys? Eddie?'

Coltart, who had seen off a large Ploughman's lunch with Stilton cheese and a Waldorf salad, looked as though he was fuelled up for a further few hours. In lieu of coffee, which he didn't like, and smoking, which he detested, he chewed a plastic toothpick supplied by the landlord, presumably in an attempt to civilize his customers. 'It's a possibility, sir,' he rumbled, 'that she drove to Ullsmouth under her own steam, parking her car where you found it because she mightn't want anybody who knew her husband to see it. I imagine she'd have access to her husband's boat, so there'd be nothing strange about her going on board and dropping the keys on the table where you found them.' He was screwing creases around his green eyes in his thinking aloud. 'She's meeting somebody there on the boat, her boyfriend probably, and waiting for him to come. When he does, something happens. Perhaps they quarrelled about her being pregnant and she gets clobbered. He panics then, knows that he has to get shot of her body and probably heaves it over the side into the water . . .'

'I should have mentioned that,' Rogers interrupted him. 'He'd have to carry her to the water's edge and wait a bit if the tide wasn't in. Otherwise it's a hundred yards dash across a mess of stinking mud.'

'All right, sir,' Coltart said phlegmatically. 'He gets rid of her somehow and then finds he's lumbered with her car. Having his own in which he arrived, he can't drive it away. It needn't have entered his mind that he ever should. All he can do is to remove the registration plates identifying the car, not thinking of the keys of course, and then taking off to wherever he came from.'

Waiting for a few moments in the silence that followed, he said, 'That doesn't sound too likely, does it?'

'It's as much a possibility as anything I can think of myself,' Rogers smiled at him. 'In fact, apart from overlooking the tax disc that had been taken from inside on the windscreen, and that the car would have to be relocked after it had been taken – which it was – it isn't bad at all. David?'

Lingard shook his head. 'Not so soon after I've eaten,' he said. 'You've worked it out yourself?'

'Have I hell,' Rogers grunted. He came back at Coltart. 'I've read your note about the Kyberd enquiry; do you think he is, or isn't, having a break for the good of his health? His partner seemed fairly definite about it.'

'Major Jarvis thought not, in a general sort of way. He certainly didn't believe he'd gone off on his usual holiday and my check at the hotel supported him up to a point. And the

116

point is that there's nothing to stop a man having a change now and then. Certainly if he wasn't well and despite the major thinking he'd been cold-shouldered out of his little job as a key-holder. I thought he was a nosy old coot who was only holding back on me because Kyberd was a solicitor and solicitors know all about things lik slander and libel.'

'Not only that, but they're over-sensitive about them and don't have to pay out vast sums in legal fees to be able to sue you to hell and back,' Rogers said feelingly. 'What do you think about the possibility of his taking off for an extended dirty weekend with Mrs Gosse who is his client, and who was, coincidentally, missing during much the same period as he seems to have been on his break.' He had his doubts about that, but he was asking, not saying.

Coltart's sandy eyebrows expressed clearly his distaste of all things carnal. 'He could be,' he agreed. 'If so, he certainly wouldn't want Major Jarvis to know, would he? I don't suppose he'd be going to his usual hotel with a spare woman either. And he couldn't tell the major where he was without all sorts of necessary explanations.'

'True.' Coltart had made a point that had removed a fragment or two from Rogers's doubting. 'And I can't think of a law that says you have to give out strong hints about your sexual profligacy to a neighbour just because he holds the house key for you. Which, incidentally, I want you to collect from him today. He might be nosy enough to creep around the house if he believes there's something fishy about Kyberd's absence. And,' he added thoughtfully to both men, 'wherever Kyberd's gone, his partner's going to need to do a little explaining.'

If – and it was a reasonably big if – Mrs Gosse had gone off with Kyberd, then Durker must know or suspect and that would explain his reluctance to give Rogers any information. To Lingard, he said, 'Have we heard from Wilfred what killed Gosse?'

'It's what we thought. Death due to a combination of shock and multiple and simple fractures of the skull with non-fatal fractures to the cheekbones and mouth parts. In other words, whoever it was tried his damnedest to pulp him and wasn't far from doing it. Wilfred says that the stick you waved at him was almost certainly the weapon, the beak part being quite capable to tearing the strips of flesh from his face. He also believes that the first few blows were delivered when Gosse was standing facing his attacker, who, he thinks, must have been taller than Gosse. But who isn't? Then, having knocked the poor devil to the ground, he gave him more whacks on the head and face until, we can suppose, the stick broke.'

'A guess at the means and motive, David?' Rogers poured himself more coffee from the jug on the table. He had need of it, feeling his lack of sleep and having to hold back involuntary yawning – to him a sign of weakness – behind closed teeth.

'Woken up while in bed by the sounds of an intruder, coming down the stairs, sudden confrontation with "What's all this, then?" and him being feloniously bashed.' Lingard was theorizing confidently. 'I'd say by his own walking-stick, not yet having heard of even upper crust housebreakers taking theirs with them. Entry only theoretically possible by an insecure window that would have had to be closed and latched from the outside after exit, which is virtually impossible, or by using an improperly acquired key to the back door. Both, I admit, verging on the slightly improbable. Motive?' He cast his gaze around the bar as if searching for it there. 'Theft of something or other? Papers? Incriminating photographs? An object of which we shall for ever be ignorant? Something, anyway, connected either with Gosse or his wife. I haven't let go a thought that whoever it was could have been known to Gosse and recognized, sealing the poor chap's death warrant so to speak.'

'If it's the back door key as it seems to be, it'd have to come from Mrs Gosse's possession, wouldn't it?' Rogers suggested. He turned his mouth down. 'A dead Mrs Gosse?'

'You're reading my mind.' The elegant Lingard had, inconsiderately in Rogers's irritable opinion, taken a full pinch of his Attar of Roses snuff and inhaled it with an exaggerated show of euphoria.

'Has this Passion Hawkins of ours uncovered anything about the Gosses yet?' Rogers had often wondered if he himself had a nickname, and, if he had, how revealing it was of how he was seen by the department.

'I've got it on paper, but most of it's domestic and shop trivia of the most ordinary. She was employed in the shop until Gosse took her unto his bosom and married her. The girl on whom Hawkins had presumably sacrificed his manhood had known her and had worked with her. She said she was a bit of a lass one way and another, and popular with men which, to my innocent mind, means only one thing when it's said by another woman; though all that was some time back, when she was into the potholing and microlight activities you've mentioned. Hawkins's informant also . . .'

Rogers interrupted him. 'Just a moment, David. You've reminded me. Forget Kyberd for the moment, who anyway mightn't be the man Mrs Gosse was infatuated with. Couldn't the man have been a member of one of the organizations running those things? A few enquiries at each might dig him out for a proper inspection.' He frowned, pulling at his lower lip with finger and thumb. 'Caves,' he said. 'Park Dominus. The airline pilot who was killed six years or so back and dumped in the Gawp Gut cave. We hadn't thought of that, had we?'

Lingard looked bewildered. 'I remember him, of course I do, but what's he to do with Mrs Gosse?'

'Not him,' Rogers said impatiently. 'Not necessarily Gawp Gut either. But if Mrs Gosse was ever involved with another potholer and he happens to be the one who killed her and had problems about hiding her body, I think he'd be driven to do it in a cave rather than in a canal.'

Lingard was doubtful. 'While people don't go swimming in the canal in winter – not at any time if they've any sense – they do go potholing at any time. A body would have been tripped over by now, surely?'

'Gawp Gut is a blind cave, something much like a largish sock, and I was told that it wasn't often climbed, if at all, because it didn't go anywhere.' Rogers knew it from personal experience, having been down it to view Dominus's body. Being a five-star claustrophobic, he had suffered, now preferring to think about it only when he had to; in daylight and with other people in his view. 'There must be at least a couple of others that go nowhere and I'm sure they'd be worth having a look at. I know Dickersen who runs the caving club so I'll twist his arm myself to get a search moving. You sort out the

Plattsmoss airfield end for the microlight part of it, and don't forget that we once had a woman dropped from one of their aircraft.' He changed course back to Gosse. 'You were saying something about Hawkins's informant?'

'So I was.' Lingard, having replenished his nostrils with his fragrant snuff, held out the tiny ivory box to Rogers, then as suddenly withdrawing it. 'Mustn't put temptation in your way, must I, George?' he said flippantly, putting it back in his waistcoat pocket. 'I was about to say that Hawkins reported that the girl he was chatting up or worse said that it was the talk of the shop that Gosse had been giving one of his married lady customers the freedom of his boat at Ullsmouth. Then a few weeks back a man they all thought must be the wronged husband visited him in his office and there were overheard angry words. Of course, they could have been arguing about anything and he needn't have been the woman's husband, so don't be all agog. Nobody knows the name of the lady and we have only the most sketchy and useless description of the man.' He grinned and jerked his head at Coltart. 'He could almost be our Eddie here, other than he was better-looking.'

Coltart, not appreciative of Lingard's flippancy and not liking him to excess anyway, grunted his scorn deep in his chest.

'You've cleared Henbest, I suppose?' Rogers wanted to go.

'He's as clean as a goldfish's bot,'Lingard answered. 'I'm probably being a mite naïve, but if you told me that he was on the short list for an archbishopric you wouldn't surprise me a bit.'

'Not the best of recommendations if you'd ever known any bishops-in-waiting,' Rogers told him cynically. 'If there's nothing more then we'd better get stuck into doing something useful.' He caught the eye of the much too good-looking youngster wearing a limp bow tie who fetched and carried the food, nodding his wish for the bill. 'Dutch,' he said to Lingard and Coltart, managing to look wolfish and in no mood to subsidize the feeding, even temporarily, of a couple of bachelors who must be choking on folding money. 'Unlike you two, I've an expensive ex-wife and her bloodsucking live-in boyfriend to support.'

He hadn't felt able to unburden himself on that subject before, but his resentment against the two for supplementing their income for what seemed all eternity with half his salary had finally pushed him into it. That he had not heard of her lover's genitals shrivelling and blackening was not for any lack of his earnest wishes to that end.

17

Before Rogers left Headquarters to see Durker – a subdued Durker whom he had advised by telephone of his coming in terms not allowing a refusal – he had decided against his earlier resolve not to attend at a brief press conference in the duty inspector's office. Liz Gallagher was one among the handful of reporters who attended, the only one not asking a question, though each of the others was patently determined to milk Rogers of the blood and shock/horror arising from Gosse's savagely inflicted death.

To his short-lived irritation, her presence there had initially made his heart thump as if momentarily out of kilter. Nothing in the dark and serious stare she directed at him showed anything of what might be considered the new-born intimacy existing between them. Nor, he admitted to himself, would anything be showing from behind his own impassivity as he passed out carefully vague snippets of information, but he still felt a tiny glow of resentment that what they had shared together had produced nothing more than an impersonal and discomfiting scrutiny. He supposed that it was what he had wanted and what he had got, a necessary camouflaging of their relationship; yet, perversely, he was finding it unpalatable.

Leaving Lingard to finish off the conference, he thought that it might be a good idea to deprogramme a disturbing Liz Gallagher from his mind before he found himself in too deeply to withdraw in a civilized, tidy and disciplined manner.

Durker was standing, apparently returning a law book to one of the shelves behind his desk, when Rogers was ushered in by the over-lipsticked girl who excluded non-fee-paying policemen from being worthy of a smile. He looked depressed, perhaps nervous – if solicitors could ever show nervousness – and briefly exposed his abundance of teeth in a greeting; which, Rogers thought, was something. Understandably, no hand was offered for shaking, since they were already declared antagonists.

'Take a seat, superintendent,' Durker said, sitting himself at his desk. His large, good-looking body was now dressed more appropriately in a dark-blue suit and white shirt, though the maroon silk tie he wore with it suggested to the detective an unwitting early morning expression of mental unease. Sitting forward with his elbows on his blotting pad and his fingers interlocked, he looked set to give Rogers, seated opposite him, a dose of his legalistic pomposity, accompanied by the wafting odours of whisky and toothpaste.

Rogers, determined on keeping his initial questioning low key, said pleasantly to the spectacled, pale-grey eyes fixed on him, 'I'm wondering if you've been in touch with Mr Kyberd? You said you'd speak to him about an interview.'

Durker frowned. 'So I did. I also said that I would contact you when I had a positive response. Are you saying that you've news of Mrs Gosse? That you've evidence to support your suspicion that some harm has befallen her?' He was speaking down to the detective again.

'You haven't spoken to him then?' Rogers was now frowning himself, his intent to a low key questioning stillborn.

Durker hesitated. 'No, I haven't. I probably shall when I consider it convenient.' Tension emanated from him, at variance with the manner of his speaking.

Rogers, sensing it, decided to exploit it, though he knew of the trouble he could be bringing on himself, most of which could affect whatever career prospects he might have entered on his record sheet were he to be wrong. 'I don't consider the matter of your convenience comes into it,' he said sternly. 'I have demonstrable gounds for believing that Mr Kyberd left his home under circumstances that must be considered highly suspicious; so suspicious, indeed, that I've already laid on enquiries at Luggate Heights.' There was an unexpected twisting in Durker's face that made him pause, though when nothing was said he continued, 'Unless you're prepared to be open with me, I shall be forced to take into my reckoning the coincidence or otherwise of both Mr Kyberd and his client Mrs Gosse being missing from their homes over the same period. Also, there is . . .'

He stopped, astonished at Durker's reaction to what had seemed to him not all that cataclysmic a statement, not sure of which over-the-top emotion was racking the man. It could have been a raging anger, though Rogers couldn't believe he had the backbone for that. His face was suffused a dull red as if his shirt collar were choking him, his teeth bared in what looked to be agonizing pain, and his hands now fists that clenched and unclenched on the desk. Breathing heavily and visibly struggling for control, his face slowly losing its distortion and returning to its normal colouring, the patiently watchful detective wondered what might be coming now.

When Durker spoke, his words were clearly despairing. 'I can't do it!' he cried, with the pink dampness of tears in his eyes, 'I can't tell you!'

Rogers, one of whose tenets was that a man never cried for himself, only for others, held a measure of contempt for him. 'You can't do what?' he demanded.

Durker was looking away from the detective, his emotional spasm apparently worked out. 'There's nothing you can do about it; nothing that need be your concern,' he said shakily. 'You'll not be receiving a complaint about it and until you do, you can do nothing.'

'But the fact that you say it isn't my concern does still upset you, doesn't it?' Rogers wished fervently that he had an inkling of what the daft bugger was talking about. That it had to do with Kyberd and Daphne Gosse was a certainty, but it was seemingly about much more than a few unethically dirty nights together of a solicitor and his client, and it behoved him to be cautious in his guessing. 'You know, of course, that my enquiries are bound to uncover what you appear to be so anxious to conceal?' His swarthy face was forbidding, his voice authoritative. 'And when anybody is that anxious about hiding whatever it is, then it has to be something very serious.'

He couldn't tell whether what he had said had made an

123

impact, other than that Durker was wordlessly withdrawn, chewing at the knuckle of his thumb and frowning in deep thought. The detective was now content to wait it out in a silence that must be becoming oppressive to him.

When Rogers was beginning to think that he had lost Durker stumbling about in the inner spaces of his own skull, he surfaced, muttering, 'Excuse me,' and lifting the handset of an internal telephone. 'Clarice,' he said into it, 'I shan't be wanting you again today, so you may leave now and finish off what you are doing tomorrow morning.' Replacing the handset, he said with little trace of his earlier pomposity, 'You are right in assuming that I am keeping from you a matter of some seriousness, though I certainly deny that I am a party to it.'

'You're referring to something your partner's done, I take it.' Rogers was beginning to see light. 'And as a consequence he's skipped it?'

There was indecision in Durker's expression, then a sort of flabby resolution. He said, 'I've been placed in the dreadful position of trying to resolve what appears to be a deficit in our clients' funds.'

'A substantial one?'

'More than can be replaced even were I of a mind to.' He looked chapfallen enough to have been confessing his own sins.

'You didn't answer my question about your partner,' Rogers said.

'I'm not naming names until I know for certain. There is a loyalty I wish to observe, an obligation.'

'You have one to your clients as well as to the Law Society,' Rogers said bluntly. 'Have you done anything about that?' He shook his head at the foolishness of his own question. 'Of course you haven't. How much was it?'

'I don't know. I'm not sure. There are documents missing, books . . . in any event I'm quite sure that it can't be any of your business at this stage.' He was verging on being distraught, a picture of muted defiance in abject misery; from where Rogers sat, most of it appearing to be for himself and probably justifiably so. 'Whichever way, I'm ruined professionally, though I've done no more than to try and straighten matters out.' His eyes were brimming with held-back tears again and he wiped them with the back of his forefinger. 'He is the senior partner you know, and I respected him. Now that he's left me to be held responsible for what he's done, I shall be struck off, finished, for without the documents he's destroyed or taken with him who can tell?'

Rogers was almost tempted to advise him to seek the advice of one of the more discreditable criminal barristers, who could so easily and deceitfully transmute the smell of manure into the most fragrant of perfumes. 'Innocence must always convince against a false accusation,' he said sententiously, though knowing damned well that it seldom did. Durker wasn't winning any sympathy from him by his blubbing in the face of adversity, and he thought cynically that it hadn't taken more than a few words for him to ditch overboard his fine sentiments about loyalty and obligations and to run scared. 'I'm here,' he said, 'and if you wish to make a statement of complaint in writing about it, I'll see what we can do about finding where your partner is.'

Durker shook his head vigorously. '*No!*' he said with more emphasis in his voice than before. 'Not until I've reported to the Law Society. Then you can do what you wish, for I shall be finished.'

'Putting aside Mr Kyberd's sins as you may,' Rogers told him, 'I have still to consider Mrs Gosse's well-being. Would she be with him?'

Durker was looking at him now, his pale-grey eyes pink-rimmed and watery behind the spectacles and showing in them a strong dislike of the detective. 'I don't believe it to be in the best interests of this firm to give you any more information at all, superintendent,' he said, his voice firmer, his put-on pomposity beginning to re-emerge. 'However, having given you so much, I will say that Mr Kyberd probably allowed himself to be indiscreetly over-friendly with Mrs Gosse. Perhaps too much so for a properly ethical relationship between them.' He looked down at his hands resting on the desk. 'There was an occasion when she first came here for a consultation when she – well, I believe that she made it quite obvious that she would have preferred me to deal with her problems, though, at the time, I was unable to. What I mean is that she was a lady not backward in indicating where her preferences lay.' He looked as if he was sniffing inaudibly his distaste for her. 'I'm afraid I didn't like her. I thought her too pushing.'

'In what she said? Or suggested?'

'Not at all. It was in the way she looked at you.'

Rogers smiled inside himself at his naiveté. 'Perhaps Mr Kyberd saw her in a different light.' Dropping Daphne Gosse, whom he was now seeing as a woman of many parts, he said, 'I presume you had words with him about the stolen funds?'

Durker looked shocked. 'I didn't know until he'd gone. When he hadn't returned after a day or so I became suspicious and checked on the accounts.'

'When was he last here?'

Durker tightened his lips as if about to refuse to answer, then took a diary from a drawer in the desk and flipped pages. 'On Friday the eleventh of this month. A fortnight this coming weekend.'

'And the next day when he didn't turn up at the office you started to worry?'

'We're not running a shop, you know. This office is closed on Saturdays and Sundays. When he failed to arrive here on Monday I telephoned his home and kept on telephoning all day. In the afternoon I went there, getting no answer to my knocking. I looked in the garage and saw that his car wasn't there, so I knew that he had gone somewhere.' He shrugged his dejection. 'I checked again during the evening and night – there was still no answer. The following day it was the same, and I was sending Miss Franklin up there now and then to see if his car had been garaged.'

'And after only two days you suddenly thought, "Ah! My respected senior partner being missing, he must have been stealing from the clients' accounts"? Is that what you're saying? Not that he might have gone off somewhere for an entirely different reason? Such as wishing to spend a few days with Mrs Gosse and not having you being too curious about his private goings-on? It's all a little odd, don't you think?' he said, shaking his head as if perplexed.

'There's no need for you to be offensive, superintendent,' Durker said with a show of spirit. 'It's obvious now that I did

suspect Mr Kyberd of something beforehand. I'd already become aware that certain bank transactions were being kept from me and I hadn't the moral courage to ask for an explanation. That he then went away without telling me confirmed my suspicions, and I was able to do a more comprehensive checking of our records.' He was back to gnawing at his thumb, probably realizing that despite the talking the dark-grey cloud hanging over his head wasn't going to go away.

'And trying to make up your mind to report it to the Law Society, I imagine.' In a way, Rogers felt sorry for the man. Behind his degree in law and his physical bigness, he was wet. 'Would you have any idea at all where Mr Kyberd might now be?'

'No. It must be clear to anybody thinking about it that under the circumstances he was hardly likely to tell me.' That had been a rare excursion by the solicitor into sarcasm.

'True,' Rogers said almost cheerfully. He was getting Durker to talk, which was his objective and, where a solicitor was concerned, no mean achievement. 'He has a passport, of course?'

'I believe he has. He's talked of touring France in the past.' He hesitated, indecision in his expression. 'It may be fanciful, but I believe that he might still be here. In the locality, I mean. Last Monday morning when I returned to the office, I had the distinct impression that my papers in the desk had been interfered with, that somebody had been sitting in my chair.'

'You're not certain though?' Rogers questioned, staring hard at him.

'Who could be? I am meticulous in my habits and, on closing the office, I leave my papers neatly in a manner which is my own and which he doesn't share. On Monday, I found them clearly to be not. Fussy as it may seem, I leave my chair flush against the desk. On Monday, I found it askew, evidently having been sat in. Whoever had been in had had to use a key and, apart from myself and Miss Franklin, only Mr Kyberd has one. It speaks for itself, doesn't it?'

'If you can trust your Miss Franklin, it does,' Rogers conceded. 'There was nothing stolen?'

'I do trust her and there has been nothing stolen or taken

127

away that I am aware of. But that's never easy to be sure of when it's a matter of documents, is it?'

'If you say so. What does she think of Mr Kyberd's absence?'

'I told her later that I'd heard from him, that he was suffering from a minor nervous breakdown and had gone away for a necessary break. It didn't sound very convincing, but it was the best I could do and she appears to have accepted it.'

'Was Mr Kyberd's office visited?'

'It must have been, I suppose. I looked at once, naturally, but saw nothing to suggest it.' He had given up gnawing at his thumb and was now manipulating one of his gold-coloured desk pens in his fingers. 'I was so sure that he had been here that I wrote a short note which I left on his desk at nights, expecting that he might come again.'

'To what effect?' Rogers, never in the business of wholly believing what he was told, was wondering how much of all this he could accept.

Durker hesitated, then pulled open the drawer from which he had taken the diary, retrieving a slip of yellow paper. Reading through it with his lips pursed and again hesitating, he then handed it to the detective.

Taking it, Rogers saw that it was handwritten in ink and read:

Hugh, It is clear that you have returned here again to be reading this. You must know by now that in your absence apparent discrepancies in the funds account have come to light. I am deeply shocked and distressed and need to find a way of protecting the firm by avoiding the necessity of disclosing the state of affairs as they stand to the Society and then, inevitably, to the police. I am pleading with you to return and to help me avoid what would be humiliation and disaster for us both. Michael.

Rogers said, 'If he did come again, you obviously failed to persuade him.'

'I'm sure he didn't come. I put odd documents and items where they would have to be moved by anyone coming in and they haven't so far been disturbed. Whatever it was he was looking for, he probably found first time.'

'You must have some idea of what he was looking for,'

Rogers put to him, trying to hold Durker's gaze from doing its sliding-away act.

'Only that it would be concerned with the . . . what we've been discussing. I rather believe he must have found and taken them, for I've looked myself and can't find them.' He sounded as though he was about to tighten up on any further disclosures. 'I'd be obliged if you'd leave now that you have received my more than adequate co-operation. And I do remind you strongly that I have not made a complaint about what has yet to be proved, nor about a man who has yet to have the facts put to him, and you therefore have no authority to enquire further into this matter until I make an official complaint.'

Rogers stared hard at him. The bloody man was crack-brained if he thought this was going to be the end of his interest in Kyberd. 'I understand what you say,' he acknowledged coldly, 'but don't be misled into thinking that you've been doing me a favour. You wouldn't have told me anything if you hadn't sometime to disclose the theft of your clients' funds to the Law Society. You, in my opinion, are on the brink of committing a serious criminal offence by delaying the reporting of your partner's apparent theft. Were I you, I'd look up Archbold's *Criminal Pleading* for the definition of the concealment of a crime and start worrying. And don't think that you've neutralized me by refusing to make a complaint. I shall have enquiries made to locate your partner, if only on the basis that Mrs Gosse is suspected of being with him.'

Surprisingly, the silent Durker had taken the flak reasonably calmly, though what was showing in his eyes would never have been taken for affection. While strafing him, Rogers had been considering whether or not to add to his burdens, deciding that he should. 'I don't quite know how it might affect you or your partner's professional relationship with Mrs Gosse,' he said almost conversationally, having expended most of his irritation, 'but her husband need no longer be considered a respondent, now being dead.'

He had always liked the word dumbstruck and Durker now illustrated it completely, with his jaw dropping, his mouth opening in astonishment, before he was able to say stupidly, 'Dead? How can he be dead?'

'Because last night somebody hit him on the head hard enough to make sure that he was.' Rogers stood from his chair, poised to leave at the first question. 'It's still very much under wraps so I'll say no more.'

Durker also stood, clumsily pushing back his chair and saying angrily, 'If you are suggesting, even by implication, that this must somehow have something to do with Mr Kyberd, I warn you to be very careful, superintendent.'

Rogers was curt with him. 'I hadn't suggested that at all. You did, so don't charge me with your own mistaken assumptions.' He had wanted to get a better description of Kyberd from him, but had left it too late and could now only anticipate an angry refusal. Instead, knowing he should not show how he felt but being bloody-minded about it, he glared his own anger at the solicitor, turned away from him and left the office, at least exhibiting enough restraint not to slam the door behind him. It all amounted, he considered, to a lack of calming nicotine in his bloodstream.

18

Once given his possible occupation, it was easy for Lingard to identify and find the offensive designer-bearded man with the forename of Simon, described by the headmaster of St Boni-face's School. Enquiring anonymously by telephone of the local Polytechnic College of Art produced the name Simon Urquhart and the address of his studio in Pennyfarthing Lane. A check on local records produced nothing more than three road traffic convictions for unlawful speeding and one for reckless driving, to all three of which he had pleaded Not Guilty, and seven on-the-spot fines for parking offences. All of which suggested to Lingard a man either arrogantly stubborn or anti-establishment, or both. Not having, for obvious reasons, asked at the college whether Urquhart was stubble-bearded or not, Lingard couldn't be certain that this was his man until he had telephoned him, told him who he was and said that he understood him to know a Mrs Daphne Gosse and therefore wished to call on him on a matter of importance concerning her. If it was convenient, naturally.

Urquhart – his voice fitted the detective's conception of him as being arrogant – said that he was working, but would see Lingard only so long as whatever he wished to say didn't last all bloody afternoon.

Pennyfarthing Lane led off the Old Market Square in the centre of the town. It was a dead end thoroughfare with three black-painted iron bollards at its entrance denying access to its multicoloured tiling to anything on more than two wheels. The narrow squeezed-together Georgian buildings in its short length each had its ground floor occupied by a boutique, an art and craft shop, a pottery, a fine arts gallery, a tapestry-weaving centre or another of the same kind. It looked a dangerous place to visit while holding a credit card.

Urquhart's name plate, modestly inconspicuous considering how his words had sounded over the telephone, was on a door between a herbalist's and a perfumery store, both breathing out sweet fragrances into the cold air of the lane.

Lingard climbed leg-achingly up two steep flights of unlit stairway to reach another door displaying Urquhart's name. The man who opened it to his knocking wore an Oxford-blue shirt and trousers with a patterned pale-blue handkerchief knotted around his throat, and was the living reality of Henbest's description. He looked as if he hadn't shaved for a week, and there was a lifting of one side of his upper lip suggestive of a built-in dispraising sneer. But, by God, Lingard accepted, he possessed a forceful, good-looking masculinity that any woman not purblind or lesbian would wish to get very close to. Taking his time and ignoring Lingard's introducing himself, he stood there, his darkest of brown eyes self-assuredly appraising the detective from his tan-coloured camel hair coat down to his hand-built shoes and socks. Seemingly satisfied – he had spent time on Lingard's silk shirt – he said, 'You'd better come in, hadn't you?' closing the door behind him.

Lingard hadn't much liked the man on his first sight of him, though, as he admitted to himself, he wasn't being paid to like or dislike people. Keeping Urquhart waiting in his turn, he looked around the studio with deliberation. It was a bare-boarded room with two closed side-by-side inner doors and a large skylight in the high sloping ceiling, three night-storage heaters making the air in it uncomfortably hot. The furnishings consisted of a cushioned high wooden chair for his sitters, an elderly gold-coloured *chaise longue*, a bench holding paint-stained pots, jars of brushes and an untidy mess of discoloured cloths and squeezed-out paint tubes. A number of sketched on and unfinished canvases rested against one of the walls. A large wooden easel held a canvas showing the completed head of a red-haired woman, her electric-blue draped shoulders in the process of being painted. Close to the easel was a standing headless dressmaker's dummy fitted with the dress being painted in on the canvas, and a small table holding a palette of colours, two or three tubes of paint and brushes. Lingard, knowing something of painting styles and noting the sitter's long and slender neck and sharp-planed features, thought with some imagination that it was likely that one of Urquhart's grandmothers could have had a fruitful love affair with the Italian painter Modigliani.

He smiled chummily at Urquhart who had turned away from him to pick up the palette and brushes and stand at his easel. 'Don't let me hold you up with your painting,' he said. 'We can talk while you're doing it.'

'So I intend,' Urquhart told him, unresponsive to the smile, but sounding reasonably civilized about the situation. He was laying blue paint on fascinatingly bare shoulders with short strokes of his brush. 'What is it that's so important about Mrs Gosse?'

'She's been missing from her home for the past three weeks.' Lingard was already anticipating difficulties.

'So?' The eyebrows had lifted, nothing more.

'With your having an association with her, you . . .'

'*Had*,' Urquhart interrupted, correcting him. 'Get your facts right.'

'My apologies. With your having had an association with her, you might be able to help in suggesting where she might be.'

'That's easy, I can't.' He looked from his painting to the detective. 'If that's all there is I won't keep you.'

Lingard, holding Urquhart's challenging stare, took out his snuff-box and pinched Attar of Roses into his nostrils. 'It isn't, actually,' he said equably. 'I thought that having known Mrs Gosse you might tell me something about her. Something that'd help us to find her.'

Urquhart had resumed his painting. 'What I know about her isn't a subject I propose retailing to coppers.'

'That sounds very gentlemanly of you,' Lingard said with heavy irony. 'Though possibly not where it concerns your threatening her outside St Boniface's School a little while back. In September to be precise.'

'Screw you.' He hadn't looked from his canvas, still intent upon laying on colour and narrowing his eyes in doing it. 'Who in the hell d'you think you're talking to?'

Lingard was unruffled. 'I thought somebody reasonably civilized. I'm mistaken?'

'You could be.' He wiped the brush he held in a scrap of rag and turned to face the detective. 'I didn't know that Mrs Gosse was missing and, at the moment, it's not anything that particularly interests me. Because I want to be rid of you I'll answer those questions I think are your business to ask and which won't be misinterpreted enough to drop me in any crap that may be lying around.'

'That's fair enough, though usually said only when you've something to hide,' Lingard told him, ready to get nasty with a man who was getting up his nose. 'So what were you and Mrs Gosse fighting over at the school?'

Instead of answering immediately – and Lingard had thought he would object to his first remark – Urquhart threw his brush down on the table and strode over to the canvases stacked against the wall. Pulling one out, he returned to Lingard and displayed it to him. It was a head and shoulders portrait of a young dark-haired woman, possibly of Spanish descent and of considerable attractiveness, wearing a white fur around a neck that appeared to have been elongated in the Urquhart style. 'This,' he said forcefully. 'She commissioned it and then told me she didn't want it, didn't want to pay for it either.'

Unsurprisingly, her representation in paint hadn't looked much like that shown in the enlarged photograph Rogers had given him, but this, Lingard knew, was what made the difference between the lens of a camera and the brain and eye of a man with a paint brush in his hand. 'And you were threatening to break her arm or whatever because of it?' He put contempt in his words. 'Doing your own debt collecting?' He paused. 'However, it happens that I don't believe you. I presume your association with her was something a little more intimate than painting her?' When Urquhart stood silent as if waiting for him to leave unanswered, he added, 'Hardly a circumstance in which you'd push for payment, is it?'

While talking, Lingard had been recording visually the man's physical features for his future recall. It was mainly a reinforcement of Henbest's description, adding to it that the painter possessed the bullet head, thick neck and sloping shoulders of a professional boxer; not a man to irritate unnecessarily, he judged; the dense beginnings of his beard giving him a piratical appearance to go with it.

'Maybe I was protecting the lady's virtue,' Urquhart said mildly in a sudden reversal of mood. 'And I'll tell you why if it'll get you off my back. If it doesn't, I'll be forced to chuck you out.' He bared his teeth in what was either pleasurable anticipation or a warning. 'I've your promise?'

Lingard, a practitioner of the painful art of kung fu and certainly not chuckable out by even an athletic and short-fused painter of women, smiled as if hearing something amusing and replied, 'Tell me, I'm sure it'll be interesting.' Though he didn't yet know the reason, he wasn't at all taken in by Urquhart's change of attitude, for mildness sat ill on his features.

'So be it, but interesting it isn't,' Urquhart said. 'I'd painted her, as you've seen, and the truth of the matter is that I did it about a year ago at the time I was separated from my wife and kids and badly in need of a woman's company. Daphne and I met apparently by chance – I've never been certain that she hadn't deliberately arranged it – and were catching up on an old affair we'd had way back and which I'd all but forgotten.' He grimaced as if to suggest that he wasn't a man who wanted that to happen to him. 'There was nothing serious about any of it, just something casual and matter-of-fact for me to keep in practice and it died the death in a very short time and not too

134

long after I'd finished the painting. I'll admit I was a bloody fool to have had anything further to do with her for, attractive though she was, she'd always been a screwball. Somebody you could always depend on to do something mad and therefore on the dangerous side to be too close to. Anyway, the painting. She said she didn't wish to take it with her, said that her old man would go spare if he knew and would guess there'd been something between us.' He shrugged his resignation. 'We can nearly always see there's no ending to what we intended to be a short-term affair, so I shouldn't have been surprised when she rang me here and asked me to meet her over something important and very hush-hush. I was back with my wife by then and I still am, and the prospect of having anything to do with her again was a bit off-putting. Still, I did meet her out of school as she'd asked me . . . did she tell you that, or the old boy who came out to see what all the rumpus was about?'

'She's missing, remember?' Lingard reminded him. 'So she'd be in no position to tell me anything. What had caused the hard words between you?'

'She started by trying to butter me up about how she'd missed me, how I was the only man who'd treated her as a woman and not just a thingummy to go to bed with.' His expression was wholly scornful. 'Holy Hell! She couldn't have meant it, and I knew she was going to put the hook into me for something I would rather not do. Don't think I'm armour-plated and fireproofed against the bagfuls of sex a woman like Daphne's capable of using to get what she wants, I'm not. But it did make me angry because she knew I'm a soft number for women like her and she was using it.' He gave his brief grin again, patently not to be taken as a sign of amiability towards the detective. 'She told me that she was leaving her husband because he was a violent bastard who'd made life so unbearable for her that she wanted to get out, but still stay locally for two or three days though not where he might find her. I guessed what she was after, of course.' He jerked his head at the inner doors behind him. 'She knows this studio's a part of my town flat because she's stayed here on an occasion or two. When I told her that it was breaking my heart to say it, but not bloody likely, she came the heavy stuff about would it be my wife who

135

was coming between us and holding me back, and had she found out about what we had meant to each other in the past . . . bitchy stuff like that.'

He looked derisive, almost as if seeking Lingard's understanding that that's how it was with women. 'That's when I became angry with her because I knew exactly what she meant. She was putting the black on me to let her use my rooms and I wasn't having it. I couldn't, anyway, with my wife likely to bob in when she came into town to do the shopping. When the old boy joined us, he was my saver and I told her that I'd think about it – worry about it, I actually meant – and then left her. Thank God I never heard from her again and, if she stays missing, don't count on me being too unhappy about it. When I say that nothing of what I've told you was out of character for Daphne, you'll think what a half-witted pratt I must have been to've had anything to do with her after the first lot.'

'Aren't we all,' Lingard agreed with him, refilling his nose with more snuff. 'You've seen her since?'

'You give me a pain, chum. You weren't listening.' His stare, now hostile, bore down on the nonchalant detective who took it imperturbably. 'I remember distinctly saying that I'd not heard from her again.'

'So you did,' Lingard murmured, having had his own reasons for asking. 'Just as well, perhaps, in view of what happened. While you were exercising your undoubted charm on her, how did you really find her as a person? Emotionally, I mean.' He did his own bit of hard staring. 'That is, of course, if you think you can confide in a copper.'

'I said that I'd chuck you out if you didn't get off my back,' Urquhart growled at him, 'and you don't have a lot of time left in which to get the message.'

'I'm on the way out,' Lingard said agreeably and smiling, recognizing that this was a scenario necessary for the painter's touchy self-respect. 'You were about to tell me what kind of a woman your Mrs Gosse was.'

'She's not my damned anything,' he retorted, 'and if you have to know, I didn't like her all that much. She was too earthy, had no finesse and was an extremely hot-blooded woman who could get in a fine old passion. She also had a temper that sometimes resulted in this.' He beat his fists in the air like a woman hitting a taller man's chest. 'Much as I imagine her type would.'

'You mentioned a previous affair you'd had with her. Tell me about that.'

Lingard received the full force of Urquhart's scorn. 'Do you mean how many times we did it? How long it used to take and whether she liked it or not? Are you one of those guys who get a hard on at hearing about it second-hand?'

'Don't measure my hang-ups by your own,' Lingard told him unruffled, pinching snuff elegantly and inhaling it into his nose, then flapping stray grains away with a fox-red handkerchief. 'I've always known that one man's sexual squalidness is another's pleasurable enlightenment, but that's not what I'm after. Tell me how and where you met her without being too damned offensive.'

Urquhart was apparently even less subject to reacting to fanciful invective than the disciplined Lingard. He said, 'I met her when we were both idiotic enough to be caving hereabouts and happened to be members of the same club. That was ten years or so back when she was Daphne Naylor and it was open season for us both. It went on and off for about eighteen months until I got fed up with sharing with the competition and I backed off. Satisfied?'

'And that was it until she just happened to want her portrait painted?' Lingard allowed disbelief to colour his question.

'Wrong.' Urquhart turned and moved towards his easel, picking up palette and brushes, though turning his head to reply to Lingard. 'I'd seen her about the town on occasions when all we said when we were on the same side of the street was something like "Hi!" in passing, and I later heard that she'd married that pathetic chemist chap, or, more probably, his money. It wasn't until this summer that we bumped into each other in the Sam Johnson Coffee House. As I said, I rather think she'd seen me and followed me in. I was on my own and sleeping here at the flat and she was her usual self, so it seemed convenient that we finished off the morning up here. Later on, I suppose to keep her happy and give her an excuse for coming here should she want it, I offered to paint her and she sat for me. That wasn't any big deal either. Eventually, of course, we got fed up with each other and that, so far as I was concerned, was that.' He broke off eye contact with the detective, appearing to be addressing the painted woman in front of him. 'And that's my lot with you, too. It's now get out time, so shove off and shut the door behind you.'

Lingard levelled his gaze at Urquhart's back, deciding that he was wholly bullet-headed. 'Before I go,' he said. 'That pathetic chemist chap whose wife you've been crawling all over was killed last night – banged on the head with foul intent by an as yet unknown person probably coveting his wife, his ox or his ass. Something like that, we imagine. You're interested?'

Urquhart was paddling his brush in a blob of blue paint he had squeezed on to the palette and long moments went by before he froze into a rigid stiffness, a tendon prominent in the side of his neck. Then he slowly turned, his face showing nothing, but his narrowed eyes saying it all. 'You bloody tricky bastard,' he whispered, dropping palette and brush on to the table and taking a step forward with clenched fists. 'You've been saving that up, haven't you; trying to catch me out in something you've got in your nasty little mind.'

Lingard's daunting blue eyes stared at him coldly. 'If there's any catching out that's been done, you've done it yourself. And if you're about to do what I think you are, I promise that you'll spend tonight in a police cell.'

Urquhart returned the unwavering stare for as long as it took Lingard to take out his ivory box and inhale his Attar of Roses. Then he made a harsh grating noise in his throat and turned, walking stiff-legged to one of the inner doors and opening it. Lingard had a brief glimpse of a refrigerator and part of a cooker before he closed it behind him, all the more impressive because he didn't slam it as he might have been judged entitled to.

Were he so minded, there were two things Lingard could do to sidestep the impasse in which he found himself. Either would undoubtedly involve him both in violence and in later disciplinary proceedings. A third course of action, which would resolve nothing, would be to walk out of the studio with his interview unfinished. It hadn't been too long or too successful, not yet giving Lingard any assurance that Urquhart wasn't lying through his teeth.

Calling out a fairly cheerful 'Good afternoon' to the door through which he had gone, Lingard left and descended the stairs, uncertain whether or not it had been significant of anything other than bloody-mindedness that Urquhart had first refused to discuss Mrs Gosse and then been almost garrulously willing to do so later.

19

Rogers, chairbound in his office and having had a fast read through the contents of his IN tray, was cerebrally active in assembling, where possible, hitherto dissociated facts and theories in some sort of order, leaving any disparate items to dangle in an investigational limbo. It was nothing he enjoyed, being a brain-aching and frustrating endeavour he would happily have discarded in favour of being outside and dealing with those lying, malevolent, fornicating, brutish and unscrupulous specimens of *Homo sapiens* he regarded as his customers.

In truth, he thought he was getting nowhere with the investigation, and that was bringing forebodings of a failure he was finding increasingly difficult to disguise with an appearance of optimism. Without a pipe between his teeth, he seemed to have lost the habit of applying a benign contemplation to the resolving of his problems. Above all, he felt disordered, the inside of his mouth tasting as exciting as tepid distilled water; sure that his nerve-endings, imagined as tiny pink and overly sanitized threadworms, were shrieking out their need for the anaesthesia of tobacco smoke. Pushing his re-emerging addiction aside was, he thought, as great an act of will as might be that of a monk repulsing a temptation of the flesh.

Coltart had obtained Kyberd's car registration number routinely from the national licensing centre and Rogers had prepared and circulated a message to his own and surrounding forces.

Confidential. Not for disclosure outside receiving forces. Whereabouts sought for interview – Hugh C. KYBERD, solicitor, approx. 45 yrs, about 5' 10" and stocky build, brown hair thinning on top, brown eyes, pointed nose, clean shaven. Believed in possession of his Rover 2000 saloon, metallic green with black roof covering, registration number B1273PQ. Is absent from his home and may be accompanied by Mrs Daphne Gosse, née Naylor, subject of Missing Person circulation of 23 November. Enquiries at hotels requested. Refer any information to D/Supt. G. Rogers, 07444–620404, Ext. 7.

Among the papers he had read was a preliminary report from the Forensic Science Laboratory referring to the receipt there of a Model 3001 Printmaster portable typewriter (Exhibit D) and an octavo sheet of paper (Exhibit E) purporting to be a note from a Clifford Gosse. Examination had shown that the machine and the note had in common a faulty alignment of the letter *S* key, with minor mutilations evident in the letters *d* and *y*. These defects, the report said, could prove with certainty that Exhibit E had been typed on Exhibit D, and, if it were necessary for any proceedings to be instituted, a comparison table would be prepared.

Which would be fine, Rogers thought, were there anybody in the frame against whom he could contemplate proceedings. That it pointed to the dead Gosse's having typed the note, or, less probably, his now missing wife, wasn't of much help, for it made no sense that either had done it. Not to him, at least. He strangled a yawn about to happen, realizing that, having been up and about since half-past three that morning, he was now tired as well as being deprived.

A report from Sergeant Magnus was equally unenlightening, though it might have a later promise held in it. Magnus had lifted a number of finger impressions from the bedrooms, bathroom and kitchen of the Gosse residence, identifying most of them as having been made by Gosse when compared with inked impressions taken at the mortuary from the dead man's fingers. The fewer, smaller prints he had to assume had been made by a woman, he guessed by Mrs Gosse, unless her husband had had the unlikely habit of having other women use the second bedroom. He had searched for and found finger impressions in the cabin of the bilge keel cruiser *Ephedra* and in the interior of Mrs Gosse's Mini car. These he had compared with the fingerprints of Gosse, identifying several in the boat's cabin, but not in the Mini. None of the fingerprints found in the house and assumed to have been made by Mrs Gosse were found in the cabin, though Magnus had found three so far unidentified prints made either by a woman or a young person. Conversely, the only fingerprints he had found in the Mini had been identical with those assumed to have been made by Mrs Gosse, though there were smears which appeared to have been made by leather-gloved fingers.

Ruminating on the fact of the larcenous Kyberd and deciding on some action – any action – rather than sitting on his backside and thinking about it, he looked up the solicitors' office telephone number and dialled it. Durker answered, noticeably not happy at hearing Rogers's voice.

'On reflection and having regard to what I've been told,' the detective said with a put-on brusqueness, 'I've decided that your partner's house shall be searched. I can't think you'd want me to spell out the grounds for my decision over the telephone. You've a key, I imagine?'

There was a long moment's wait before Durker answered. Then it was, 'You'll do no such thing, superintendent,' being more authoritative on the telephone than when being bearded in his office. 'I refuse on Mr Kyberd's behalf to permit it. You have no grounds you may use for this and I'll not hesitate to take proceedings against you should you proceed with this serious and unlawful trespass.'

'In that case you leave me no choice, Mr Durker, but to go before a magistrate and apply for a search warrant, which I can do immediately.' Rogers was about to leave the solicitor with a no option situation on his lap. 'It would then, as you know, be necessary for me to swear on oath a summary of the facts I have and the substance of that which you told me this afternoon in order to justify it. My being forced to disclose this in order to get the warrant certainly won't be in your interests or your partner's.'

There was another long silence while Durker apparently

worked that out. When he spoke, his thin and reedy voice was that of a man whose throat had seized up at the reminder of the potential disaster waiting for him from the Law Society. 'That,' he croaked, 'will not be necessary, superintendent. I do not have a key, but I do insist on being present.'

'I already have the neighbour's key, so there's no problem,' Rogers said cheerfully. 'In an hour's time – say five-thirty, if that suits you.' He closed down, not giving Durker the opportunity of bloody-mindedly disagreeing with an arrangement he had no intention of changing. Nor caring much whether Durker would be there or not, just so long as he could get it done before he returned to his apartment to get back some of his lost sleep.

With the darkness of the coming evening encroaching against the cone of light given out by the desk lamp, Rogers closed down the venetian blinds; then remembered that among those things not done he had yet to call Dickersen, the president of the High Moor Speliological Club. He was still speaking to him when Lingard entered the office. He gestured to him to sit and wait, finishing his conversation and replacing the receiver.

'I'll tell you about that later,' he said to Lingard, trying to read signs of achievement in his face. 'I hope you've dug out something useful?' He looked up at the tobacco-smoke-stained ceiling in simulated entreaty. 'Dear God, I hope that some bugger has, because if there's anyone who needs it, it's me down here.'

'Get up off your heathenish knees, George,' Lingard said. 'You'll get no help there, and I think only a smidgen of it from me.'

Rogers thought that there was almost an affront in his second-in-command's looking as immaculate and freshly-scrubbed as he did so late in the day. It always suggested to him that Lingard had sneaked off while on duty to refurbish the elegance of his image. Rogers leaned his presently unimmaculate self back in his chair – it did its usual squeaking noises, as if it housed a colony of mice – and folded his arms, listening closely to Lingard's detailed account of his interview with Urquhart. Despite his concentating, he was having a little trouble in preventing his eyelids from drooping.

'His having been potholing with Mrs Gosse seems to be an interesting connection,' he said when Lingard had finished, 'though I must say I feel a little doubtful about the likelihood of her being found in one after having words with Durker this afternoon. That's something for later, however. How does their coupling weigh with you? Significantly?'

'Significant to a degree or two, I think,' Lingard replied, a little discouragingly. 'But no doubt, as Urquhart said, there were others in the potholing mob sharing in the goodies she had on offer. So it's a matter of who can tell, and I can't. Not at the moment, anyway.'

'You make him a womanizer?'

'That for sure. If I had a wife who needed her portrait painted, he's the last one I'd commission to do it. I don't think the *chaise longue* in his studio is there just to sit on, so all in all I don't believe he'd get in too much of a lather over any one woman. I'm also inclined to accept that Urquhart's first go at dodging the flak was the average married man's pusillanimous attitude when somebody mentions him in connection with another woman.'

Apart from the largely merited gibe about married men, Rogers wasn't in agreement with that, but Lingard was the one who had interviewed the man and his opinion held the most weight. 'He sounds to me,' he said, 'a man who'd lay one on you given half a provocation.'

'Or none at all. He's certainly got what I'd call a violence of the tongue, but somehow I can't equate him with using a walking-stick on Gosse, short on temper though he seems to be.' Lingard was visibly searching in his mind for what he had to say, poking fingers through his blond hair. 'Not even being near to pretending I know anything about psychology,' he said, 'I am of the opinion that while he may be somehow connected with Mrs Gosse's being missing, he knows nothing about her husband's death.'

'You're sticking your neck out, David. Justify.'

'Egad, George, so I am, and so I will.' Lingard wasn't at all put out of countenance. 'Before I sprang it on him – agreed, not too diplomatically – he'd been using words and phrases I wouldn't believe any man with a killing on his mind would use.

He'd have been more careful before barging along with the attitudes he did.'

'I wouldn't quarrel with that,' Rogers said, but sounding as if about to do so, 'though it wouldn't be the first time by far that a bit of side-stepping with a touch of openness was used to camouflage guilt. More so as he chopped you off at the knees when you did tell him that Gosse had been murdered.' He pulled at his lower lip in doubt. 'I don't know. I suppose in itself that could equally be an argument for his not being involved. Keep your interest in him going, David, and we'll see. Not all homicidal intentions come from cuckolded husbands. It has been known for those who objected to their wives being rogered by the passing traffic to have had life made difficult, even dangerous for them, one way or another. Is that your lot?' He yawned behind clenched teeth, disguising anything that might have showed by coughing.

'I'd like your say-so to call off the organized search for Mrs Gosse,' Lingard proposed. 'The troops have covered as much ground as can be expected of them and the canal's been a dead loss from the beginning. That is, unless we're interested in the loads of old junk that've been heaved into it, and having our underwater search squad go down with galloping ptomaine poisoning or worse.'

'Finish it,' Rogers said. 'I've already heard that divisional chief superintendents are bitching about us keeping their chaps off the beats. We've only the caves to do, which, when done, should satisfy our detractors-to-be that we've used maximum endeavour.' He smiled. 'After that, we'll have to see what develops from our not knowing what to do next.'

'Are you accepting that she's unfindably dead? Or missing of her own volition?' Lingard was packing his nostrils with his Attar of Roses with Rogers not too far from asking him for a pinch or two.

'That's the problem, isn't it?' He thought that that had stuck out a mile. 'My interview this afternoon with Durker didn't help all that much.' He told him what had emerged from it, referring to his notes when necessary, so that Lingard had a clear picture of the nature of Durker's responses to his questions.

'He sounds an awkward cove,' Lingard commented, raising his eyebrows, 'but why the doubts?'

'He fell in too easily with my suggestion that his partner might have been unethically having it off with a client, that they could have gone away together. Mind, as Kyberd's partner he's bound to be roped in up to a point in whatever trouble there'll be over the clients' funds, and I imagine that this must affect whatever loyalty he says he has for him. He must already feel hard done by, so why shouldn't he add a further bit to the infamy Kyberd's earned himself already, when I'd virtually put the idea into his mind? On the other hand,' Rogers said, exaggerating his ambivalence for the sake of argument, 'why wouldn't Kyberd take an apparently delectable and free-loving client with him to whichever Shangri-La he'd decided to hide in?'

'Which is why you've circulated them as having toddled off together hand in hand,' Lingard pointed out, holding back on his own opinion.

'I've no option, have I?' Rogers grunted, pushing back his shirt cuff and checking the time. 'I've to meet Durker in half-an-hour to look over his partner's house, so there might be more to come.' He cut it short to change the subject. 'Dickersen,' he said. 'I was on the phone to him when you came in. We're organized for a small search party, with Coltart and a DC to go with it in case they have some sort of a result. Dickersen says there're only three rarely-used caves suitable for the disposal of unwanted dead bodies; rarely used, I suspect, because they're dangerous even for daft buggers like potholers. There's Gawp Gut, which we already know about because of poor Dominus having been dumped in it, and then there's High Rift Pike and Blind Dog Hole. High Rift Pike is higher up on the moor than the other two and not accessible by a track, so I asked him to do the other two first as it was certain that a car would have had to be used. A search shouldn't take long because it's a fair bet that, if she is in one of them, her body would only be below where it was dropped or pushed or whatever from the entrance. That's how it was with Dominus and I don't see how dealing with another unhelpful dead body could be any different.'

He stood from his desk with an effort he usually reserved for lifting heavy weights. 'With a bit of luck,' he said, only three-quarters humorously, 'I might fall over tonight and break a leg or something. I could do with a couple of days recuperating with my feet up and nothing more to worry about than how attractive would be the district nurse sent to look after me.'

20

With the appearance of the moon only a glimmering promise from behind the black bulk of the moor overhanging Kyberd's house, the evening was a bleak and shadowed darkness. Rogers, arriving ten minutes early by intent and parking his car in the drive, braved the sea wind scything coldness against his legs and the deep need in him to go somewhere else and sleep, to walk briskly around the house. He examined meticulously the windows and doors, seeing what his handlamp could illuminate for his understanding through the glass of the conservatory and the window of the garage – all without any discernible profit – until moving headlights showed a car being turned into the drive.

Durker, heavily overcoated against the cold and apparently having no need for spectacles outside his office, loomed with an unsolicitorlike hulkishness in the darkness. He said 'Good evening' in a reasonably civilized manner in reply to Rogers's greeting, then said without further politeness that he proposed to enter no further into the house than inside the main entrance door, and that he required the detective superintendent to make a written note of it.

Rogers, unsurprised by the complexities of any lawyer's thinking, said drily, 'For a solicitor, aren't you putting a lot of trust in my not running off with your partner's furniture?'

Expecting no answer and getting none, he strode to the door of the house, unlocking and opening it. It was icy cold in the entrance hall and filled with an atmosphere of brooding empti-ness and silence, Rogers using the beam of his handlamp to locate a light switch. There were three copies of the *Times* newspaper and a scattering of delivered letters on the floor. Picking the letters up, he shuffled through them, finding them all addressed to Kyberd and appearing to be personal or commercial correspondence. The earliest date on the news-papers was the tenth of November, suggesting that Kyberd had left the house on the ninth.

Durker, who had followed him in, stood blinking, his lower-ing expression reflecting his feelings about his forced co-oper-ation. Handing him the letters, Rogers said, 'If you've no objection to reading your partner's personal mail, perhaps you'd go through these and pass on to me anything you think might help find where he is.'

Leaving the hall, he entered each ground-floor room in turn, switching on the lights and walking around it with the hand not holding the handlamp kept firmly in his overcoat pocket, as a precaution against inadvertently leaving his fingerprints and confusing a possible later search. Ignoring what was manifestly domestic and unlikely to tell him anything useful about the enquiry in hand, he looked for evidence – as he had with the newspapers – of either an ordered or a hurried departure on the part of Kyberd. And, as a matter of routine in similar cases of flawed humanity suspected of having detached large sums of money from their rightful owners, he looked for signs indicative of a possible despairing, occasionally vengeful, intention of suicide.

Rogers had to admit that, for a man separated from his wife, Kyberd was of extraordinarily tidy habits, putting himself to self-confessed shame. Despite this neatness, the sitting-room, dining-room and kitchen all showed – only God knew how – the lack of the civilizing hand of a woman. Though the rooms were handsomely furnished and equipped, there was no over-kill to suggest the excessive spending of easily acquired wealth. All that he had seen so far illustrated the habitat of a man who lived on his own; the solitary place setting on the dining-table underlining the bleakness of it, the refrigerator in the kitchen containing – as did Rogers's – the few oddments of convenience food kept by a man who ate out more than he ate in. There were no photographs of him or the wife who had left him. Strangely enough, despite the reprobate solicitor's having apparently chosen to tread the primrose path with a stolen small fortune and one of his more fetching clients, Rogers had, in his professional tour of the ground floor, so far formed a quite favourable impression of how he imagined him to be. And that, where a solicitor was concerned, was highly unusual.

Passing Durker, who had now put on his spectacles to read Kyberd's mail, Rogers received a cold-eyed stare of suspicion as he started to climb the broad banistered stairs to the upper floor. There were two bedrooms with bathroom *en suite*, and two rooms empty of furniture. In the larger of the bedrooms he found the double bed unmade, with a man's green-and-black striped pyjamas and a woman's blue nightdress lying where they had been dropped on to the disordered sheets. Opening the doors of the wall-length wardrobe revealed only a few items: a man's several suits in dark grey or black, casual jackets and trousers, a lightweight overcoat, a raincoat, ties and shoes, all looking a little lonely among the rows of largely empty hangers.

In the adjoining bathroom he found a tortoiseshell comb with black hairs in its teeth and a partly-used lipstick in a shade of red he was unable to put a name to. Though there were soaps and plastic bottles and aerosols of deodorants, bath oils and splash-on lotions for men, there was no shaving gear or tooth-brushes and paste. A wicker basket for soiled laundry contained among other articles two white shirts, two sets of underwear and two pairs of socks.

Rogers made a sound like 'H'm' from behind a closed mouth and moved to the second bedroom and its bathroom. Presum-ably used only for accommodating whatever guests, other than female intimates, a solitary solicitor might entertain, neither contained anything but its furniture and furnishings.

Returning to the hall below, Rogers saw that Durker held the letters bundled in one hand. 'There's some quite convincing evidence that your partner has recently been entertaining a woman in his bed,' he said expressionlessly. 'Might you believe her to have been Mrs Gosse?'

Durker had tightened his mouth at that. 'I don't believe it. What is your evidence?' Not bothering to hide it, he was distinctly hostile.

'A nightdress. A tube of lipstick. Neither, I assume, for use by your partner. Would you want to see them?' Rogers had long lost any wish to be agreeable towards him.

'No, I do not,' Durker snapped.

'As you wish, though it doesn't allow you to draw any conclusions that I'd care to listen to. And I did ask if you believed the woman to have been Mrs Gosse.'

'I heard you and I propose not to indulge in speculation.'

Rogers wanted to tell him bluntly that he couldn't give a damn for what he chose not to indulge in, that he was merely being given an opportunity to comment on the situation, should he wish. And, because Rogers was still tired, with grit behind his eyes and his nerves on the twitch, he tried hard not to show the rising irritation he felt. 'It's up to you,' he told Durker, forcing a little amiability. 'Was there anything in any of the letters likely to help?' He had known the answer to that before he asked it:

'I've no intention of discussing any of the contents with you.'

It was difficult for the detective to equate the grey eyes glaring with so much dislike in them with those he had seen brimming with tears of wretchedness earlier that day. 'Thank you for your help,' he said, with no trace of irony or sarcasm, opening the door for Durker to leave. 'I shall keep the key until the question of whether or not Mrs Gosse was here has been settled. Should I wish to come here again, I'll let you know.'

Durker, turning and walking away into the darkness, said nothing in reply to that, leaving Rogers confirmed in his thinking that he had been dealing with a man big on bulk but small on brain and short on courtesy. Switching off the light and slamming the door secure, he waited in the outside cold that seemed only minimally more frigid than it had been inside the deserted house until he saw Durker's car passing through the gate and into the road. Returning to his own car, he followed him out, heading for the silent emptiness of his own unshared apartment, which he had never, even in the occasional forgetfulness of euphoria, been able to call a home.

Reaching it with an emotion immeasurably short of nostalgia – he noted that it was now close to being half-past six – he climbed unnecessarily steep stairs to the second floor of a building deserving of instant demolition for its graceless rectangularity. Inside, as he had often not too exaggeratedly described it, it appeared to have been designed for an agoraphobic bachelor dwarf with no itch to swing a cat. It had a small sitting-room with a dining area that made normal furniture in either appear gargantuan, an even smaller kitchen, a bedroom to which it might not be wise to invite an oversized girlfriend, and a shower room that reminded him of a damp and windowless telephone kiosk.

Making himself a cup of mahogany-coloured instant coffee, he fell asleep half-way through drinking it in his easy chair. Awakened by the ringing of the telephone he sometimes hated with a deadly intensity, and falling about on leaving his chair to answer it, he was informed by the Headquarters switchboard operator that an Elizabeth Gallagher of the *Daily Echo* had called, wishing to speak to him. Finding him out of office, she had asked for his unlisted telephone number and would be calling back for it if he agreed.

Rogers, still half-adrift with sleep, said, 'Give it to her and if she's going to ring me, not for fifteen minutes.' Lurching to the kitchen to make more coffee, he checked his wrist-watch for the time – it was twenty minutes to eight – wondering for what reasons she would want to talk to him at this time of the evening and thinking of only one. And thinking that with an off-duty mind, he accepted that even an overriding need for sleep should never stand in the way of a shared immorality. If that were it, then he had to make himself more presentable and sweet-smelling than he was now.

When he answered the telephone the second time, he had washed, shaved, made up the bed he had left in confusion when he had got out of it sixteen hours before and had, despite his unrefreshed tiredness, orchestrated himself into the mood to entertain an obviously still interested lady journalist.

'I find you a very difficult man to get hold of,' she had started, her voice striking him as being curiously odd. 'Are you on your own, and is it convenient for you to speak to me?'

'I am, and yes, of course it is.' He was suddenly cautious, having the shadow of an apprehension of trouble. 'I'm glad you called.'

'Last night,' she said abruptly. 'I'm dreadfully sorry, but I had to be honest about it and tell my husband.'

For a moment he thought she must be joking, then seeing her serious unsmiling face in his mind he knew that she wouldn't be. 'Your husband?' he echoed stupidly, thinking that his blood should be running cold and wondering why it wasn't. It had so run in his youth, in a comparable situation, when a girl about whom he had been rather serious told him that she thought – thank God wrongly – that she was pregnant. 'I didn't know you had one. Why didn't you tell me?'

'You never asked.'

'For God's sake! Why should I ask? You were spoken of as Miss Gallagher, weren't you?'

'Only by you, and then it didn't seem important. After you'd invited me to your apartment, it was too late to explain. Would you not have, had you known?'

She was a bloody cool number, that he had to admit. A typical woman in asking him questions he had difficulty in answering. 'I think I might have given it an extra thought or two,' he said, not wishing to offend her no doubt unfathomable feminine susceptibilities. He had really wanted to say that if there were any guilt about her making a domestic drama of it, it had to be all hers, but was intelligent enough not to do so. 'Why the sudden outburst of morality?' he asked her. 'Or do you always creep into the confessional afterwards?'

'You must know I don't,' she told him composedly. 'I was home later than usual and he was suspicious. He was angry as well and I couldn't lie to him; I never could and I've never wanted to.'

He said, reasonably lightly considering that to which he was being subjected, 'Your husband. Presumably he's the standard issue of misunderstood husband, six feet plus, built like a gorilla and without a thought in his head unconnected with tearing off my arms?'

She sounded offended and about to put him in the wrong. 'I didn't give him your name, only that you were a policeman. Nothing more.'

'Given that the poor devil won't have to be too bright to find out who I am, does he propose doing anything about it? Do I now have to trot around wearing a bulletproof waistcoat while looking apologetic?'

'That isn't really funny, you know. He's a very gentle and understanding man normally, and if he's angry it's with me and not with you.'

'I am not comforted,' he said with heavy irony, 'but thank you for letting me know what I've done. Is there something more?' Despite his intention to be civilized about it, he knew that he was sounding pompously dismissive.

She was hesitant now, seemingly hurt. 'I thought . . . I don't believe we need be unfriendly. And we may possibly be working together again.'

She was making him feel an uptight prig and, because he had lost a lot of his capacity for being bloody-mindedly rude, he sought refuge in what he knew to be misapplied humour. 'It's no big deal,' he said almost affably. 'I knew beforehand that something like this would happen to me when I made the mistake of giving up smoking. Shall we let it lie on the table for a while? I'll still see you about professionally, I imagine?'

There were long moments of silence before she said softly, 'Yes, of course. I can see now that it's not been of any particular consequence and I'm sorry I bothered you with it.' She disconnected from him, replacing her receiver gently it seemed, and leaving him listening to a dead line, as baffled as he had ever been by the incomprehensibility of women.

Back in his chair, this time with a stiffish whisky, he thought about what he had said. Why had he been so bloody inept in his handling of his end of it and, above all, why had she made him now feel himself to be a shabby, satyrish third party in some sort of a sexual triangle? It needed only her so-called gentle and understanding husband – for whom he was sorry – to ventilate his anger in a letter of complaint to the Chief Constable for him to see in the circumstances the disciplinary offence of discreditable conduct and to do something about it.

Rogers was trying hard to push the problem to one side so that he could get back to his interrupted sleep, when his telephone bell rang again. It had to be her or, perhaps, her husband, he thought gloomily, lifting the receiver he should, if he had any sense, have left off its cradle. The voice of Chief

Inspector Rees-Williams with its Welsh intonations lifted his ailing morale when it reported to him that Detective Inspector Coltart had called in by radio with an urgent message for him. The body of a woman, thought to be that of Mrs Daphne Gosse, had been located in Blind Dog Hole.

You lose one, you win one, Rogers told himself. While feeling sorry that the ending for Daphne Gosse had been what sounded to be a nasty death, he contrarily felt unusually elated that his intuition, were it that, had done its stuff just when most needed. Before closing down, he asked for a patrol car and a driver who knew where Blind Dog Hole was, also ordering the routine call-out of those required to attend at the locus of a discovered murder.

As he got himself ready with a comparatively small whisky taken against the coming chill of the night, he found that he could push his tiredness back into stand-by, while the problem of Liz Gallagher had reduced itself in his revitalized consciousness to a minor irritating itch. That it would return in full measure the following day, or the day after that, was something he would fret about when it did.

21

High up on the treeless, rock-strewn Great Morte Moor, Rogers thought the noise of the car's jolting progress along the narrow track to be an anachronism in the almost primeval and desolate landscape. Visibility through the windscreen showed a superabundance of moonlit sky luminous enough to blot out the stars. If his driver knew where he was going in this featureless wilderness, Rogers certainly did not, being by preference a flagstoned-path man and in one of his phases when he thought himself mostly immune to the attractions of what he considered to be a manure- and silage-smelling countryside.

The first signs of man's existence on the moor's vast prominence were the CID van, a Range Rover and some dark figures standing several hundred yards downhill of the track and close to a serried mass of upthrusting limestone boulders, seen luminously ashen in the moonlight. Descending the steep slope to the scene proved less of a rough ride than it had been on the track, though Rogers did push hard on the flooring and hope that neither the engine nor the brakes would fail.

His first impression on climbing from the car was of his own insignificance in the overwhelming silence, of the remoteness of where he stood and of how bloody cold and windy the night was up there. Threading his way through about fifteen feet of narrow passage between chest-high outcrops of rock, in imagination carrying or dragging the body of a woman, he reached a small clearing of dead bracken. Waiting on his arrival were the squat figures of Dickersen and two of his team, all dressed in yellow oversuits and orange helmets, and the huge Coltart with a DPC whose face was familiar but his name forgotten.

Nodding to Coltart, he held out his hand to Dickersen, the top of whose helmet only just came up to Rogers's chest, and who was rough-hewn behind his pebble-lensed spectacles and rat's-nest of a greying beard. Of a weatherbeaten toughness, he had a bone-crushing grip for the friendly shake he was receiving. 'Maurice,' Rogers said, holding back on wincing, 'I'm grateful. This is the second one you've found for us.'

'Aye.' Dickersen was smoking a stubby pipe with a badly charred bowl, its acrid-smelling smoke rising in small wind-blown streamers. 'The poor lady's down there all right.' He nodded his helmet at a darkness of deep shadow that was apparently Blind Dog Hole.

To the detective, it was similar in size and shape to a coffin, and enclosed on three sides by overhanging boulders. A wide rusty iron gate with no apparent purpose for being there was propped close to them. 'Dropped down, of course?' he said.

'Aye, no question of that. It's a twelve-metre pitch to a ledge and Arthur who was going to be lead man says she's on it. Below that there's another pitch to a roof fall, and we're lucky she didn't finish up there, or you'd have had it.'

'Why? Too far down?'

'No. There's rock instability with too high a risk of collapse.'

'You went down to see her?'

154

Dickersen pulled a face. 'I looked down at her from a rope. That was enough for me.'

'I don't blame you,' Rogers assured him. He moved across to Coltart. 'Have you got anything for me?' he asked.

'Mr Sawyer over there . . .' – he pointed a thick thumb at one of Dickersen's colleagues – '. . . went down and he described her to me. Slim, he said, and a good looker. About thirty and has black hair. That and Mrs Gosse being missing seemed to fit.'

'You didn't see her yourself?'

'No, Mr Dickersen said it's too much trouble and too risky for us amateurs,' Coltart growled, wooden-faced. 'You apparently have to hang on a rope to see her.'

'He's persuadable,' Rogers told him. 'You've heard from Headquarters?'

'Everybody's been notified and they're on the way. Except Dr Twite, that is. He's out somewhere, and nobody knows where.'

Without being censorious about it, Rogers had a good idea of what the amorous, gormandizing pathologist might be doing during the hours of darkness. With the body of the presumed Mrs Gosse being thirty-odd feet down a pothole in the middle of nowhere, a location unlikely to be visited by Twite should he be able to avoid it, Rogers decided to short-circuit his at-the-scene examination. Apart from Twite's only too likely refusal to dangle his overly fat bulk on the end of a rope, there was little chance of his arriving for hours.

'Get back to Headquarters on the radio,' Rogers instructed Coltart, 'and ask them to post a man outside Dr Twite's house, advising him on his return of the imminent delivery of a female body to the mortuary and that I'd be incredibly grateful if he'd attend there urgently on his return.'

Treading through the dead bracken to Dickersen, he said, 'We can't contact the pathologist we need, so I shall be going down myself to have a look at her.'

Dickersen took his pipe from a mouth that showed disapproval. 'Are you daft, mun? Since when have you been able to do a rope-down? Able to work a self-lock descender? Or a jammer?'

'Never, thank God. I don't even know what you're talking

about and I suspect you know it.' Rogers had had this non-hostile trouble with Dickersen six years ago at Gawp Gut and he accepted that it was motivated by a concern for the safety of his constabulary-owned skin. 'Daft or not, I've got to see her as she is.' He grinned. 'Over your unconscious body if you like because I'm bigger and nastier than you can ever be. Have you still got your climbing ladders?'

Dickersen pushed the pipe back into his mouth. 'You're not going to listen to me, you booger, are you?'

Rogers smiled at him. 'I knew you'd see it my way, Maurice.'

He waited while Dickersen made loud metallic noises from inside the body of the Range Rover, stamping his feet on the hard ground against the creeping cold. In truth, as a claustrophobic, the last thing he wanted was to put himself through the terror of being in a confined space, made worse by darkness, and unable to escape from it without exhibiting what he considered to be a shaming pusillanimity. He looked around at the vast openness of the moonbright sky, at the lunar-like landscape uninhabited by man for as far as he could see, trying to assess how much of a bloody idiot he was even to think about going down into the suffocating darkness; and knowing that it was more than eighty per cent pride that was making him do it. That Coltart had joined him and was doing what Rogers called looming, was an assurance that he could show nothing of this even by the twitch he knew would surely come.

With Dickersen producing two rolled-up ladders of wire cable and alloy rungs and giving them to Sawyer to join up and to tether at the lip of the hole, the third man of the team, introduced as Nigel Thompson, was asked to get out of and to hand over his helmet, his oversuit and webbing harness.

'Are you telling me I've to get into that outfit just to look into a hole in the ground?' Rogers demanded, not believing it would do anything but aggravate his feeling of being entombed.

'It's either that or you're on your own and can use your fingernails for all I'll help you,' Dickersen growled, poking the stem of his pipe in Rogers's direction. 'I've not the time to attend inquests on bloody fools who don't find out that caving can be dangerous until they're dead. The oversuit'll fit you if you take your coat off and I'll help you on with it and the harness. I think you'll be able to manage the helmet on your own,' he added, humorously sarcastic.

Submitting with a meekness unknown to his subordinates to Dickersen's superiority on his own dungheap, Rogers allowed himself to be equipped with the only slightly shorter Thompson's gear, grunting his discomfort as the harness was strapped tightly around his thighs and waist. Before jamming the helmet on his head and buckling its chinstrap tight, Dickersen lit the acetylene-gas lamp clipped to its front. When Rogers turned his head, so the hissing white beam of light would follow to whatever he looked at. Uncomfortably encased against disaster though he might be, the waterproof fabric, webbing straps and plastic and metal fastenings, in which he felt stiff and inflexible in movement, gave him no confidence.

Leading the detective to the dark cavity between the boulders – he was already regarding it as the entrance to an abyss – Dickersen unhitched a coil of nylon rope from his shoulder and tied it with a complicated knot to a snap-link on Rogers's harness. 'Now listen to me, mun,' he said, his craggy face showing that he was actually enjoying this. 'Immediately below this opening there's a lump of rock that'll push you out to a vertical pitch. You'll have to sort of slide your belly over the ladder which'll be flush to the rock at that point. Don't worry too much or panic; that's a lifeline tied to you and we'll have hold of the belay. You won't be going anywhere that we can't haul you back from. You've been on a caving ladder before, so remember you can only fit one of your big feet on to a rung at a time. And unless you want to finish topside down, keep close to it; hug it tight, think it's a girlfriend of yours if you've got one. You look a bit flabby to me, so rest in between times and don't hurry or you'll run out of steam and then we will have to haul you up.'

He stabbed his pipe-stem at Rogers's chest. 'Remember,' he said. 'While you're on the rope, I'm the boss. 'I won't speak to you unless I think you're in trouble, but if I yell "hold", stop whatever you're doing and freeze. No looking up, nothing. Got it?'

'I hear you,' Rogers agreed with a false air of unflappability, then saying ironically, 'This potholing's a great fun thing, isn't it? If I wasn't here enjoying myself so much I could be sitting with my feet up in front of a fire and missing it all.'

Dickersen actually smiled and said, 'Don't booger it up by falling on Arthur, will you. He's roping down first to be on hand if you need him.' He stretched an arm and jerked his thumb downwards at Sawyer who, already fastened to a fixed line leading into the hole, dropped on to his belly and slithered feet-first from view down the ladder.

When a shout came echoing up from the depths, Dickersen handed the free end of the lifeline to Coltart. 'Tie that round your middle. You'll be the anchor, so just think of what you'd have to answer for if you happened to let your gov'nor drop.'

Rogers didn't feel like laughing at that one and, on Dickersen's instructions, laid himself face-down on the ladder with his legs in the hole. Finding a rung with the tip of his shoe, he slowly lowered himself into the darkness below him, looking up at the moonlit sky that had never seemed so desirable to stay with.

With the carbide lamp on his helmet illuminating only a small disc of the coffee-brown stone in front of him, he let himself down around what seemed an overhang until he hung vertically over space, his nose inches from the rock face. Already feeling the sides of the shaft pressing in on him, he was trying to convince the pessimistic part of his brain that his shoulders weren't going to be trapped immovable as he feared, that it was unlikely the ladder had hitherto unnoticed flaws in it that would signal 'destruct' and send him plummeting down into unknown and unreachable depths.

Outside the light of his lamp there was a blackness tangible enough to be felt, a dense silence broken only by the scraping of his oversuit, the thin hissing of his lamp and the rapid pounding of blood in his eardrums. The brushing of an unknown something against his back was, he hoped, only the rope by which Sawyer had descended before him. 'Mad,' he muttered to himself, feeling that he had already been down there hours and referring to anybody mucking around in potholes for something to do. 'They must be bloody mad.'

Glued to the ladder by will power after the dozen or so blind gropings with his feet for further rungs below him, he peered

cautiously down between his legs, seeing the glimmering of
another lamp and an indistinct shadowy form that could be a
prostrate body. That his nose could now detect the sickly smell
of death's corruption was nothing to give him confidence in his
own continuing survival. Swinging on the unstable ladder had
brought his knuckles and kneecaps in painful contact with the
only half-seen wall and he was now in a mood to wonder why
in the hell he had been so stupidly insistent on seeing the body
in situ. Dickersen, he concluded, shouldn't have been so bloody
amenable to the argument he wished now he hadn't made.

When he descended into the ambit of a light that shone on
the lower parts of his legs, he knew he could accept that he had
arrived. And he thought it a good thing too, for the overtight
harness he was wearing was putting at risk his already suffering
genitalia. Down another four or five rungs and he could see
Sawyer crouched, apparently double-jointedly, in a small
chamber in the rock face. In the disc of Rogers's light he looked
down-puttingly calm, almost cheerful.

'You got here then,' he said, his voice loud in the confined
space. 'She's right under your feet, so don't go down any
further. Let me pull you in.'

Rogers, looking down to below his feet, saw the body of a
woman lying on her back. As Sawyer reached out and pulled
him over, he could see that she was lodged against an outcrop
of rock in a short slope that dropped into the blackness of a
further shaft into which the lower part of his ladder had
disappeared.

With no ceremony, Sawyer pulled him in to join him
crouched in the chamber, twice jerking hard at his lifeline.
'That,' he said, 'is to tell 'em you've arrived safely.'

'Can't you just yell up?' Rogers queried, feeling Sawyer
gripping the rear part of his harness in a reassuringly strong
fist.

'It's the drill,' Sawyer told him, ignoring his previous call up
the shaft. 'Shouting in some caves can bring down a rockfall
and us with it. You just have your look at the poor lady and I'll
get you back up the ladder.'

Rogers was measuring the distance the body lay from where
he crouched and it seemed too near the drop into the lower

shaft for his peace of mind. 'What do I do?' he asked. 'Just jump down to her?'

'Not unless you want to finish up hanging in that pitch behind her.' He was close behind Rogers and speaking directly and moistly into his ear. 'Do it this way and don't worry about falling. I've got a good grip on you and you're still on the lifeline. Lean forward as I go with you and grab hold of the rung that'll be at your eye level. You'll be pushing the ladder away from you, but I'll be holding you back and you'll be fair and square over the lady.'

That wasn't quite as Rogers had imagined, though in imagination it had been bad enough. 'I'm a thirteen-stoner,' he said, putting carefree insouciance into his voice despite a dried-up mouth, 'so I hope you can hang on to me without rupturing us both.' He took a deep breath and pushed himself forward towards the ladder, grabbing the highest rung he could reach and finding himself suspended face-downwards at an angle of forty-five degrees, his toes still on the solid rock and his harness held securely by Sawyer.

His head, he found, was hanging no more than five feet over the body and at right angles to it. With the illumination from Sawyer's lamp added to his own, he studied her. Recognizably Daphne Gosse from her photograph, she was looking up at him from sightless eyes. She was dressed in a green hip-length oiled country jacket, its zip fastener ripped open to show a fawn polo neck sweater and a tweed skirt, one brown-stockinged and shoeless leg being twisted sideways at a grotesque angle. Her black hair, disordered and lank, rested partly over the side of her face exposed to him, but not concealing a bloodless pink gash that bared the bone of her forehead. The hands, clean of stains, were tightly clenched and, so far as he could see, there were no visible signs anywhere of the means of her death. Light-brown smears of dried soil and grit contrasted with the waxen pallor of her flesh and fouled the oiled material of the coat. Though her features were set in the emptiness of death, her half-closed eyes dulled to non-expression and barely reflecting the light shining on them, there was no doubt that she had been an attractive woman. Rogers, hanging achingly over her and fearful that his cold and tiring fingers might lose their grip

160

on the ladder – and the ultimate horror – allow him to fall on her and have his flesh touching her cold dead flesh, nonetheless felt depressingly sad at the futile waste of her dying. High-spirited and reckless as she was reported to have been, he could easily imagine her to be waiting in the wings of wherever she now was, intent on exacting revenge on her murderer when he or she suffered the final chopper. He rather hoped she was, just in case he buggered up his end of the job down here.

With Sawyer hauling him back into the chamber, he was already thinking over the changed basis of his investigation, the connections and disconnections going on in his brain making, as yet, little sense. Daphne Gosse, found dead in a pothole, almost certainly having been murdered, was about to pose a quite different problem from that which had existed until now. Earlier, while the possibility of her death had always been present, she could only be factually regarded as a woman who had fled from an overbearing husband to find whatever it was that she wanted and sought in the company of a dishonest solicitor.

The only physical thing of possible significance he was taking back with him, and which he could have guessed anyway, was that because the gash in her forehead had manifestly not bled, it had to lead to the conclusion that she had been dead for some time before being dropped to her lonely interment. And by what means she had died would be determined by Twite, for he himself had seen nothing pointing to it in his brief scrutiny of her body.

On his climb up the ladder, helped by somebody at the top – probably the tremendously strong Coltart – hauling on his lifeline, he remembered that he was supposed to be suffering from claustrophobia and therefore, quite logically, began to increase his rate of climb before cold sweating panic overtook his hurrying heels.

22

Being pulled from the pothole into the glare of floodlights burning white holes in the blue moonlight and finding his human winch to have been Coltart, Rogers saw that most of his initially required staff had arrived, together with the Murder Wagon and the Coroner's Officer complete with his coffin shell and body bags. So had an even more frigid wind that made his eyes water and cut into exposed flesh like invisible razor-blades. Shedding the uncomfortable helmet, harness and oversuit, and putting on his heavy coat, he resumd his professional *gravitas* together with the sang-froid of a man who did this sort of thing every morning before breakfast.

'Have we heard from Mr Lingard or Dr Twite?' he asked Coltart. It wasn't calamitous that his second-in-command hadn't arrived, but until he was told by Twite from what trauma Daphne Gosse had died, that in fact she was actually and legally dead, he would be stumbling around virtually blind.

Coltart, looking as if the brawn in his huge body had been frost-bitten, said, 'I'm told Mr Lingard's on his way. Dr Twite returned home while you were down in the cave and he says he'll be standing by ready to attend at the mortuary, but only if you get the body there before midnight.' Coltart creased his face into the semblance of a smile. 'After that, he said he'd be in bed and staying there until the morning.'

Rogers thought it sounded as if Twite had had an unsatisfactory evening either with his latest grass widow or with the presentation of his late meal, in either event a man best approached with careful politeness. 'We've a fair bit of leeway,' he pointed out, 'if we can get hold of a stretcher and have Mr Dickersen and his chaps haul her out. Incidentally, I'm sure it's Mrs Gosse down there and that she's been murdered, so in the meantime I want you to organize a sufficiency of men as searchers. Have them go over the terrain here with whatever lights we can get hold of to pick up any tyre marks not our own, or anything foreign to the scene that may have been dropped. You can stay up here and repeat the performance at first light, when the place may look less like a public car park.'

Seeing Dickersen sitting in the cabin of the Range Rover where he had gone to wait after Rogers's emergence, he walked over to join him. 'Move along, Maurice,' he said, 'I'm icing up out here.' Climbing inside to share the shadowed warm fug of tobacco smoke, he said, 'I've come to butter you up into giving us a little more assistance. I've somehow to get the body up and out for the pathologist to do his stuff on her tonight. It's possible?'

'She's the one you were looking for?'

'She is, and I'd like you to have a good look at her when she's brought up. I'll tell you then. It's possible? I mean bringing her up tonight?'

'Aye. It's all the same down there whether it's daylight up here or not.'

'I'd like her body bagged and hauled out on a stretcher, Maurice. Can you hang on here while I send for one?'

'No need, mun. We're ancillary to the Cave Rescue Organization . . .' – he jerked his pipe to the rear of him, coming perilously near to stabbing it in Rogers's eye – '. . . and we've all the hardware we'd need back there for getting a body out, dead or alive.' He looked at the detective searchingly, his hard mouth obviously held back from smiling, his eyes wicked behind his glasses. 'You were all right down there? I could have sworn I heard some middling groaning and fetching and bad swearing coming up at me.'

'The groaning I'll admit to,' Rogers conceded nonchalantly. 'The harness you made me wear was too damned tight and was doing a long drawn-out job of neutering me.' Steering clear of any discussion of his performance as a caver, for even in retrospect the thought of the shaft brought a toe-curling fear, he said, 'I've one of my sergeants waiting to photograph the body as it lies and also needing some help in putting it into the body bag he'll have with him. Will you see him down?'

Dickersen took his pipe from between his teeth and nodded. 'Aye,' he grunted, opening his door and starting to climb from his seat. 'I'll be getting the stretcher.'

163

'Before you do,' Rogers said, 'why the old gate propped up near the hole?'

'Animals,' Dickersen told him. 'The poor beasties tend to fall into holes in the ground and that's fatal one way and another. Where it's needed and where we can, we put in removable barriers against it.'

That put Dickersen in Rogers's personal pantheon of the kindly and compassionate, and while he was audibly moving metal equipment in the back of the Range Rover, Rogers left his seat and moved towards the Murder Wagon parked outside the limestone outcrops. The ginger-haired Sergeant Magnus, whose supreme happiness appeared to be an untiring search for latent fingerprints and cast body hairs that were waiting to be found and photographed, was organizing his equipment in one of the coach's cubicles. 'I understand you've experience in caving and potholing, sergeant,' Rogers said cheerfully, deciding exaggeratedly that what he had done for Merrie England, so could the sergeant.

'I have, sir?' Magnus knew well enough not to query the quite imaginary assertion, guessing what was in his superintendent's mind. 'You mean you want me to go down?'

'It's better than hanging around up here in the cold, isn't it? She's almost certainly Mrs Gosse and almost certainly has been murdered, so I'll want some shots of her as she is, as she was found. And take a body bag with you while you're about it and see that she's not banged about or handled too much and that we don't lose anything from her we might regret later on.' He could see that Magnus, patently a man indifferent to heights or depths, couldn't give a damn where he went, just so long as he could find the virtually unfindable and then expose film on it.

'In this cold weather, I'm thankful she wasn't found in the canal,' was all that he said.

When he left the coach, Rogers went into the cubicle assigned to him as an in-the-field office, lighting a butane gas heater against its ice-box interior. He had to give some time to thinking, to make whatever connections his tired brain would allow in asking itself questions. How long had Mrs Gosse been dead and had her going preceded or followed her husband's death? And, whichever it was, why both? If she had gone off with Kyberd, as was apparently supposed, she certainly hadn't gone far. As, it was equally apparent, Kyberd hadn't, if his partner Durker's supposition was correct. It was odd to think that even now he might be in the area, waiting to do whatever it might turn out that he needed to do. Given all that, what motive could there be for her being killed and her body disposed of down a pothole? Though not dismissing the notably absent Kyberd as her lover and subsequent murderer, he was unable to imagine the connection between the stealing from clients' funds and her death, though between the theft and her joining him on a moneyed primrose path, he could. Then there was her froggish husband, who had seemed to be on the losing end of everything. Why was he, presumably out of the running for his wife's affections, bludgeoned to death and an attempt made to burn down his home? A solid motive or two for either of the killings wouldn't come amiss. And then there was the emotionally unbalanced Durker, who hadn't actually said that his partner had absconded with Daphne Gosse but, fair enough, had fallen half-heartedly into agreeing, though without actually saying so, with what had only been a chance-shot question by Rogers himself.

Having spent time in this form of investigational meditation – in between the surfacing of involuntary images of an excessively nubile Liz Gallagher, to whom he could not now claim a proper title – without any inspirational truths emerging, Rogers was scowling his frustration when Lingard came in. Well-scrubbed and glossy, immaculately shirted and suited, he again made Rogers, who had after all been in what might be called the deep end of the investigation, feel downright scruffy and soiled.

'Stap me, George,' Lingard drawled, 'I've only to take a few minutes off for a spot of dry-cleaning in the sauna when the ceiling falls in and nobody can find me. Do I see that we're exhuming Mrs Gosse?'

'I believe it's her, but I'm not taking bets on it yet,' Rogers said; then filling him in with what information he thought pertinent. 'I've a special job for a man of your talents with women needing consolation. Miss Naylor, of whom you know, is the only relative we can call on for an immediate identification before Wilfred starts on his butchery. See her straight away, will you – better take a WDC with you – and, if she's not too upset, see if she has anything more about her sister she's now willing to tell us.' He added, straight-faced, 'While she's over-endowed with bosom and has an extremely attractive body, I should warn you against getting into a lather about her because she's almost certainly lesbian.'

'No doubt one of the reasons for your not seeing her yourself,' Lingard said drily. 'Incidentally, on the way in I noticed that the body was being pulled up, so I'll take in whatever there is there before leaving.'

'And as I saw her under some difficulty,' Rogers told him, standing from his chair, 'me, too.' Weariness was creeping up on him, the bone-aching sort that made him feel he was already in his eighties, and not a good thing at this stage of his investigation.

Coincidently with the body's being lifted slowly to the surface by Dickersen and Coltart – it resembled an upright and plastic-swathed Egyptian mummy – Rogers and Lingard reached the entrance to the shaft. When it had been swung in and lowered gently to the ground in the small half-circle of those drawn to look silently at the disquieting countenance of violent death, Rogers crouched at the side of the stretcher and unzipped the plastic to expose the pallid face in its frame of disordered black hair. That simple act transformed what had been a packaged shell void of identity into a recognizable though inanimate Daphne Gosse again, the subject of so much of Rogers's attention during the past two days, her now fled personality the colouring of his earlier thinking. If anything could be read into flesh from which the inner glow of life had gone, her features, starkly illuminated in the full glare of the floodlighting directed on them, reflected what had been a possibly highly-strung, probably neurotic and dominant attractiveness. What-ever she had done, pity – to Rogers, a sometimes useless and unhelpful emotion – would inevitably affect his thoughts of her. Little of which, he would be the first to admit, had been expended on her unpleasant husband.

Straightening his aching legs and standing, he beckoned to

166

Dickersen to come nearer. 'Have a good look at her, Maurice,' he said. 'I believe you might know her.'

Dickersen, his forehead creasing beneath his helmet, looked pebble-lensed down at the dead face. 'Aye, I might. I've seen her face before, but the name Gosse isn't familiar.'

'Does the name Daphne Naylor help?' Rogers suggested.

Dickersen did more peering, crouching and looking at the face in profile, then returning upright. 'I've got her,' he said slowly, scratching at an already dishevelled beard. 'She was a member nine, ten years back. A bit of a handful, I recollect, and we had to ask her to keep to above-ground chores or leave. And leave she did.'

'Why exactly?' Rogers reached down and covered the face that would probably haunt him for a week or two.

'She was a dangerous woman to partner in caving and she eventually ran out of people willing to go down with her. I mean she was dangerous because she couldn't or wouldn't conform to caving disciplines.' Although all but Lingard and Coltart had now moved away from the body, Dickersen spoke in a conspiratorially low voice, as if being overheard was as dangerous as the activity he was talking about. 'She seemed to me to be one of those people without any fear and that meant she was bloody daft with it, a certainty that she was going to get herself trapped in a choke or drowned in a sump one day, and probably take sombody with her.'

'You'd also know, wouldn't you, if she'd been particularly close to any other member? Or members?' Rogers had been watching his guileless eyes magnified behind the lenses, seeing in them the awareness response to his question.

'Aye, that I would,' Dickersen agreed. 'And she was.' He was frowning, manifestly casting his mind back. 'A newspaper chap and an artist. Fowler and Urquhart. Not both at the same time though. At least, not that I'd heard. But they did have a bust-up in the bar and the committee nearly chucked them out. She'd been thick with the two of 'em at one time or another and she was the reason for the trouble.'

'She'd been caving with them?' Rogers had seen the lifting of Lingard's eyebrows at Dickersen's words.

'Aye. Off and on, of course. There were others, but not like it was with those two.' He grimaced. 'At one time I thought that they were having a go at it when they were supposed to be caving, but that was probably a dirty way of thinking.' He looked down at the covered body, Rogers thought just a little sadly. 'She was a pretty girl. She knew it and used it as you'd guess.'

'Was this bust-up you mention a fight between the two men?'

'That it was.' Dickersen shook his head, whether in admiration or in disapproval it was difficult to judge. 'A real stand up and knock down fist fight, with nobody wanting to stop it. Urquhart was the one left standing, being as I recall a hard man and the most evil-tempered booger of the two.'

'Now I know why caving's supposed to be dangerous,' Rogers said. 'Neither of them is with your club now, I imagine?'

'Not for years. They come and go, like.'

'Was this particular cave operational then?'

'It was used, yes. Then we had a roof fall about eight years or so back that we hadn't the means to open up, and it's been left like it since.'

'Maurice,' Rogers said. 'I'm going to give you some names. It doesn't mean that any of them are necessarily connected with this business, but I'd like you to tell me if you know anyone I mention. More especially, if any one of them is or was a member of your club, or known to you as a caver.' He paused, listing them in his mind before giving them out. 'Frederick McCausland. Jarvis – that's the surname only. Michael Durker. Virginia Naylor – she's Mrs Gosse's sister. Hugh Kyberd.'

Rogers hadn't seen any recognition in Dickersen's eyes and he had thought only briefly before shaking his head. 'No,' he said. 'I'd remember way back easily enough, and I'm sorry I can't help there.' He looked in turn at each of the three detectives regarding him with impassive intentness, then said to Rogers, 'If that's it and you've finished with us, we've got homes to go to. I'd like to get cleared up and leave.'

'My grateful thanks, Maurice.' Rogers held out his hand for shaking, wincing in anticipation of the bone-crushing grip. 'The Chief Constable will be writing his appreciation of your help in due course.' He smiled his own warmth at him as he left, turning to Lingard. 'That was a little something your chum

Urquhart thought fit not to tell you, eh, David? Would you care to have a go at him? To sort him out one way or the other? We can't afford not to now, can we?' He could see the Coroner's Officer and a PC waiting with a coffin shell near them and he decided that he could leave now with a clear conscience.

'Definitely not,' Lingard replied, in the act of recharging his nose with tranquillizing Attar of Roses. 'When, naturally, I've finished with not getting too involved with your over-bosomed Miss Naylor. You've some idea of a motive?'

'You possibly more than I. But I do understand that unwelcomed importunity in a woman and short-tempered violence in a man can be a health hazard for the woman. I imagine you'll want to hang on at the mortuary to find out what killed her, and when?'

'Of course.' Lingard's features had become almost predatory. 'I'll have him if he's our man. I'll smell out whatever guilt's hiding in him.'

As Rogers knew, that was no idle threat. Lingard could, with his affably relaxed but penetrating questioning, get more of a believable response to it than would a more formal interrogation. It was probably the only gleam of light that Rogers could look forward to, though he had to admit to himself, if not to Lingard, that it seemed to be only a very tiny gleam.

23

Rogers, having parked his car outside the mortuary, walked to where he saw Lingard's Bentley glimmering a glassy-green in the moonlight. 'It's either freeze out here or freeze in there,' the elegant detective said as he climbed from the car, 'and I thought I'd prefer to do it out here.'

'Miss Naylor's been?' Rogers asked as he about-turned to head for the mortuary entrance.

'And gone,' Lingard said, walking with him. 'She came under her own steam in the sportiest car I've seen in years and driven by a Miss Finche-Roche who looked to me as if she was a retired

Rear-Admiral. There was a lot of stiff upper lip and a tear or two when Miss Naylor said 'Yes, that's my sister, Daphne,' with the Finche-Roche side of whatever it is being handsomely supportive. I had a brief chat with her on her own afterwards – she hadn't known about Gosse's death, incidentally – but there wasn't much we couldn't have guessed for ourselves. She said that she wanted to help us in our investigating her sister's death and now wanted us to know that she had been a pathological liar – or words to that effect – that she just couldn't help it, not even with those she loved, and that we could treat as fantasy anything we heard about which we had doubts. Including, she thought possible, the pregnancy she mentioned.'

'A damned good time to tell us.' Rogers had seen a few oddities of potentially useful information about Daphne Gosse flying out of the nearest window. The more simple was the information which remained, the more difficult it would be to resolve. And only he and God knew how little there actually was. 'It's probably knocked a few holes in my thinking,' he said, believing that to be the understatement of the day.

Lingard, pausing at the door, said, 'Something before we go in, George. After Miss Naylor had gone, the attendant and WDC Lauder undressed Mrs Gosse between them and found that she had no underclothing on at all. No pants, no body stocking or vest, no bra, nothing.' He smacked his gloved hands together. 'In this weather, too.'

Rogers frowned. 'A sexual attack?' He shook his head. 'That's a damned stupid thing to say, though we'll soon find out. There must be a reason other than that, David, and if there is it's beyond me at the moment. You've an idea or two?'

'Nothing,' Lingard said, 'and I've been thinking about it in top gear.'

Rogers opened the door and they entered the dim blue lighting of the subterranean passage leading to the mortuary proper. Part of it was stacked with the refrigerated body storage drawers that hummed and occasionally rattled in their chilling function, the two men passing them with echoing footfalls.

The room into which they entered felt sub-zero and was lit coldly by strip lighting. With the walls a combination of glossy white paint and white tiling, it was furnished with ice-blue

170

melamine worktops. Two single-legged stainless steel necropsy tables, glittering from the prophylaxis of frequent scrubbing, occupied the centre of the room. Daphne Gosse lay on her back on one of them, a dinner-plate-sized lamp casting shadowless light on her pallid nakedness, a black hose hanging from the ceiling to the table dribbling water against her flank.

A tan-coated girl attendant with an initiate's fraught look about her waited at one of the worktops, Daphne Gosse's clothing in clear plastic bags and a camera and flashgun at her side. Rogers waved a hand at Twite, whom he could see putting on a green gown in the adjacent changing room.

Going to the packaged clothing and smiling 'Good evening' to the attendant, he carefully removed each article from its bag, unfolding it and examining it. It was all there as he had seen it on the body in the shaft; the oiled jacket, the sweater, skirt, tights and one shoe. The only pockets were those in the jacket and they were empty. While the clothing was badly stained, it appeared to be mainly from contact with natural surfaces in the shaft during her fall into it. He could see no bloodstaining on the fabrics.

When a rubber-gloved and linen-capped Twite came in from the changing room, Rogers and Lingard were standing where they could watch or not watch the body being examined, their buttocks supported against a worktop. 'You owe me, old son,' Twite said to Rogers, amiably enough for a man kept from his bed. 'I wouldn't have done it for anybody else.' He had already been put in the picture in detail over the telephone.

'There's only one thing I didn't mention, Wilfred,' Rogers told him. 'Her sister said she was three months pregnant. You'll check?'

'I'd hardly miss it if she were.' He was selecting the instruments he would need from a wall cabinet. 'Why no underclothes?'

'There's an obvious reason for no pants when a woman is otherwise fully dressed,' Rogers said, being careful not to say anything likely to embarrass the girl attendant, were she to prove embarrassable. 'It happens often enough, but rarely the whole lot in one go. Can we get some idea of the time of her death first?'

171

'Done on my arrival, and it's not going to be easy. Being left in a cave and then exposed to cold night air, not yet knowing how she died, doesn't help much.' He was now standing by the body and looking up at the ceiling as if for an answer. 'I'd say somewhere between fifteen and twenty-five hours, but don't hold me to it yet. Rigor mortis is still present and that could have been retarded by the low temperatures.'

'So probably, if not certainly, sometime during the previous night? The same night as her husband?'

'I'd say extremely probably, for she's certainly what you would call freshly dead.' Twite pushed his face forward at the girl attendant who put a cigarette in his mouth and then lit it with a gas lighter. He put the instruments he was holding at the side of the body and peered intently in turn at the eyes, the interior of the mouth and the gash on the forehead. Then he repeated it, saying 'H'm' and 'Ah' from a closed mouth, occasionally jerking his head to scatter cigarette ash to the floor. Bending to be nearer, he scrutinized the body surface inch by inch, pressing dead flesh with the tips of his gloved fingers as if reading braille and then, to finish, forcing open the tightly clenched hands. Staightening his back, his belly wobbling visibly beneath his gown, he pursed his lips while the girl took the cigarette stub from his mouth and put it in a disposal bin.

'Preliminary stuff, old son, and off the cuff,' he said, though sounding wholly satisfied. 'The laceration on the temple was caused post-mortem, more than probably during her fall into the cave. As were more certainly the smaller cuts and grazes. There're signs of lividity around the mouth and she's bitten her bottom lip and tongue. Her hands are contracted in a cadaveric spasm, and the post-mortem staining indicates that she's been on her back at least for the first few hours after what was, from whichever cause, an asphyxial death. And,' he added, 'I suspect that I'm going to find that the lady was pregnant.'

'With no sign of how it was done?' Rogers, who could still regard the body as being that of an attractive woman, had been wondering by what omnipotent order of justice she had been doomed to become a pathetic ruin under the pathologist's cavalierly-wielded scalpel. He needed to make some sort of sense of it for his own peace of mind. Repeated attendances at the post-mortem examinations of women and children were making him more sensitive than less to the sickening repugnance the process could inflict on him. Men seemed not to matter as much and any suffering a violent death were made less of a tragedy, Roger's expended pity the less, were he convinced that they had, in some measure, deserved it.

Twite had smiled at his question. 'I imagine you mean the asphyxiation and not the pregnancy,' he said. Never having shown that he had entertained similar thoughts about the subjects of his form of surgery, he would have considered Rogers foolish in doing so. 'That's what's puzzling me. So far at least, I've seen no marks of a manual or mechanical obstruction being applied over the air passages, and I doubt there could be any inside.' He picked up a scalpel and held it poised, manifestly thinking. 'You've no suspicion that she could have drowned?'

That surprised Rogers though it should not have, a picture of the boat *Ephreda* at Ullsmouth coming instantly to his mind. 'Her car was found abandoned near the boat moorings at Ullsmouth, so she could have been. You think she was?'

'Perhaps no more than you do, but we'll soon know.' He beamed at Rogers and then laid a rubbered forefinger along the spine of the scalpel he was holding, leaning over the body and placing its point under the chin.

This was the initial cut against which Rogers had never yet wholly steeled himself. He said, 'I forgot. A telephone call to make. Don't wait for me.' That he knew he was acting like the usual run of whey-faced probationers on their blooding-in failed to deter him from pushing himself from the worktop and striding to the door. Seeing the electronic flash from the girl attendant's gun reflected in the wall tiles, he accepted that he was deserting his post just as the real action was starting. Leaving by the door and searching for a saver, he considered that having now seen Daphne Gosse and the body of her husband, both within nearly twenty hours of continuous duty, enough was enough. He would reject its inadequacy later, but it would do for now.

Stationing himself in the shadow of a wall in the bitter cold outside and wondering, bleakly humorous, if unmarried men

173

of forty years with hang-ups were acceptable to the French Foreign Legion, he kept his eyes on two small ground-level glass-brick windows which, in the mortuary, were set close to its ceiling. He saw reflected through their thicknesses the regular flashing of the electronic gun. They would tell him that Twite's examination was continuing, their cessation that he had finished.

Occasionally stamping his feet and beating his gloved hands together, he gave his mind to thinking about what he knew from experience would be Twite's near certainty that Daphne Gosse had drowned, and his assessment of the time elapsed since her death. Something unidentifiably illogical was engaging his mind and not, so far, being helped by his thinking.

Time passed and, newly awakened sensitivities or no, he knew that he would have to return. Blinking as he entered into the comparative brilliance of the mortuary, he saw that Twite was still bloody-gloved with the body – at which he glanced at only briefly – but appeared to be at the final stages of his examination. 'Sorry about that,' Rogers said. 'Unforeseen delays.'

Lingard winked an understanding eye at him and Twite said, as beamingly as he had before, 'It's all right, I've kept it warm and waiting for you.' He pursed his lips and made a kissing noise at the attendant. She, having apparently discarded the camera and showing no signs that she had been unduly disturbed by viewing the evisceration of a body, came to him and, placing a cigarette in his mouth, lit it. 'Two things first,' he said. 'The lady was pregnant – being no obstetrician I can only guess that the foetus was somewhere around three months in its development – and there are no signs of sexual interference. Not ruled out, of course, but you'll have to wait on my microscope for a definite answer.' He nodded in the direction of the nearest worktop. 'The poor little tadpole's in that kidney dish if your interest extends to it.'

'Not really,' Rogers assured him. 'Only the act, not its consequences. Was she drowned?'

'As you may see if you do happen to look,' Twite said banteringly through a cloud of cigarette smoke, 'I've opened up the chest cavity, about which I shall particularize, even if in

174

doing so I have occasionally to descend to using your constabulary patois. Bulging lungs, moderately congested and containing an abnormal amount of lightly bloodstained fluid, as did the bronchioles, though not the bronchi. A little frothy slime in the respiratory passages as a whole; I think only the residue of a greater quantity. Taking that into consideration with bloodstained fluid found in the pleura, the right side of the heart being dilated and containing blood, the evidence of petechial haemorrhages in the eyes, the bitten lips and tongue and the cadaveric spasm shown by the clenched fingers, what say you?' He was jovial in his knowingness.

'It was then?' Rogers accepted that the question had been largely rhetorical, for he knew well the physical appearances of a death by drowning. 'Do you know whether in the sea or the canal?'

'Consider the clenched fingers, old son.'

'I have.' That was something else Rogers knew. The approach of death by drowning could cause a final spasm resulting in the hands grasping and retaining material such as small quantities of seaweed, sand, gravel, river plants or mud. 'Holding damn all,' he muttered, disappointed and frustrated, 'though it isn't an absolute, is it?'

'No. An indication though.'

'It'll mean a laboratory analysis, I imagine? A day or so I can't afford.'

'At least, though I'm certain that it's not sea water.' Twite was smiling fatly as if enjoying Roger's disappointment. 'There is something else that might short-circuit it. That is, if you've the stomach for it.'

'Don't think I haven't, Wilfred,' he growled. He could see that both Lingard's and the attendant's eyes were on him, guessing that something probably unpleasant – and, he thought, no doubt deserved – was about to descend on him. 'What is it?'

'The chest cavity, old boy. Put that beak of yours over it and sniff. Smell what's there and tell me what it is, or what it might remind you of. Close your eyes if it helps.'

'You're not serious?' He looked from Twite's face to Lingard's for the laughter he was sure would come, but which did not.

'I am now. I can't tell you what, but it's my own opinion I'm putting forward and it's such that it needs confirming by another's. David did it, but unfortunately found everything there smelling of snuff. If you want to convince yourself where she drowned it's all you'll get to help you for a day or two.'

'It's true, George,' Lingard drawled. 'You'll need to do it to be satisfied. Even if you chuck up it'll be worth it.'

Realizing that he had to do it or lose face, Rogers positioned himself at the side of the table. Closing his eyes against the ghastliness of it, he leaned over the body and breathed in through his nose. He did it twice, praying that he wouldn't puke, then lifting from it swiftly and turning away.

The others were watching him as he struggled to rationalize what his nose – normally only used seriously in identifying the odours of food or a woman's perfume, but now probably as tired as the rest of him – had told him was underlying the smell of raw flesh. He felt that he was about to screw this thing up.

'Well?' Twite said with a touch of impatience. 'You must have smelled something.'

'I don't think it'll be what you want.' He was about to be irritable. 'Not with the other I was smelling.'

Twite was about to be irritable himself. 'Out with it, man. I smelt it and thought it unlikely.'

'Something scented and I don't think it could have been on her skin. Only faintly though. Like soap. Or perfume. Or bath oil, though it's stretching it a bit to think it could still be there.' The expression on the pathologist's face told him that their noses had been as one. 'Of course!' He was confident now. 'She drowned in the bath and swallowed it.'

'Bath oil, I'd say, wouldn't you? It'd need to be strong to survive in flooded lungs. It isn't certain, naturally, but it'll give you something to work on.' Twite was immensely pleased with himself. 'Wasn't there a Victorian gent who drowned a couple of his wives while they were having a bath?'

'George Joseph Smith, who wasn't a Victorian though he did drown three of his wives, if not more,' Rogers said, reasonably familiar with the case. 'He grabbed their ankles and jerked them under while they were soaking in the bath, being hanged for it only once sometime in nineteen-fifteen.'

'It makes the absence of underclothing comprehensible,' Lingard suggested, 'though it doesn't explain why she was dressed at all.'

Rogers, knowing of man's vagaries under the pressures of panic, wasn't thinking that too important a matter. 'I imagine if you're to carry a woman you've just murdered from indoors to a car outside, it'd be less visible or suspicious for her to be clothed rather than unclothed to anybody happening by. Better clothed *en route* to the pothole, too, unless she's going into the boot. Or, of course, whoever it was may have had some sense of decency in not exposing the naked body of a woman to public view, though that should be good for a laugh in many a cemetery.'

Only minimally interested in anything not anatomical, Twite moved from the table towards the changing room, stripping off his gloves as he did so. 'Bed for me,' he yawned, 'and you'll get my report when I'm up again. Which won't be for a long time.'

'I'm grateful, Wilfred,' Rogers said, straightfaced. 'If we get a positive result during the night from what you've told us, I know you'll be anxious to be informed of it right away.'

It wasn't quite clear what Twite said in repartee as he went through the door into the changing room, but it wasn't complimentary and it couldn't have been anything to which his young girl attendant would be accustomed.

On the way out – only Rogers knew how much he needed fresh air, cold as it was – and having arranged to confer with Lingard back at the office, he realized what a bloody fool he had been for at least the past few hours. As a convinced believer in the monitoring activities and the higher intelligence of his basement-housed subconscious mind, he accepted the rightness, the sweetness, the logicality of its thinking now being pushed up into the flawed, day-to-day working of his clapped-out brain in its hour of need. It had all to do with the ability of his nose – nothing that he had ever thought remarkable – to refer to his memory of past and present odours and to put it on hold in his subconscious mind until it decided that it could be passed on. As befogged with tiredness he drove through the darkened streets to Headquarters, he did wonder what, in the total absence of any incriminatory evidence, he could do about it.

<h1 style="text-align:center">24</h1>

Having refined the logic of his earlier thinking while taking into account that a smell was an external stimulus judged subjectively and little more, Rogers was managing to retain a cerebral high against the sapping by fatigue of his physical condition.

Sharing his theory – in the sober daylight to come it might not amount to much more than a fanciful one – with Lingard, they had agreed over cups of canteen coffee on a tactic that had its flaws, but which seemed the only one with any promise of success.

'Tonight, about two-ish,' Rogers said to Lingard from where he was sitting, feeling crumpled and grubby, at his office desk. 'It has to be tonight and I must be supposed to be still grubbing about in Blind Dog Hole. So, without actually saying so or being too explicit, you've to imply that Mrs Gosse – well, if need be, only say a body – has just been found. There should be no peace for the wicked, so if the wicked's in bed so much the better. If so, apologize for the undoubted inconvenience of your call and say that I shall be there for an urgent and very necessary interview in one hour from the time you are telephoning. You don't know why you were told to arrange the meet and you can't suggest why, other than it all sounded extremely important.'

'You're wanting me to simulate a quite uncharacteristic thickness?' Lingard, his yellow hair only slightly astray, his eyes still blue-bright, sounded a little put out. 'Stap me, George, it won't do my image any good.'

'We need to suffer in the cause of justice,' Rogers said, staring at him. Then he smiled and tapped his fingertip on his forehead. 'All I'm asking is that you act as if you're dim up here; that you're unwittingly letting out that there's heavy stuff happening, that you're rather unsuccessfully bottling up what might be catastrophic tidings. It won't affect innocence, but it'll certainly provoke panic stations in the guilty.' He looked at his wristwatch, hiding a yawn behind closed teeth. 'On its own, the timing of your call should be enough to ring alarm bells. You're happy?'

Lingard, about to drink from his coffee cup, grimaced. 'As happy as anybody is who has to wait on the sidelines, I imagine. I'd prefer to be in with the action.'

'I'd prefer you to be here, David. Given that I'll be wading in fairly deep waters, you'll be a bigger help in the event of a problem by staying at the open end of the radio and taking your notes – if there are any. Nor would it do you any good to be with me should I drop an almighty clanger. I'll have a couple of our bodies in the vicinity to cover me if there's a break for it, or things become dangerous.' He grinned again, though it made his face ache. 'Not much chance of that, I suppose, unless there's a try at clobbering me à la Gosse.'

'And Mrs Gosse?' Lingard asked. 'Do we get a strong whiff of her involvement in the killing of her husband?'

Rogers hadn't yet worked out Daphne Gosse's part in the circumstances leading to her husband's death and subsequently to her own. He hadn't, he admitted to himself, simply because his subconscious wasn't yet coming up to scratch about her. This shadowy entity, whose existence he took seriously, though mostly helpful, was not always forthcoming when needed, being often obstructive or downright disobliging and leaving him to flounder alone after the truth.

'It's all speculation at the moment,' he answered Lingard, 'but it wouldn't surprise me. As an accessory though, not the one actually doing the dirty work. She typed that note for certain. Necessarily, I'd say, if she was planning her disappearance. A bit of intelligent forward thinking wouldn't come amiss if she wanted her husband to be suspected of the foul play bit – which he was up to a point – while she went absent and joined her lover; already, it seems, a putative father.' He thought about that for a moment or two, then said, 'Your friend Henbest suggested that she could be paranoiac. Perhaps that was a part of it, though I'd guess a small part. In any case, why should she not spread the word that her husband was wanting to murder her if it could eventually cause hot coals to be poured on his head?'

Lingard said, 'Why not, in fact, if the thought of his being murdered just happened to be in her mind at the time? That already it was being considered by the two of them?'

'Not impossible, David,' Rogers agreed. 'It'd be odd though, wouldn't it? She being the author of the fiction that foul play was suspected and then becoming the victim of it with a vengeance.'

'My opinion exactly,' Lingard said. 'If that were proved to be so, getting her come-uppance could be beautifully apposite.'

'But sad.' Rogers was thinking of the ruination effected by Twite's scalpel. 'The little I saw of her pre-PM, I thought her an attractive woman, though what I'd heard about her wasn't all that good.' It sounded like his requiem for her.

'Egad, George,' Lingard disagreed sharply. 'I saw her too, and I'd say as attractive and caring as a snake.'

'Nevertheless, we haven't any evidence of her connivance in anything but trying to put an unloving and possibly brutal husband under deep suspicion of having murdered her, and nothing that wouldn't be disapproved in time,' Rogers reminded him equably. 'That, I feel, in a lesser degree, isn't so uncommon a happening in a marriage that we can't accept it for the time being.' He pushed back his shirt cuff to check the hour. 'And time to bolt our hare, David. Give me ten minutes to get in place before you ring, and make certain that all pocketphones are kept off the air once I start doing my stuff.'

As he put on his heavy coat he wondered whether Daphne Gosse's pregnancy might not be the motivation for her death, then decided that where contemporary mores were concerned, an unwanted pregnancy was a near enough non-starter for murderous action being taken against the mother-to-be; more often a reason for a dying of desire coupled with a financial handshake, and not for a drowning in a bath.

180

25

With the moon now behind its vast bulk, the moor cast a dense shadow over the town; its streets and roads, with their lamps extinguished, flooded with a blue-black inkiness. This suited Rogers, who was standing in the deeper shadow, virtually indistinguishable from the brick gate-pillar behind which he stood. He had buttoned up his coat to conceal the white of his shirt, only the pale triangle of his face and the glitter of his eyes betraying his presence. He carried a switched-off pocketphone clipped to the outside of his coat pocket. His nose was detecting the scent of a cigarette drifting from where one of his concealed DPCs was having a surreptitious smoke. There were no passing cars, the residents of the lightless and silent street seemingly unconscious in sleep.

Opposite the waiting Rogers rose the block of apartments known as Craven Court, its ornamented façade of stone facings and wrought iron – so much of what could be seen in the darkness – suggestive of expensive leasings. At its side was a covered-in hardstanding giving space to three parked cars and a shooting brake. Bearing in mind his assumption about why Daphne Gosse had been dressed after her naked death, he was confident that the boot-less brake would become the object of his later interest. The only windows in which he thought he could see subdued glimmers of light were on the ground floor, the floors above being, as at this time of the morning he would expect them to be, in darkness.

Not all the thoughts occupying Rogers's tired mind were concerned directly with the man for whom he waited; he would focus those to the exclusion of all else at the proper time. Now, trying to disregard the chill creeping upwards from his frozen feet, he was endeavouring to make mentally assimilable Daphne Gosse's battered-wife behaviour, her pre-planned leaving home and whatever it was that followed and led to her death. He had arrived at a partially satisfying answer – that is, resting on his initial postulation being proved correct – when he heard the muted sound of metal against metal coming from near where the cars were parked.

Checking the time on his wrist-watch – it was twenty past two – he unclipped his pocketphone, switched it on and tapped three times with his fingernail on its miniaturized microphone. From behind his muffling hand he heard Lingard say, only just audibly, 'I hear you, Nightstart – Over,' and Rogers, sending back twice the series of three fingernail taps, indicated that he would now be on transmission and required radio silence on its wavelength.

Clipping the instrument back on his pocket, he silently moved the few steps from the pillar to a position from which he could see the side of the building and, dimly, the densely black rectangle of a doorway. Even as he began to cross the street, he saw a flitting shadowy figure carrying what appeared to be suitcases and approaching the shooting brake.

The man was quietly loading them into the rear of the brake with what he must have felt an agonizing slowness, when Rogers appeared as if from nowhere at his shoulder. 'Good morning, Mr Durker,' he said with careful politeness. 'Am I mistaken in believing that I had an appointment with you here for much later on?'

Durker, wearing a heavy tweed coat and a Russian-style fur hat, had dropped the suitcase he was holding, shocked into sudden limpness. He uttered a groan as he turned his head to take in what was, for him, the awfulness of a stern Rogers. 'I . . . I . . .' he whispered slack-jawed, his face paper-white, his fingers clutching at the edges of the brake's roof as if to hold himself from falling; a man clearly seeing his worst nightmare being realized.

'I . . . I was coming up to see you,' he finally stuttered from shaking lips.

As much as he could in the darkness, Rogers studied the big man. Durker was in that physical condition when, with fear supervening, the heart would pound suffocatingly, the legs weaken to bonelessness and, possibly, the sphincter muscle shamefully lose control. He had visibly lost any self-possession he might have had, now disintegrating into a shaking funk.

Knowing that only guilt could unman him and panic his mind, the detective decided to hit him straight away with unsettling words.

He said harshly, 'With two suitcases? Obviously not prepared to be here when I was supposed to call?' Realizing that his interrogation, loud enough for the listening Lingard to hear and record, might be echoing into the quietness of the sleeping street, he reluctantly softened his voice, though keeping in it the edge of accusation. He wanted from the solicitor only the merest verbal indication of a guilty knowledge. 'Your partner,' he said. 'He was there first, wasn't he?' These words, only having meaning for Durker were the guilt to lie on him, committed Rogers to nothing.

Durker, his agonized eyes on the detective, released his hold on the roof's edge. 'May I sit?' he managed to get out.

'Yes.' Rogers waited while Durker sat himself slumped on the tailboard. 'You were about to tell me which of them was there first.' Grim-faced and emanating establishment authority, he yet had it in him to say in his mind, *Dear Lord, if only for this once, please don't deliver unto me a dumbstruck awkward bugger who's taken a vow of perpetual silence.*

Durker, now an ill-defined shape in the darker shadow of the brake's interior, was a long time silent before he said, 'To do that thing couldn't be normal, could it?'

Rogers thought that he had seen the sparkle of tears in the hardly visible eyes. He again opted for the ambiguous and said, 'I won't know until you tell me.'

'I wasn't myself; I know I wasn't.' His voice was steadier as though what he had said had given him a substance with which to feed an explanation he felt was needed. 'She made me, you know. It wouldn't have happened otherwise.'

'You put your partner down there first, is that it?' Rogers, having smelled decomposing flesh in the Blind Dog Hole, and later noting its absence from the recently dead Daphne Gosse, had had the two facts subconsciously evaluated, giving him a delayed answer to the problem of the missing Kyberd. He thought that he should have recognized it sooner. 'How long before Mrs Gosse?' he persisted.

'I don't know.' His head could be seen being shaken. 'I can't

183

think. Two weeks? Would that be right? She told me to and took me up there.'

Rogers hoped that Lingard had heard and recorded that damaging admission, though even the short distance Durker was from him could be against it. He stooped and reached for him. 'Come out, Mr Durker, and lock your cases in the car,' he said firmly, his voice proportioned between being friendly and being officially impassive. 'We'll finish our talk in my office.'

Not sure whether he was dealing with the human equivalent of a ticking bomb, Rogers stood close behind him as, without demur, he used his key in a shaking hand to lock his cases in the brake. Then, holding his arm almost companionably, he led the docile – he believed still stunned – Durker to where he had parked his own car in the street. Putting him in the passenger seat, in much the same attentive manner he would use in escorting a woman he was taking out to dinner, he pressed down the lock button before closing the door and rounding the car to get in on the driver's side.

Durker said, 'May I smoke?'

'Of course.' Rogers had unclipped the pocketphone on taking his seat and placed it without subterfuge, its red on-light showing, in the open glove compartment, mentally keeping his fingers crossed against some fool of a PC breaking radio silence against orders. 'Make yourself comfortable while we talk,' he said.

Well aware that he needed much more from Durker, and being unwilling to return to Headquarters and the nullifying and restrictive procedures of booking in a prisoner, he had already decided on what, despite a flagging brain, he had to do. Too, he thought that he might have been holding the solicitor's professional abilities in too high a regard.

When Durker appeared to be settled with his cigarette – to which his fingers were imparting a distinct trembling – Rogers asked softly, 'Did you kill your partner because he'd discovered that you'd been stealing from clients' funds?'

His mumbled reply came so easily that Rogers could hardly believe his ears. 'It was an accident. I didn't know what was happening . . . a kind of blackout in my head, I think.'

'And now's the time I'm sure you'll want to unburden

184

yourself for your own peace of mind; to explain the deaths of both him and Mrs Gosse.' Rogers was now at the point where the guilty, and in his opinion, only the guilty, more often than not made the decision to refuse to say more. He had no real choice if he wanted what was said by Durker to be admissible at a trial, and he said, 'As you should know, it's now that I'm required to caution you that you are not obliged to say anything unless you wish to do so, but what you do say may be put into writing and given in evidence.'

When Durker, still a largely undefined blackness in the interior shadow, remained silent, puffing jerkily at his cigarette, Rogers made his bid for more talk. 'You mentioned having a blackout. Would you like to tell me about that?' Looking sideways, he had seen tears brimming in the eyes staring through the windscreen at the outside darkness.

Starting with a jerk of his head, Durker spoke slowly, giving a relieved Rogers the impression of a man numbed in spirit picking his way through a mind of which he was not wholly in control. 'I meant to put it back, though they all say that, don't they?' He did a brief giggle, surprising Rogers, who glanced at him sharply. 'But I did. I honestly did, though I was never given the chance. And it was all recoverable with time. Hugh . . . Hugh who I'd liked and admired did an audit on the accounts quite unknown to me. I was in my apartment with Daphne – Mrs Gosse – when he unexpectedly called. She went into the bedroom so that she wouldn't embarrass me, and Hugh, not knowing she was there, accused me of a theft that I'd never really committed.' He turned his head to Rogers. 'You do appreciate the position I was in when it happened?'

'Yes, I certainly do,' Rogers replied. Now that the sweat of fear in Durker appeared to be more under control, he was sensing the beginning of an attempt to rationalize and to defend what he had done.

'He shouted at me, said that he was handing it all over to the police . . . being quite unresponsive to my trying to explain it to him. It made my head feel as if it was swelling and I couldn't see properly. When he went to leave I had to stop him, to try and convince him that I had only borrowed the money and that I could get it all back without anybody knowing about it. He wouldn't listen and that made me try to hold him back. He was terribly angry with me and hurting me with his struggling, and he had somehow got his head trapped under my arm.' He swallowed audibly, then began breathing with small rasping sounds. 'That was when everything went blank and I really don't remember what happened until I saw that he'd fallen on to the floor in some sort of a fit. While I was trying to revive him, Daphne came in from the bedroom.' He paused and Rogers could see him biting at his mouth and frowning. 'That was it. She said "Oh, my God, what's happened?" and I explained that Hugh had lost his temper – which she had heard, of course – and had apparently dropped unconscious. She looked at him and felt his pulse and then said that he'd had a heart attack and was probably dead.'

This was something that hadn't occurred to Rogers. While he didn't necessarily believe him – far from it – a failure of the heart or similar under stress was a possibility and a not inexplicable occurrence. 'You said that Mrs Gosse told you to take Mr Kyberd's body to Blind Dog Hole, and that she went with you. Is that so?'

'Yes. She took over because I was naturally distressed and she made me agree that it would be better for us both if we took him from the apartment and hid him. We had been intending to go abroad anyway and she didn't wish this to prevent us. She said she had climbed the cave some years back and it was no longer visited because of an accident. So she came with me and we hid Hugh there.'

'You mean you dropped the poor bastard down there,' Rogers wanted to rasp at him, but said only, 'There was nothing stopping either of you from getting a doctor to him, was there?'

'I lost my head and she said nobody would believe me.' He turned down the window a few inches – Rogers had moved to restrain him before realizing what he had intended – and tossed his cigarette butt out, a tiny comet of glowing red ash in the night. Then, putting a hand over his eyes, he leaned forward. 'I respected Hugh,' he whispered. 'I wouldn't have hurt him deliberately, and on my own I wouldn't have done that to his body.'

'What went wrong between you and Mrs Gosse that she

finished up dead in the same cave as your partner?' Rogers, feeling so mentally and physically weary, was wondering how much longer he would be able to keep this up, convinced now that he was dealing with a man he considered to be a murderous psychopath and one who might easily turn on him in an unsolicitorlike frenzy.

Durker straightened in his seat and resumed his looking through the windscreen, now fogged up with condensation from their breathing. 'Did you know that she had drowned?' he asked.

'Had she? You tell me.' He hadn't wanted Durker to say that, though that he was continuing to talk surprised even the detective with his experience of the weirdness of human nature.

'I'm sure she was. When I came back from the office I called out to let her know I was home and there was no answer. I thought that she'd gone out and I was terribly shocked to find her in the bath with her head under the water. I hadn't any experience of that sort of thing, but I lifted her out and gave her the kiss of life.' He shook his head as if in despair. 'It was too late . . . I knew she was dead, poor girl. I've been thinking about it since and it could have been a stroke or – I hate to say it – suicide. I mean, we loved each other so it couldn't have been anything else, could it?'

'You certainly appeared to be having a run of bad luck,' Rogers commented. 'Other than, of course, knowing that she was taking with her some of your more dangerous secrets. One of them, such as knowing about your thefts from clients' funds.' Neither expecting nor receiving an answer to that, and becoming even more convinced that he was dealing with a psychopath short on intelligence as well as pity, he murmured, 'You'd think there would have been a note, wouldn't you, were it suicide? Some indication of an unhappiness with life that you would have undoubtedly already put forward? And which you haven't.'

Getting no reply to that either, he pressed on. 'Mrs Gosse was your client, of course, and not Mr Kyberd's?'

Durker stiffened in his seat and Rogers braced himself in anticipation of whatever it was in his mind to do. Whatever it was, Durker had held the question to be significant, though there was no other response. He said, 'I'm sorry I told you differently. Hugh passed her file to me after the first conference with her.'

'You and she were in correspondence? Initially, at least?'

'Naturally,' Durker said warily.

'Having told me that she was your partner's client, was it your intention then to retrieve any letters from you to her after she'd left home without them? You'd have been sunk, wouldn't you, had they been found?'

'No, it was not!' His denial was explosive.

'You're so sure?' Rogers said, putting disbelief into his words. 'And here I've been believing that you broke into her home – possibly having been told where the letters had been left – and that you were disturbed by Mr Gosse, a man somewhat short-tempered who would, no doubt, have objected to your presence in no small measure. I imagine that there was nothing accidental or suicidal about *his* death? Nor, I'm sure, did he die from natural causes. No?' he queried when Durker remained silent, appearing to have decided to remain so. 'Perhaps later, when you've given some thought to the circumstances of his death and what we may have learned from them.'

With his eyelids feeling as if there were grains of sand behind them and what he could only imagine to be dark patches developing in his thinking, Rogers wanted this interview over with. He had already obtained more from Durker, a man who could have been expected to keep his mouth closed, than he might have reasonably anticipated, and what he hadn't got would have to wait. That what he had obtained was largely a contrived if confused stab at blamelessness mattered little just so long as it tied Durker by association to the deaths of Kyberd and Daphne Gosse. The matter of Kyberd's missing Rover, of Daphne Gosse's dumped Mini at Ullsmouth and that of her nightdress and lipstick found in Kyberd's house were already clearly explicable to him in terms of tracks being covered and the loading of suspicion on to a missing dead man. They were of relative unimportance and for sorting out later, when his batteries had been recharged. Which, at the moment, did not seem to him to be much of a possibility.

Durker was now hunched in his seat, clearly withdrawn into

himself and not about to cause trouble, and Rogers wasn't intending to provoke it by using his handcuffs. He turned the ignition key and started the engine, then switched on the headlights and pulled out from the kerb, hoping that he could reach Headquarters without falling asleep at the wheel and demolishing himself or one of the local authority's lamp-posts. As for Durker, he thought that the Devil might well be able to look after his own.

26

To be awake, dog-tired and physically depleted at five-thirty on a dark and cold November morning can rarely be anything but an occasion of pessimistic gloom. Rogers thought so, and he was beginning to believe that he was becoming an authority on the depressing effects of it. At the moment he was a conscious but collapsed bundle of flesh, bone and crumpled clothing in an easy chair. Having returned to his apartment, hoping for an hour or two's rest in the chair before starting again, he had first made coffee then exhumed the pouch of tobacco he had buried in the linen cupboard against such a moment. Retrieving one of the pipes he kept in the kitchen's cutlery drawer for reasons he had chosen to forget, he stuffed its bowl with tobacco and had his first smoke after many months of suffering deprivation. Though the tobacco was stale and dry and virtually unsmokable he enjoyed it, thinking how much pleasure there could ensue from occasionally being weak-willed and hedonistic.

None of this made him less than frustratingly unhappy about Durker who, refusing to say anything further, now occupied a police cell, having been provisionally charged with the comparatively piddling and not yet substantiated theft of funds from his firm's clients' accounts, and with the even less serious and archaic misdemeanours of disposing of the dead bodies of Hugh Kyberd and Daphne Gosse, upon each of whose bodies a coroner's inquest was required to be held. As the facts now stood, Durker's verbal statements – almost certain to be routinely challenged by his defence counsel as being inadmissible, even though recorded at the time by Lingard – were yards away from implicating him in the two deaths. Durker, he considered, must be under the protection of an efficient, if morally dodgy, guardian angel for, in addition, he had – and Rogers knew with a cold certainty that he had – managed to bludgeon Gosse to death and to set fire to his house without leaving behind the smallest trace of incriminating material.

Coltart and a generously understanding Dickersen and his team had returned to Blind Dog Hole and were already reported to have found the decomposing body of a middle-aged man in its lower depths. When it had been raised to the surface and identified as that of the missing Kyberd, then Twite would be persuaded from his bed to perform an examination of it and to discover by what means death had lain claim to him. It was Rogers's firm belief – By God, it had better be! he told himself – that Kyberd's body would show the evidence of what must have been Durker's murderous attack on him. And he, Rogers, already feeling half-dead, would have somehow to prise himself from his chair in that hour or two's time to continue the task of metaphorically fitting a rope around Durker's neck.

The scented bath water detected in Daphne Gosse's body and to which he had earlier pinned a shining hope or two now meant nothing, for Durker had unintentionally or cunningly made it of no importance, frustrating Rogers's planned questioning by freely admitting that she had been in his flat and had drowned in the bath. Whether Twite would be able to dredge anything from his previous examination of her body to show that she had been drowned by violence was doubtful, but Rogers had to be optimistically expectant that he would. Something good, surely, had to be dealt out to those generally held to be on the side of the righteous.

And then, though nothing to do with Durker, there had been the letter. On his return to his apartment he had found it in his mail box inside the front door. The envelope was lilac-coloured and had *George* written on it in a strange but unmistakably feminine hand. Initially, he hadn't been pleased to see it and had tossed it unopened on to an occasional table. He thought exaggeratedly that it wouldn't have surprised him too much had it exploded.

It was still unopened as he sat there and, after his sanity-sustaining pipe of tobacco and in between fretting about Durker, he had reached the only conclusion he logically could on its manner of address and its delivery by hand. That conclusion was that he could reasonably assume that Liz Gallagher wished to continue their association, and, in doing so, indicating that she and her husband were far from happily mated; knowng that very few who were shopped around for casual sex. That Liz had told her husband she had fornicated with another man seemed an excess of unnecessary openness, which might confirm some kind of a discord to already exist between them.

In his weighing up of what he might do, he thought reasonably seriously about the hole in the ozone layer and global heating, of coastal erosion and the pollution of the seas, of the seemingly systematic destruction of wild life, and then· the continuing destruction of the rain forests. Against the threat of the earth's seemingly approaching its death throes, his adopting a sanctimonious and priggish attitude towards going to bed with a married woman might appear so absolutely of no consequence that it would be laughable. And, dammit, having been through that particular marital hell himself, who was he to hold back from a woman, probably neglected physically and unhappy, to whom he was attracted? Admitting his pusillanimity in not opening the letter, he knew that he would do so when he had finished with Durker. Were its contents to confirm his considered assumption, then he would do something pleasurable about it.

'Given the time,' he muttered to himself, clasping his hands together and relaxing his body for what he anticipated would be no more than a catnap. 'Always supposing that I'm given the bloody time.'

	DATE DUE		
JUN 2 5 200			
OCT 1 4 2003			
APR 2 4 2004			
JUL 2 1 2004			
AUG 2 8 2007			
DEC 1 5 200			
DEC 1 5 200			